Op...

Ali Baba was merely a █████████████ ....ed
upon the hidden lair o ██████████████ ..ow
he's off on a riotous adv....... with the likes of Aladdin and
that other Sinbad—while evading dangers both magical and
murderous . . .

DON'T MISS THESE HILARIOUS
ADVENTURE SERIES
BY CRAIG SHAW GARDNER . . .

The Ebenezum Trilogy
"A lot of fun!"
— Christopher Stasheff, author of *Warlock and Son*

"A slapstick romp worthy of Laurel and Hardy!"
— Marvin Kaye, author of *The Incredible Umbrella*

The Ballad of Wuntvor
"A bizarre, witty, delightful fairy tale for grown-ups!"
— Mike Resnick,
author of *Stalking the Unicorn* and *Soothsayer*

"A delightful, very funny, superbly off-the-wall entertainment."
— Lionel Fenn, author of *The Quest for the White Duck*

The Cineverse Cycle
"Awfully silly!" —*Locus*

"Wildly funny . . . entertaining." —*S.F. Chronicle*

"Two thumbs up!"
— Esther Friesner, author of *Harpy High*

A BAD DAY FOR ALI BABA

CRAIG SHAW GARDNER

ACE BOOKS, NEW YORK

This one's for Dancing Girl
(This cha-cha's on me.)

This book is an Ace original edition, and has never
been previously published.

A BAD DAY FOR ALI BABA

An Ace Book / published by arrangement with
the author

PRINTING HISTORY
Ace edition / September 1992

ISBN: 0-441-04676-2

Ace Books are published by The Berkley Publishing Group,
200 Madison Avenue, New York, New York 10016.
The name "ACE" and the "A" logo are trademarks
belonging to Charter Communications, Inc.

PRINTED IN THE UNITED STATES OF AMERICA

10 9 8 7 6 5 4 3 2 1

◆

An Introduction,
*in which we are once again ushered
into the world of marvels.*

Ah. Many of you have come back for another of our tales.

Those of you who were here before know of my compatriot's story of the two Sinbads, full of marvels and dangers, but a tale in which all comes right in the end. Yes, yes, dear fellow, except of course for that unfortunate business with the Queen of the Apes. But that is all behind you now, or so we shall all most fervently hope. You appear, quite frankly, to be almost completely recovered.

But on with the business that brings us all here. Today I will tell you a second tale, one filled with such wonders and terrors that it shall make brave Sinbad's previous story seem like the slightest of rumors whispered in the wind.

So it is that I, too, shall return to that time before time, when Baghdad, whose towers seem to be made from the light of the sky and the colors of the dawn rather than common mud and clay, was the greatest city in all the earth. But this is a tale of other lands as well, with dark and forbidding forests so large that they hold trees equal to one hundred times the entire population of Persia, places so great that they might hide the best and worst of men and beasts. And my tale shall travel even farther still, past great and searing deserts, where lurk those wild things banned from all the cities of men, and where both man and beast might go made from heat and thirst.

But my story is more than a simple catalogue of the strange and the terrifying. It is the tale of a certain man, of humble bearing and modest occupation, named Ali Baba, and how a chance encounter led him to great wealth and even greater danger.

Aha! I hear certain of you cry. This is the tale of the Forty Thieves! And yes, this is the tale of the Exactly Forty Thieves, and how they fell upon hard times with their Greater Caravan

Redistribution Program. What, do you ask, do I mean by *exactly*? And what did the thieves do to all those caravans?

Perhaps you do not know the true story of the forty thieves, after all, including the interference of certain djinn and items of exceptional magic. Perhaps you would be better served if you ceased your chatter and began to listen. Perhaps you have even guessed that my name is indeed Ali Baba, and, especially you noisy lot in the back, perhaps you forget that I once was one of the most talented of woodcutters, and have retained a facility for the exacting use of exceedingly sharp instruments.

That is much better. A storyteller needs to hear his own voice. I shall begin.

And please, this time, no giggling during the dramatic passages.

♦ ♦ ♦

BOOK THE FIRST:
being
ALI BABA'S STORY

✦

Chapter the First,
in which we find there is more to a woodcutter's lot than a pile of logs.

Every man, it is said, has his destiny, and it is a wise man who accepts what is written for him. Ah, but there is a catch upon that very line, for what man can find that scrap of parchment upon which his own destiny is writ?

So it was that a certain poor woodcutter did eke out his existence in a certain city in the most distant corner of Persia, ignorant of the great events that were soon to shape his life in unexpected and even extremely unlikely directions. And that humble yet industrious woodcutter was named Ali Baba.

Now, Ali Baba was the younger of two sons, and when his father had passed from this world, the elder bequeathed all of his earthly goods upon the older of the two, whose name was Kassim. This was, of course, the accepted custom in that place and time, as it remains today. And the younger son did well to accept this, for his father was not a wealthy man, and the humble should not become bitter because custom should turn against them.

But this newfound wealth was not enough for Kassim, and the elder brother squandered those coins like a man might pour water into the desert sands, until he, too, was forced to seek employment. And even in this regard was he none too prudent, for he fell in with certain bad company, and began to run certain errands and perform certain services for a certain house of extremely low repute. But still did Ali Baba keep silent, and continue to go about his menial business without complaint.

So it was that Ali Baba pursued his woodcutting, day in and day out, collecting vast and back-breaking quantities of wood in the wild forest beyond the city, receiving calluses upon his palms and splinters in his fingers, facing constant threats from wild bandits and wilder beasts, so that he might eke out the most meager of existences. And Kassim, who appeared to do what little labor was

expected of him in the middle of the night, would loll about the
house during the day and call to his many servants for scented
water to cool his brow. But Ali Baba thought little of his brother's
lot, even though his brother happened to live directly next door to
Ali Baba's poor hovel, and although his brother's actual lot was
far larger than the pitiful few feet of property that Ali Baba, his
wife, and the one single servant that they could afford were
crowded upon, and further that Kassim seemed to have loud and
vociferous gatherings that lasted far into the night, depriving Ali
Baba of much-needed sleep.

But still did the modest woodcutter not object. So humble and
hardworking was this man, in fact, that he barely noticed the
dozens upon dozens of petty affronts and nagging oversights on
the part of his less-than-perfect brother that *might* cause him to
object. Of course, should I dwell upon this unpleasant matter,
there is one small example that happens to come to mind. It is a
certain incident concerning an evening pleasant in all respects. At
least it was pleasant at first, before the actions of the jet-black
stallions of Kassim's superior (whose true name was Goha, but
whom all called One Thumb, since the thumb which once rested
upon his left hand rested there no more, having been separated
from the remainder of his flesh by a particularly sharp scimitar
during a particularly heated discussion concerning the disposition
of certain women of that household over which he held dominion)
as they wandered away from Kassim's gateway. And these
stallions did happen to poke their heads through a space in Ali
Baba's fence, and they further did happen to sample the finest
young vegetables from the man's small yet tidy garden. And
further, in the manner of horses everywhere, as did they eat, so did
they defecate, so that their offal covered the usually spotless stone
path that led to Ali Baba's gate. Therefore, when Ali Baba arose
the next morning, even before the dawn, so that he might drive his
mules the incredibly great distance into that portion of the
dangerous forest where the best wood might be found, he
discovered these twin disasters.

But was the noble woodcutter upset at the loss of his vegetables,
without which he would be hard-pressed to feed his household a
balanced, if undeniably meager, diet? But was the humble Ali
Baba embittered because his front walk was now heavily soiled
and odoriferous?

Well, we shall leave such questions for the sages, for at that
exact moment the unassuming Ali Baba, truly a prince among

paupers, did indeed espy his brother, Kassim, traversing his nearby gate. And so meek of manner was the woodcutter that he did not wish to draw the degree of attention to these recent upsetting matters as some might have found necessary.

"Good brother!" was instead his greeting.

"What is it now?" Kassim responded shortly. "Can you not see that I am a busy man?"

And indeed, Ali Baba was uncertain whether he wished to make his brother busier still. Yet did he feel that such business, once begun, was best done with. So it was that he stated: "There are two things that have come to my notice." And with that statement, he pointed at the vegetable garden, a patch of ground where vegetables now grew no more.

His brother glanced hurriedly at the disturbed earth. "From the looks of your garden, it is wise that your primary trade lies in woodcutting," was Kassim's jovial reply.

But was the meek Ali Baba prepared to stand idly by and silently accept his brother's ill-considered humor? Perhaps not, for the woodcutter further stated: "But the deed was done by Goha's horses." And, as proof of this statement, he pointed to the overly fragrant mounds upon the walk.

At this Kassim frowned, and wrinkled his large and ill-shaped nose. "Why has this not been removed? It is bad enough that you must live in such close quarters. You should be careful that your habits do not further sully the neighborhood." And with that his brother wheeled about, and marched away with that imperious stride so cultivated by the well-to-do.

But was the simple Ali Baba, so much purer in spirit than his brother in so many ways, put out in the least by his brother's selfishness and lack of understanding? But was the righteous Ali Baba ready to take this earthenware cup that is now in his hands and smash it into bits against this nearby tent pole? Was the always courteous Ali Baba about to take this parchment before him and shred it into tiny pieces, wishing each piece were a part of his brother's—

Oh, dear. You must excuse me. I was temporarily carried away by my tale. Why are you shifting your position? You are certainly not considering leaving. I am but setting the stage for the great events to come. Perhaps Sinbad is correct, and I should tell the tale more directly.

Where are you going? I have not even told you about the Curse of the Contrary Wishes, or the awesome discovery I made upon

National Djinni Day. And I have not breathed the first word about the Palace of Beautiful Women.

Ah, that is much better. I believe I have done enough to set the stage, and shall proceed—yes, most rapidly—to the point at which the true action began, and I realized that my life would be changed forever.

What is that? Oh, yes, the Palace of Beautiful Women. Well, I shall comment upon that eventually.

♦

Chapter the Second,
in which we again attempt to determine
wherein lies the truth of the tale.

So it was that the hardworking Ali Baba found himself chopping the most sturdy wood from the darkest part of the forest, a place so dense with undergrowth that it seemed to be twilight at noon, and every shadow appeared to produce a further shadow of its own. Ali Baba was understandably disquieted by his surroundings, but he also knew that the wood that he cut would bring a good price at market, so that he might provide adequately for his wife and children.

The sun shifted beyond a nearby hill, and the afternoon became no brighter than the onset of evening. The wind increased in volume, bringing with it the growling cry of some forest predator. Ali Baba redoubled his efforts, wondering if any amount of effort might be worth the loss of his life. It was little wonder, then, that he jumped and hit his head upon that tree branch when he heard the approach of a great many horses.

Did I say a great many? He quickly ran from the path as the earth shook with their approach. As they passed his hiding place within the dense forest thicket, Ali Baba further heard the sounds of coarse laughter and the sort of language one did not generally associate with the upper echelons of polite society. So full of entirely understandable trepidation was he that he almost completely forgot about the bump upon his head, and remained as completely still as a living being might within his place of concealment.

But still did the shaking of the earth become greater, so that Ali Baba could no longer distinguish between the movement beneath his feet and the quaking of his own form at what transpired. For, just beyond the thicket, he could now see the horses gallop past in twos and threes. And upon every horse there rode a man clothed in robes as dark as a storm at night. Ali Baba silently counted as

9

they passed, and when he could see nothing more but a dissipating cloud of dust, he had enumerated fully forty horses and forty riders.

Perhaps, he thought, his most prudent course of action would be to turn away and gather together his mules (which he had tied to a group of trees at some little distance), and thereupon he and his mules should remove themselves from the immediate region as quickly as their legs could carry them. But, as the wise man has often said, scrutiny may squash the swiftest Simba. So it was with the woodcutter, who, as he absently rubbed the tender spot atop his head, knew that he might never rest until he discovered what such a group of fearsome men were doing in this remote corner of the forest.

Therefore, in order to learn further the ways of the coarse and the dark-robed, Ali Baba turned himself about, and saw that all forty men had stopped their steeds in a nearby clearing by the side of a steep hill. Having dismounted, all pulled bags of foodstuffs and waterskins from one side of their horses. But then, with a signal from the man at the front of their ranks (who Ali Baba reasoned must have been their leader), the thirty-nine remaining freed those bags from the other side of their saddles. And, from the way these bags clanked as they hit the dry earth, and the effort that it took for the forty men to carry these sacks, Ali Baba guessed that that baggage must be filled with gold and other items of value.

Some of the men did then turn around, and Ali Baba ever so carefully looked out of his hiding place to get a better idea of what manner of man carried this sort of gold. What he regarded next did not give him ease, for every man seemed to wear a great beard parted in the middle and curled to either side. What truly gave them a fierce appearance, however, was the density of those beards, with hair so thick that each beard rose almost to that man's eyeballs. Not that Ali Baba could see truly those eyeballs, for these men did squint and scowl as if each one had a less pleasant disposition than his brother.

There could be but one conclusion. This gold that these men carried could never be the result of honest labor. Ali Baba was therefore spying upon bandits of the worst sort. Once again did the woodcutter resolve not to invite any of those assembled before him for any social occasion whatsoever.

"Gather around!" their leader called in a particularly rasping and uncultured voice. "We shall pass quickly into our hiding place!"

Their leader then walked toward a large rock set at the back of the clearing, a rock as tall as three men and equally wide. It was while still facing that rock that the bandit leader spoke the following words:

"Open, Sesame!"

Ali Baba did not marvel greatly on these strange words at first, for his mind was occupied with wondering which side of that dense wood would serve as the bandits' hiding place. But to his amazement, their destination was no part of the wood at all. He instead heard a great grinding noise, and saw the great rock roll aside, revealing a deep cave within the hillside beyond.

None of the bandits before him remarked upon this occurrence at all, as if a great boulder's independent movement were as common as the spit of a camel. Instead, they once again carried their burdens forward into the newly revealed cave, groaning and complaining a bit at the weight of their parcels, and insulting each other in such a way that it fully reasserted their low breeding.

So surprised was Ali Baba at this amazing occurrence that he almost stepped forth from his hiding place. He did lean as far forward as the brambles would let him, and therefore was privileged to hear two further words from deep within the cavern.

"Close, Sesame!"

And with that, the great boulder promptly rolled back into its place to hide the cave beyond.

What was this wonderful enchantment, where great rocks would move at the simple mention of an agricultural product? Ali Baba was so overwhelmed that it took him a moment to realize how entangled he had become in the briars, and a moment beyond that to panic at the thought that he might not be able to untangle himself before the bandits reemerged. Thus did he spend the next few minutes freeing his clean but simple clothing from its briar captivity, while at the same time attempting not to picture the many sharply curved scimitars he had seen hanging at the waists of the men in black.

Yet Ali Baba's fingers were as nimble as any who earned one's keep through honest toil, and the woodcutter managed to release himself before there was any further noise from the boulder at the hillside. Yet, before he could consider what to do with his mules or those many other facets of this increasingly complex situation, the ground did once again shake around him as the great rock tumbled away from the bandits' hideaway.

"Quickly!" the leader called to the other thieves. "We must

fulfill our task, and return to the route of the caravans to collect more gold!'' He clapped to hurry the others long. ''Close, Sesame!''

Perhaps the leader had been a bit too fast in the pursuit of his goal, for this time the roll of the boulder was accompanied by a loud and extremely unpleasant scream.

''Something is wrong!'' the bandit leader snapped.

''Oh, no,'' the other bandits were quick to assure him. ''Hardly anything at all.''

The leader pointed at each member of his retinue in turn as his lips moved rapidly but silently. ''I do not see all thirty-nine of you!''

''Well, there is that, O bravest of brigands,'' one of the others admitted.

''I believe it was Number Twenty-eight,'' another ventured.

''Twenty-eight?'' another mused. ''He always was a little slow. Wonder he made it this far.''

''Twenty-eight?'' their leader demanded. ''Is he still trapped within the cave?''

''No,'' one of the others replied, ''he made it through the entranceway.''

''At least,'' another added, ''most of him did.''

''What are you saying?'' their leader asked angrily. ''Have we *lost* Number Twenty-eight?''

''Well, not precisely lost—'' another of their number answered quickly.

''No,'' an additional brigand elucidated. ''He is simply much broader and flatter than he was previously.''

''He is also,'' one of the earlier speakers added, ''far more deceased.''

With that, the chief of all the brigands stumbled backward into that last small corner of light that still graced the clearing and looked off toward the heavens, his eyes catching the last rays of the setting sun in such a way that his face seemed alight with fear. His voice shook when next he spoke. ''Then there are only— *thirty-nine* thieves?''

What, Ali Baba marveled, would be horrendous enough to make such a fearsome man know fright?

The bandit band had no answer to this question, and the whole forest seemed heavy with their silence. But that unnatural quiet would not endure for long, for their leader had become quite agitated. ''Oh, woe!'' he cried in the most lamenting of tones. He drew his scimitar and waved it about in the most reckless of fashions. "Heads will roll! Bellies will be slit! Limbs will be chopped off at random!"

The other thirty-eight ruffians looked nervously back and forth, and appeared to be extremely busy shifting from foot to foot and clearing their throats. Their leader jumped ever higher in the air, calling out syllables that might have been words had he not been so upset.

"Pardon, O first among thieves," one brave outlaw ventured at last. "We do have another option."

"Another option?" The leader waved his sword in the other speaker's direction. "I should split you in two for the very thought! Remember, when you agreed to join this band, you were told there is no discipline here but death!"

"But"—his face took on a certain ashen quality as he continued to speak—"then we should be only *thirty-eight.*" Their leader laughed bitterly as he lowered his sword. "You know how luck deserts us when we number less than forty strong!"

With that, Ali Baba heard the sound of distant thunder. Hadn't the sky been without clouds only a few minutes before?

"I bow to your superior wisdom, O cleverest of cutpurses," the man who had spoken before answered smoothly. "It is therefore of the utmost importance that we quickly regain our full complement of forty thieves so that we might once again be blessed by those dark forces which we worship."

"Easy enough for you to say!" The leader again laughed harshly, as if he still could not see the reason of the other. "But where might we find another thief on such short notice, especially in so dark and deserted a wood as this?"

"Well, there is that fellow hiding over there in the brambles." The other man pointed straight at Ali Baba.

With that, half a dozen of the bandits leapt forward and dragged the very startled Ali Baba from his inadequate hiding place.

Still was the leader not convinced. The chieftain of the bandits stared at Ali Baba, his bearded gaze a mixture of surprise and skepticism, with a hearty dose of dismissal mixed within. Ali Baba, for his part, tripped and stumbled down upon the ground before them.

"This man is not even thief material!" the leader announced. "His clothing is all threadbare and covered with brambles. Furthermore, he appears to have a bloody lump upon his head, as if he has recently been hit with a blunt object."

"A beaten man, O sultan of swipe," the bold speaker replied. "Think how prepared he shall be for the sort of discipline you might choose to dispense for minor infractions."

"Discipline?" said another with a frown. "I thought the only discipline was death."

"What? You dare to question me?" the bandit leader screamed as half a dozen of his fellows leapt upon the man who had made the offending statement. "Kill him!" He paused in thought, his scimitar again poised high in the air. "No, no, that would only prove his point. His was certainly a minor infraction, it deserves a minor punishment. We shall only cut off his thumb. No, no, the little finger. And from the left hand, too! See? From this moment forward, I shall be merciful."

Ali Baba had some trouble concentrating on the next portion of the conversation, due in large part to the screams of a certain man being shown the leader's mercy.

"But we are impolite!" the leader remarked as he turned to the woodcutter. The leader was nothing but smiles, while Ali Baba for his part was of the opinion that he was not at present experiencing the most auspicious turn of events.

"We have not welcomed the latest member of our fearsome band," the leader encouraged. And with that, all the remaining thieves, even the one who had very recently been deprived of a body portion, drew their scimitars and held them overhead while they let out a great cry.

"You are one of us now!" cried one of the thirty-nine.

"There is no escape!" added a second.

"You will know the life of a thief!" cheered a third.

"One destined to be hanged!" opined a fourth.

"Riches will flow through your fingers!" suggested a fifth.

"Before your hand is chopped from your wrist!" chortled a sixth.

"Gold dust will flow through your veins!" encouraged a seventh.

"If you should live to spend any of it!" mentioned an eighth.

And still did the encouragements continue to rain down upon Ali Baba, if encouragements they were, for they seemed equally divided between the loftiest of promises and the direst of threats.

"Quickly now!" their leader interrupted them at last. "Give our newest member his robes dark as the deepest cave and his sword sharp as an infant's anger!"

"Number One likes to talk like that," the thief who brought the robes whispered in Ali Baba's ear as the woodcutter at last rose from his knees.

"No talking so that others cannot hear, Number Seventeen!" Number One chided. "You know how much enjoyment I garner from removing tongues!"

All the thieves laughed at that. Perceiving that it was the socially acceptable thing to do, Ali Baba did his best to laugh as well. He also hurried to don the proffered robes, as he sensed already from his limited experience that any pause in the action might engender a corresponding change in the leader's mood.

The leader nodded curtly when Ali Baba was dressed. "Grow your bread thickly and quickly, and all shall be well!"

Grow his beard thickly and quickly? Ali Baba thought in dismay. Although he could chop wood the equal of any man, his beard, especially upon his cheeks, tended toward the thin and scraggly. He wondered if it would be safe to mention such a difficulty, but before he could resolve his thoughts into a suitable statement, the leader had turned away.

"If I cannot grow my beard?" he instead asked the fellow who had offered Ali Baba his robes.

Number Seventeen made a slashing motion of hand across his bearded neck. "And I do not refer to the act of shaving."

"Come, my thieves!" Number One called from where he already sat astride his horse. "The cave must be filled! There is gold to be acquired! It is time to ride! And where we travel, death and disaster are sure to follow!"

And with that all of the forty thieves minus one rushed to their horses and followed their leader at full gallop from the clearing.

It took Ali Baba some little moment of time to realize what had just occurred. A moment ago, he had been captured by a group of cutthroats and villains, and forced to join their ranks. And now, but a moment later, those same cutthroats and villains had all galloped away, leaving him alone in the clearing.

Perhaps, he thought, now would be as good a time as any to take his mules and return to his humble home. Except that it was so quiet in this clearing now. And he further was very aware of a certain nearby cave and its contents. He therefore walked up to the great rock on the side of the clearing and repeated the words of the bandit leader:

"Open, Sesame!"

And the rock did roll away, revealing a great cavern beyond. Ali Baba stepped carefully around the remains of Number Twenty-eight as he entered. But he found no mere cave within. No, instead of the rock walls and floors which he had anticipated, he found himself in the midst of rich rugs hung upon the walls and piled upon the floor, with jewel-encrusted braziers of solid gold that were still alight from the bandits' recent departure. This place looked more like the home of a sultan than a cavern carved by nature. Truly, Ali Baba thought, this place must serve as the bandits' home when they were not searching for gold. He stepped forward and pulled aside another rug that divided one part of the cavern from the next.

Why, was his next thought, would the bandits have any need of more gold than this? For beyond the hanging the cavern widened and deepened as well, although the woodcutter could only guess at the chamber's vast size, for the great majority of the space was occupied by great piles of gold and precious stones.

Ali Baba's eyes flicked from one end of the room to the other, attempting somehow to comprehend the extent of this wealth. But as fast as his eyes moved, his brain worked faster. There was so much gold in this room that surely the thieves would not notice if a bit of it was missing; say, the exact amount that could be carried by one woodcutter and six strong mules? And why shouldn't Ali Baba take some of the gold with him, for when would he ever have occasion to run into these forty thieves again? Especially if he were to remove himself from this particular part of the forest forevermore?

These were the woodcutter's noble though somewhat deficient thoughts as he dragged forth bag after bag of gold, two for each of his sturdy mules to carry back to the city. If he had but known of the dire consequences of his actions, well, he would have taken the valuables, anyway. After all, gold is gold, and that sort of riches doesn't come to a woodcutter every day. But he perhaps would have been a little less cheerful about what had so recently transpired.

He could have sworn, as he left the cave for the final time, that he heard a noise, low and rumbling, like the deepest of chuckles. But it was surely the wind, he told himself, or perhaps the murmur of an underground spring.

If he had but known the true nature of his surroundings!

But Ali Baba would learn. For in one thing the bandit leader had spoken the truth. Where rode the forty thieves, death and disaster were sure to follow!

◆

Chapter the Third,
in which the woodcutter receives
a most woeful reception.

But, at this juncture at least, Ali Baba was blissfully unaware of the calamitous consequences that were soon to follow. Instead, he led his mules back into that city which served as his home, and further to the street on which his house was located, and thence before his front gate, strolling in such a fashion that no one might suspect his mules carried other than the sort of thing a woodcutter might haul from place to place. But as he pushed open the gate, he discovered that someone had bolted it from within, and panic threatened to take him by the throat, for he did not wish to call out loudly and thus draw attention to himself and his many mules.

Ali Baba paused, and breathed deep of the evening air, and swore that he would not be undone by the gate of his own exceedingly humble home. Then it was that providence graced him with an idea: What, he pondered, would happen if he once again used those magic words that had worked so well upon the gate to that cavern in the forest?

So it was that he again spoke those words, though much more softly this time, since the hour was growing late and he wished his neighbors not to overhear him, for more reasons than one. Still, he said the words clearly enough.

"Open, Sesame!"

And with that the gate unbolted and swung open.

He quickly led his mules within the courtyard, and as soon as the last of the asses had entered, softly but firmly remarked, "Close, Sesame!" and the gate did swing shut, and the bolt was once again thrown into place, as if by magic. These, Ali Baba reflected, were indeed words of power.

However, the woodcutter had little time for reflection, for his wife ran out into their insubstantial courtyard, crying in strident tones. "How did you enter the gate? It should have been locked.

Oh, woe! Our humble home has been broken into and our few meager possessions are forfeit!''

Ali Baba felt so blessed at that moment that even his wife's lamentations could not restrain his spirit. "Ho, my beloved!" he said instead. "This courtyard is so small, you may view all of it without turning your head. Do you see anything missing from your view?''

She frowned as her eyes darted back and forth to take their inventory. "No, over there is the bucket with the hole in it, and the rake missing half its prongs. And yonder is our one-legged chicken and our sickly goat. I suppose we still do retain all our worldly possessions. Not that they amount to anything.''

At a different time, Ali Baba would do nothing but agree with her. But now he had a dozen sacks of gold and jewels that weighed heavily upon his mind.

"Come, wife," he said instead, "and do not dwell upon our poor lot in life, for our lot has changed.'' With that, he patted the nearest of the bulging sacks strapped to the mules. The sack did its part by making a satisfyingly hearty chinking sound.

His wife's reaction was, at first, every bit as gratifying as the sound of the gold, for her mouth fell open as wide as an old man's yawn. Soon, however, her wits returned to her, and with those wits some idea of what the bags contained and, even more, how those contents might have been obtained.

"Oh, woe!" she therefore announced in her best wail. "A life of doing naught but chopping wood has snapped your reason, and you have turned to robbery!'' She pulled convulsively at her ragged shawl. "All is lost when a woodcutter goes bad!''

But the addition of so much gold to his possessions had put a shine upon Ali Baba's attitude, and he could do nothing but smile at the continued fretting of his bride. "Nothing could be further from the truth, O wife. Come, let us unload the gold, and I shall tell you how I stumbled upon it.''

Once again did his wife's mouth open as the clever Ali Baba recounted his adventure with the forty thieves, and the rock that rolled to an enchantment, and the cavern that was filled with gold. And, when he was done with his story, his wife praised his feats and further praised providence for showing her husband this ill-gotten wealth so that it could be removed from those men of low breeding and given to someone who truly deserved it.

But then did the woodcutter's wife hesitate, and frown again. "Oh, woe!" she cried, looking at the dozen sacks of gold before her. "You have brought me a pile of gold, but not given a moment's thought of where to put it! Now will my frail, poverty-weakened muscles be forced to lift those heavy sacks and find someplace to hide them from inquisitive neighbors, not to mention certain authorities who might question the manner in which they were obtained!"

Ali Baba had to admit that some of his wife's worries were valid. But so filled with energy was he by his good fortune that he found himself filled with ideas as well, such as the next one that came from his lips:

"Wife, you have often complained about the unevenness of the kitchen floor, and how it has a tendency to turn into the worst sort of mud when there is any amount of rain whatsoever. What if we were to bury the gold within the kitchen's confines so that you might have a firmer foundation under your feet?"

Ali Baba's suggestion seemed to calm his wife's nerves, if only for a few seconds. "Oh, woe!" she remarked. "Then we are to bury the gold without any idea of how much you have obtained?" She wrung her hands and looked upward to the sky. "It is just like a man not to consider one's budget!"

Now, Ali Baba was a man who knew great patience. But the most peaceful river must at some point meet the mighty ocean. So it was that he stated in a somewhat more forceful voice: "But it will take more days than there are in summer to count all this gold!"

But still was his wife unconvinced. "Perhaps this is so. But there must be some way to measure all this great wealth. Otherwise, how will we ever determine the children's inheritance? Surely, if we cannot count every piece of gold within those sacks, we can at least measure its bulk and through that determine the extent of our wealth."

Ali Baba admitted that perhaps it would be wise to consider the future. He further realized that he would need to get some sleep at some point in his life, and so he acceded to his wife's wishes.

"It is a pleasure to obey so clever a husband," she replied. And, since the woodcutter's household was far too poor to own so sophisticated an instrument as a common measure, she thereupon walked over to the fence that the household shared with their next-door neighbor, who also happened to be Ali Baba's brother, Kassim.

Now, as you may recall from earlier in my tale, Kassim inherited by far the greater share of their father's wealth, and despite squandering almost all of these monies in base pursuits, had still retained a home of some size and elegance, and had further been wed to a woman who had some common association with his less-than-reputable employer.

Despite their proximity, the two households had little immediate contact, primarily due to certain misplaced ideas concerning superiority and social standing among those members of Kassim's family. Nonetheless, well did Ali Baba and his wife know that they would witness the arrival of Kassim's wife once every evening, as she would come to their common fence at that moment when she was looking for a handy place to throw the remains of her family's evening meal.

So it was that Ali Baba's wife took herself to that far corner of the yard as the woodcutter dragged the heavy sacks within the confines of the kitchen. Once there he alerted their only slave, for they were so poor that they could afford but one, that he would need her assistance in digging a sizable pit.

As he created the hiding place, it soon came to pass that Kassim's wife reached the fence where stood his wife, and, although the two women spoke at the very end of the courtyard, still was the courtyard so miserably small that Ali Baba could hear their every word. So he listened while his wife lamented that his household had no measure, and he further heard with even more interest the remarkably sultry tones of Kassim's wife as she remarked that she would see what she might uncover. He again thought, as he dug, of the shame that such a comely form and enticing demeanor as those held by his brother's wife had to be combined with such low breeding!

But his wandering mind deafened him to the true meaning beyond the other woman's words. Oh, if only he had known of Kassim's wife's subterfuge, and the dire consequences that would soon ensue! Still, were that the case, the story would end here, and be nowhere near as filled with danger and magic. But certain major players within this drama might also have remained among the living.

Ali Baba instead returned to his pit as he heard his wife explain that the digging noise must surely be coming from the next yard over. Their plot of land was so miserably small. Noise carried so well on summer evenings. But couldn't she fetch the measure for them?

Anything, came the other woman's deep-throated reply, for the wife of that strong and manly woodcutter.

Ali Baba redoubled his digging as he heard the neighbor's voice fade with distance. This had been a trying day, he realized, and he would feel better to free his mind of errant thoughts and be done with his labors.

If he had but realized that the morrow would be far worse!

♦

Chapter the Fourth,
in which we recall the importance
of a good memory.

Still it was far into the night before Ali Baba could find his rest, as he continued to dig, his wife measured, and their young slave, Marjanah, laid the gold within the ditch for hour after hour. And, even when their labor was complete, the weary woodcutter could not rest for long, for he perceived that he should still rise at first light, as was his habit, and go about his business as if he had not recently found a sultan's ransom in gold. Truly, thought Ali Baba, this accumulation of vast wealth was not all that he had imagined.

So did he arise with first cock crow, and taking his mules with him, he did depart to another forest on the far side of the city from that dense wood where the forty thieves kept their cache of gold. And, as was his fashion, he soon became involved with the cutting and binding of twigs and those other aspects of the lumberman's art, so that the day passed with reasonable speed. Still was Ali Baba greatly fatigued from his labors of the night before, so that, when he saw a cloud cover the sun, he decided it was enough of a sign of rain for him to finish his work for the day and return to his household.

So it was that, weary of muscle, blood, and bone, he and his mules returned to that home which was not so pitiful as it had been the day before. Traveling thus, he eventually came into his courtyard, where he found his wife upon her knees, wailing and tearing at her already ragged garments. Truly, he had not expected a cheerful greeting from his mate, for in his many years of marriage he had come to know her actions well. Yet he had not anticipated the dire nature of the news with which she now greeted him.

"Oh, woe!" she cried with a voice filled with anguish and regret. "All is lost! Our great wealth has been discovered!"

"Discovered?" Ali Baba replied as he for once shared the true depths of his wife's feelings. "What do you mean? Have the thieves found my residence?"

But his wife's sole response was the continued wailing and wringing of hands. And, indeed, now that the woodcutter considered his question, he realized that those forty thieves were so vile of temper and dark of disposition that they would have left neither his wailing wife nor his pitiful home as evidence of their arrival.

"We are still hidden from the thieves, then?" At this, at least, his wife nodded. But Ali Baba was still without an answer. And he realized, with the grim certainty a sailor might feel at an approaching storm, that there were other disasters possible beyond the return of the thieves; others who might covet the gold and have the authority to take it.

"Is it the city guard?" Ali Baba asked.

His wife was still so overcome with tears that she could do naught but shake her head and look aloft, gazing, the woodcutter was sure, at some power higher than the local constabulary.

"No one as lowly as the guard?" Ali Baba's throat felt as dry as the desert when a sandstorm is nigh. Who might have a greater claim upon all that gold? He remembered then those white-turbaned strongmen who guarded the palace of their sultan, men of polished sword and deadly reflex. "Could it be," he therefore asked with some trepidation, "the king's private army?"

But again his wife's head shook amidst her bawling, which appeared to have redoubled.

Ali Baba had never seen another individual, not even his wife, cry so prodigiously. This, then, must be a calamity of untold proportions. What could be worse than being discovered by thieves, the police, or the private guard of the king?

His wife paused in her display long enough to choke out two words:

"Kassim's wife."

The two words had much the same effect as being kicked in the chest by a camel. His secret was now known by his less-than-virtuous brother? His wife was quite correct. This was worse than any of those options he had previously foreseen.

"At last!" a familiar voice called from behind him. "That duplicitous individual who dares to call himself my brother has returned home."

Ali Baba did not need to turn around to know that this was the voice of his only brother, Kassim, and that he should further see Kassim standing upon the other side of their common fence. But, after taking a bitter breath, the woodcutter did indeed turn around, and he was not in the least surprised.

Still can amazement come to the most fully prepared, for a mere moment later his brother opened his closed fist, and within that fist was a shining piece of gold, identical in all ways to all those countless other pieces that now resided beneath the kitchen floor of the woodcutter.

"I believe," his brother said in a voice honed by a life of collecting debts by any means available, "that you are familiar with this. In fact, I imagine you are familiar with a great many of these. But you cannot keep such a fine secret from your dear brother, who, after all, is only concerned about your welfare. Especially when your dear brother has such a clever wife."

And with that, Kassim's wife sauntered over to her lord and master, and, for but an instant, Ali Baba wished that his own wife might walk about in such a fashion. But he banished such thoughts from his head, worrying instead how much his brother would demand from him as the price of silence.

It was then, his wife pressed close by his side, that Kassim related how his wife had discovered Ali Baba's gold. For, after Ali Baba's wife had asked for the measure, the wife of Kassim had gone to her husband and told him that she had witnessed the most astonishing thing. Why, indeed, would a household whose most prized possessions included a bucket with a hole within it and a one-legged chicken have need of an instrument to measure anything? His wife's curiosity was so piqued, in point of fact, that she decided to add a certain something to the bottom of the measure before she lent it to Ali Baba's household. So it was that she rubbed a quantity of suet on the underside of the measure, in order that, whatever that measure would rest upon, be it grain or corn or even—although plainly unthinkable—copper coins, that suet would retain evidence of what had passed above.

Then it was that Kassim's crafty wife had passed the measure to Ali Baba's unsuspecting spouse. And when the measure was returned at first light upon the following morning (for Ali Baba's wife was always conscientious in such things, in case she might want to borrow that thing again), Kassim's wife immediately walked deep within her household's palatial yard to a point where she could no longer be seen across the common fence. Assured then that her plans would not be spied upon by her neighbors, she turned the measure over to discover, to her astonishment, not grain, or corn, or even copper, but a coin of the purest gold.

She had, Kassim further explained, immediately brought the news to her husband, as was the duty of every wife. And Kassim was most distressed, for he would never suspect that his brother would hold such a rich secret from his family, especially considering how Kassim was so much more familiar with the handling of money.

As this story was told, the woodcutter found himself increasingly pressed to pay attention solely to its details, as distressing as they were. For there was also the matter of Kassim's wife to draw his awareness. Indeed, she was most attentive toward her husband. But, as she nibbled upon Kassim's ear, her eyes appeared to be fixed upon Ali Baba.

"Surely," Kassim continued, "we thought it was some oversight that he did not come to us immediately with the news."

"We know that dear Ali Baba would have no secrets from his family!" his wife added, somehow managing to talk and pout at the same instant.

The woodcutter experienced a chill that had absolutely nothing to do with the season of the year. And indeed, there was a part of Ali Baba that wished to have no secrets from this woman at all.

Still had Kassim and his wife discovered the gold, and further had Kassim the might of his master, One Thumb, that he might draw upon should anyone become difficult, and even further still was that pout that the woodcutter could not bring himself to turn away from. What could Ali Baba do but tell them the story of the forty thieves, the cavern of gold, and the words of power?

Kassim listened most carefully, and asked certain questions that would never have occurred to the woodcutter, questions that left little doubt that he was aware of the most intimate habits of thieves.

"Very well," Kassim replied when Ali Baba was finished. "I am most pleased with your admission." And, from the tonality of his speech, Ali Baba could fathom that, had his brother not been pleased, there could have been a distinct possibility of blood and broken bones, despite any considerations of familial relations.

"I have a small task that I must perform for my master," Kassim further stated. "But, upon the morrow, I shall visit this cavern, and see if you are telling your dear brother the truth." He thereupon smiled, an action which somehow reminded the woodcutter more of winter wind than summer sun.

So it was that Kassim and his wife disappeared from their side of the fence. And Ali Baba returned to the solace of his wife and his maidservant, Marjanah. Indeed, even his wife could sense the intensity of the woodcutter's dismay, for her remarks of "Oh, woe!" did not seem to be delivered with the usual force. Marjanah, for her part, remarked quite reasonably that, since Kassim and his wife had made no inquiry about the location and amount of that treasure Ali Baba had already acquired, that treasure was at least reasonably safe.

The woodcutter, alas, would not be comforted. Once a man of Kassim's moral standing discovered the location of some gold, his thoughts would not rest until that gold had been transferred to his safekeeping. And to further complicate matters, that man Kassim worked for employed many others who were of the same moral standing and thought processes as his brother. Little had Ali Baba realized when the wise men said, "Present presently, departed henceforth," they had been speaking about his gold.

But there were more miracles in Ali Baba's future than those two words, "Open, Sesame!"; for there then transpired a truly astonishing sequence of events. Although the actual story came to Ali Baba at a somewhat later time, and in a somewhat different manner, still might I now relate the exact nature of those events for the sake of continuity.

So it was that, when next the cock crowed, the woodcutter's brother, Kassim, proceeded without sleep, as was often the habit of one who performed so much of his work beneath the cloak of night, to that place in the forest that Ali Baba had earlier described. And, acquisitive man that he was, Kassim took with him a dozen mules and two fine horses to help him carry the load that he planned to so easily acquire.

Now, although Kassim and Ali Baba were truly brothers, they seemed opposed in all things beyond parentage, as if a tree might bear a pear in one season and a fig in the next. So it was that, when Kassim reached the clearing where stood the great rock, he marched straight to its middle, without first observing the surrounding area for unfriendly persons, as the woodcutter surely would. And, once in the clearing, Kassim tied his mounts to the most convenient trees, rather than secreting his animals as Ali Baba had done on that earlier day. After all, in his many years as enforcer of the will of One Thumb, he had become unused to the pursuit of subtlety. Kassim therefore completed his tasks in the easiest manner possible, and then strode forward to the great rock, saying in a voice so loud that it must have carried across half the forest:

"Open, Sesame!"

And, as magic spells do not discriminate according to the personal attributes of those who speak them, so did the boulder roll aside with an impressive, ground-shaking rumble. Kassim was much pleased that his brother had spoken the truth, and resolved to stop thinking about those punishments he had been prepared to inflict had the woodcutter's words proved untrue. He strode forward into the cavern that had been revealed, and after a quick "Close, Sesame!," for even one as careless as Kassim knew enough not to leave his back exposed, he followed his brother's direction to that room that was filled, floor to ceiling, with gold and precious stones and other objects of great value.

Kassim pulled aside the tapestry, and was overwhelmed for more than a moment. There was more gold here in this one room than he had witnessed in all of One Thumb's score of hiding places! Why had Kassim not thought to bring fifty mules and ten horses?

Still, Kassim was sensible enough not to chide himself too freely. Should he ever dispose of all the wealth he could now carry, he might always return for more. And should even that possibility fail him, he could easily extort additional large sums from such a spineless eel as his brother. So it was that he cheerfully went about his task of filling the many large sacks he had carried herein for this very purpose.

The hours fled one upon another as he fulfilled this pursuit, but all tasks must have an ending, and so it was that Kassim at last had filled every sack to bursting, and carried them from the treasure room out to the entranceway. All that was left to do was roll aside the stone and load up his pack animals, and he should be a wealthy man for the rest of his days.

He opened his mouth to say the magic words, but produced a yawn instead. So involved with his work had he been that only at that moment did he realize how great a fatigue had stolen over him. But he had no time to sleep, for the sun must be close to setting upon the other side of the enchanted boulder, and he knew from long experience that great riches were best transported late at night. He attempted to rub the sleep out of his eyes, and looked forward to the great stone, and quickly said two words before another yawn might overtake him.

"Open, Barley!"

He waited patiently for the rock to roll outside, but nothing transpired.

Kassim frowned. There was something amiss. Perhaps his fatigue was causing his voice to waver, and he was not issuing his command with the proper authority. Therefore, he repeated himself, this time almost shouting the words.

"Open, Barley!"

The great rock was as still as before. It was at that moment that Kassim had a horrible thought. Perhaps he had misremembered the magical incantation. He turned and looked fondly again upon all the gold. Could a day of counting uncountable riches cause a man to take leave of his senses?

Well, Kassim had been in far more delicate situations than this. If the incantation did not concern itself with barley, surely it was some other common agricultural product. And, now that he thought of it, that product had to be very common; so common that it would be simple to forget, even for one with as great a mental capacity as Kassim. He must then force himself to think in a more common way than was his usual.

"Open, Oats!" he therefore announced. The boulder did not acknowledge these words, either. Kassim did his best to concentrate, which seemed increasingly difficult when his head was heavy from fatigue and his eyes were full of gold and precious stones. Perhaps, he considered, he was still not being common enough.

"Open, Beans!"

No, that did not sound at all right. Kassim felt a vague sense of unease, as if, in this boulder before him, he had finally found something too large for his powers of persuasion. And yet, how many grains and foodstuffs could there be? He would therefore call out everything he knew that might come from a farm. Surely, one of them would work! He bade the stone then to roll away in the name of Rye, Millet, Chick-pea, Maize, Buckwheat, Corn, Rice, and Vetch.

Throughout it all, the boulder remained stubbornly still and silent. Kassim thought with panic that he had exhausted every agricultural product known to civilization. And even he was not too sure about the exact nature of vetch. Mayhaps, he considered in his rising panic, it was not the second half of the pronouncement that he had gotten wrong. Could it be that he had misremembered the verb part of the incantation?

"Unlock, Barley!" he quickly shouted.

As you would suspect, those words also elicited no response.

Kassim's thoughts ran as fast as a rabbit might scurry to its hole. What were other words that might mean "open"?

"Unbind, Barley! Unfasten, Barley! Undo, Barley!"

Kassim had by now begun to doubt that he could remember anything. What if barley were indeed not the correct word?

"Unfasten, Oats!" he therefore called. And then "Unclasp, Oats!" and "Undo, Oats!" and so forth and so on.

Kassim found twin emotions rising within him as one invocation after another failed to produce results. One was that alarm that he might not be able to immediately remember the correct words, and would be trapped here. The second, greater feeling soon threatened to overwhelm the first, however, and that was an anger at his brother, Ali Baba. How could that pitiful excuse for a woodcutter put his brother in such a situation? Did not Ali Baba have any family feeling? Perhaps Kassim would again reconsider his plans for his brother, and, after he had freed himself from this temporary prison, would torture Ali Baba for the inconvenience the woodcutter had caused.

Kassim's anger gave him strength. Sooner or later, he would have to speak every imaginable combination!

"Peel, Corn! Ventilate, Vetch!"

Somehow, as he shouted, the panic again overtook the anger, and he found himself calling out wildly, one empty incantation after another. "Disengage, Beans! Extricate, Oats! Unclasp, Sesame!"

And on and on he called, until he no longer had a voice, but only a whisper. Had he not called out every possible combination? When he was free of this place, his brother would surely pay for putting Kassim through such discomfort.

Then, when Kassim could cry out no more, and had at last paused to regain his breath, the boulder rolled aside, as if it had finally made the decision to open of its own accord.

It would have been a much more favorable occurrence if that had indeed been the case, but, unfortunately for the continued well-being of the woodcutter's brother, there was someone on the other side of the mystic passage. To be more direct in my description, there were almost forty someones. And, from the color of their robes and what Kassim could see of their fierce countenances behind their even fiercer beards, they did not appear to be of a particularly friendly bent.

As large and ugly as these almost forty men appeared, there was one among them that appeared even larger and uglier than all the rest. And as he strode forward, Kassim realized that this must be their leader.

"What have we found here?" the leader called out, and Kassim found himself even less happy that the other man had opened his mouth, for his teeth were revealed as jagged and rotting, as if he practiced the eating of raw flesh.

Kassim knew what One Thumb would do if he found someone in a treasure room. And, judging by appearances alone, compared to this rough bandit captain, One Thumb might be mistaken for a benevolent father figure! Kassim prepared to be run through with any number of swords.

Instead, the bandit leader paused. "Wait a moment! How many thieves do we total at this very minute?"

Kassim would not play their counting game. He was a man of action. If he were to die, it would be quickly and brutally. In this case, at least, did Kassim get what he had desired.

He ran forward, attempting to burst through the almost forty men. He knocked back the burly leader, but the chief was quick of hand and foot, and grabbed Kassim by the jaw as almost thirty-nine other men simultaneously drew their scimitars.

Thus did Kassim find a true assessment for his actions. By being trapped not only within the cave but within his panic, he had but suffered only the first part of his punishment. Death was the second.

And even worse was that final part of his punishment, which would come after death.

As Kassim waited for the judgment of almost forty swords, that descended in such a fashion that they might almost be guided by a single hand, he thought he heard another noise, originating from his posterior. Yet there was nothing to his back but the rough wall of the cave.

It was an errant thought, but the last one he ever expected. What creature might hide within the wall of a cave and chuckle?

♦

Chapter the Fifth,
in which we discover how six parts may be
greater than a whole.

Ali Baba was not a happy woodcutter. So worried was he, in fact, that he was unable to go about his daily business, and instead hid from the midday heat within whatever shade his inadequate dwelling might provide. And yet, the more he hid away from this world, the more he dwelled upon his worries. His secret was no longer safe, for his less-than-honest brother, Kassim, had pried out the whereabouts of the treasure hoard. He thought again of those thirty-nine thieves who guarded that hoard. If they had not already been persuaded to pursue Ali Baba for his earlier pilfering, he had no doubt they would become truly enraged at their loss at the hands of Kassim. For Ali Baba was a frugal man, even in the acquisition of gold. The same could not be said for Kassim.

Kassim was not the sort of man to practice moderation in any part of his life. No matter how great his prize upon his return, he and his wife would have it spent and gone before summer would follow spring.

Ali Baba found himself sweating unduly for a man who was seated in shade.

Nor was Kassim the most discreet of men, and his many friends of low repute would be all too willing to discover the source of his newfound wealth.

Alas, Ali Baba thought, what he might give for a breeze.

Perhaps if he could close his eyes and doze until his brother's return. But every time his lids were shut, the woodcutter had visions of dwindling piles of gold. Should his dream gaze turn in one direction, wheeled carts filled with riches were carried off by Kassim and One Thumb. Should his dream self turn away, it was only to witness his gold removed by those forty black-robed men of the forest.

Hour passed upon hour, and still Ali Baba could find no

solution, his problems seeming more like a pit of quicksand you might never escape. And still was there no conclusion to the tale. The woodcutter saw evening turn to darkest night, and yet no brother appeared to boast of his newfound riches. Ali Baba blinked, and he swore he saw the first faint glow of morning, but there was not a single boisterous or obnoxious sound as usually accompanied Kassim's arrival.

Perhaps, Ali Baba realized, he might have to face a completely different problem. No! His entire upbringing at his brother's side rebelled at such a thought. Surely, Kassim would have been clever enough to elude the band of thieves.

But then, even Ali Baba had been discovered by that nefarious band, and Ali Baba, unlike Kassim, was wise to the ways of the woods.

A pounding upon the fence roused the woodcutter from his reverie.

"Wake up, O noble brother-in-law," came the husky yet mellifluous tones of the wife of Kassim. "You do not wish to sleep while a member of your family is in peril." After a pause, she added in a softer tone, "And, I should think, it is such a tragedy to sleep alone."

"Sleeping?" For some reason, Ali Baba found himself the slightest bit discomfited by this exchange. He further found himself perspiring all over again. "I was not sleeping," he insisted when he recalled how to form a sentence. "Rather I was lost in thought." Now that the woodcutter had a moment to consider it, the dawn had arrived with remarkable abruptness.

"Would that I could be lost in a similar situation," the wife of Kassim murmured, then added, as if she suddenly remembered her station, "but your brother has not returned from that adventure which you sent him upon. Surely, you must find him!"

Yes, Ali Baba thought. Once the situation was presented thus, it was obvious that such had to be his responsibility. He therefore pulled his eyes away from his brother's wife and went to tell his own wife of his obligation.

"Oh, woe!" she began upon receipt of the news. "Then you need to return again to that dread forest where you previously only barely managed to escape with your head still attached to your shoulders?"

Ali Baba supposed it was prudent of his wife to remind him of such things. It certainly did little to fan his enthusiasm, but a duty was a duty. So it was, with the coming of true dawn, that Ali Baba once again set out for that enchanted and dangerous destination where first he found his fortune. This time he brought but one mule, for, were he to carry something upon his return, it would not this time be large quantities of gold.

He arrived some time later at that unfortunate clearing in the forest, and discovered that all was silence. He could see no immediate evidence of his brother, or the many mounts Kassim had brought to help carry his riches. Upon closer examination of the dry earth upon the trails leading to this open glade, he did see the regular impressions of many mules from the same direction in which he had arrived. However, overlaying these calm markings at clearing's center were the heavier tracks of a great many galloping hooves. So great was the pummeling of the earth that Ali Baba could easily imagine these tracks were made by as many as forty mounts, ridden by as many as forty men in black.

Those forty or so men seemed to have disposed of Kassim's horses and mules. So, too, no doubt, had they disposed of Kassim. Still did Ali Baba have a moment of hope as he remembered his all-too-recent experiences with the brigands, including his very brief career as the fortieth thief. He realized that his brother's current state of health—indeed, his current state of existence—might have more to do with how many thieves were presently in the band than any behavior upon Kassim's part.

And yet all was quiet again. Whatever the thieves had accomplished, they seemed to have had no desire to tarry. Did that bode ill or well for the fate of Kassim? The woodcutter looked up at the boulder that guarded the entryway to the treasure. Were there secrets about his brother hidden within there as well? Whatever the consequences, Ali Baba had to know.

"Open, Sesame!" he repeated with some trepidation.

The boulder rolled away as it had before. As the enchanted rock moved, the woodcutter stood upon the balls of his feet, ready to spring away at the first sign of any trap. But the cavern beyond the rock seemed as deserted as the clearing about him.

Yet, as he approached the cavern, what hope he held quickly deserted the woodcutter, for Ali Baba could see other signs that all had not fared well for Kassim. Firstly, there appeared to be a deep reddish brown substance upon the path within; a deep reddish brown substance that reminded the Woodcutter's extremely active imagination of nothing so much as dried blood. And, as a second point, considering the extremely porous nature of the soil hereabouts, for such brown markings to remain there must have originally been an extreme quantity of deep reddish brown undried blood. Blood, no doubt, that had once resided inside the unfortunate Kassim.

Things were soon to become even more uncomfortable, for there next occurred a certain sequence of events that convinced Ali Baba he might not be alone within these ill-lit spaces. For as he strode by the deep brown path, something flopped in the lightless corner to his left. And he had taken but one hesitant step toward that first noise when something else shuffled to his right. He froze, not knowing which way to turn as a third noisemaker stomped immediately to his rear.

Ali Baba's mind was filled by unpleasant possibilities. While the primary gold-filled halls of this place were as awash with light as they were upon his first visit, always lit, it seemed, by torches that never expired, perhaps those thieves who had attacked Kassim still hid in the dim recesses of these caverns, waiting for another luckless victim. Or, even worse, maybe the enchantments that lurked in this cave went far beyond a simple "Open, Sesame!" Ali Baba realized he should have come better prepared for the worst of eventualities. Except for some small woodcutting tools that he always carried upon his person, he was defenseless.

Another flop, a second shuffle, and a further stomp were joined by the sound of something being dragged across the earth. Ali Baba looked about in a most agitated manner, but could discern nothing in the shadows that might take the shape of a man. Still could he hear the movements in four or five directions at once. Yet all the sounds seemed to emanate from positions quite close to the floor and near the edges of this ill-lit cavern, spaces that were indeed too small to hide anyone near his full growth. But what besides a man would make those sounds? Ali Baba had a sudden image of a dozen fearsome serpents surrounding him as they inexorably approached him from every direction. He remembered that odd noise he had heard when last he left the cavern. Why had he not warned his brother of this? Perhaps more important still, why had he not warned himself?

The woodcutter decided he could make no further discoveries of a healthy nature in this present location. He therefore moved quickly toward that further chamber where he had earlier discovered the gold.

But still on that day and in that place there were to be no simple solutions, for beyond the curtain that led to the treasure, Ali Baba heard a groan.

Then was he truly encircled. Still, were he to perish, he would do so in a manner that would make his profession proud. "Beware, O any who prowl hereabouts," he called in the gruffest voice he might manage considering the circumstances. "I have a hatchet, and I know how to use it!"

To his astonishment, a familiar voice came from the other side of the curtain. "Would you so threaten your poor brother? Or at least which pieces might remain of your poor brother?"

Ali Baba quickly drew aside the cloth that separated the rooms, and saw Kassim's head resting above a great pile of gold.

"Dear brother!" the woodcutter cried in great relief. "I feared I would never talk to you again. I had terrible visions of how the thieves might have mistreated and murdered you."

"Mistreated me?" Kassim replied darkly. "Murdered me? Yes, they have done both, and that is but the beginning!"

Ali Baba was truly confounded by this most recent utterance. Whatever had happened in this cavern, it seemed to have unhinged his brother's reason.

"Come," Ali Baba replied in the most reassuring of tones. "It cannot be as bad as that. I will free you from your golden prison and we will flee this accursed place."

To the woodcutter's astonishment, a bitter laugh burst forth from Kassim's lips. "You assume, then, that I have a body beneath this mouth?"

"How else could you talk to me thus?" Ali Baba responded quickly. "Being trapped in a mountain of gold has given you a fever."

Kassim's next response was much more sober. "In a sane world, perhaps that would be so. But my head stands alone to regard my folly, and the other parts of my body can but struggle to join it."

The woodcutter could only hope that, once he was free of his enchanted prison, Kassim would stop speaking nonsense. But once again was Ali Baba aware of those noises from the other room, except for two differences. All the noises now seemed to be behind him. And all of them were drawing closer.

"How could you possibly understand?" Kassim babbled onward. "This cavern has enchantments beyond the dreams of mortals." Once more came that bitter laugh. "Not that I should speak of mortality."

The sooner he had his brother out of here and under the healing rays of the sun, the better. "Speak no more in riddles," Ali Baba said. "I shall come forward and give you a hand."

"No, dear brother," was Kassim's reply. "In but a moment, I shall give me a hand of my own. If you might step aside?"

The woodcutter felt something, a small animal perhaps, pushing at his foot. He glanced down quickly, visions of serpents once again dancing behind his eyes.

Would that it had been a serpent! Ali Baba almost leapt to the roof of the cavern. By his foot, a hand crawled across the parched earth. Following that hand was an arm up to but not including the shoulder, for the crawling thing ended abruptly in bloody flesh and bone.

"What is this?" Ali Baba cried as he felt his reason flee to that same far place where his brother's had gone before.

"It is only a part of me," Kassim replied, and now his voice took on the tones of reason. "This is how I was tortured and killed by those villainous thieves, for I have been divided into six equal parts."

"Six—parts?" attempted Ali Baba, although he felt as though his throat had ceased to furnish air to his vocal cords. The hand, for its part, continued to drag the attached arm forward toward the pile of gold.

"Two arms, two legs, one head, one torso," Kassim calmly catalogued. "My head was left upon the pile of gold to serve as a warning to any who might trespass in these caverns. The rest of my parts have been scattered hither and yon throughout the cave."

"They left you littered about the cave?" Ali Baba asked in disbelief. Such an action did not appear to be in the best interests of good housekeeping.

"Their final act," Kassim remarked, the tone of his voice echoing the woodcutter's disbelief. "After they were done with me, the thieves appeared to be in an uncommon hurry to be gone again."

Ali Baba recalled that occurrence on the day before, and how quickly the thieves left after they had captured him. The brigands appeared to rush from conquest to conquest, although in this chamber alone they might have enough gold already stored to live in luxury for a hundred generations. Thus, he thought, was the madness that could come with great wealth.

Now, though, he must face quite another type of madness. He looked again to that part of his brother that could still communicate.

"Apparently," Kassim answered before a question could be asked, "nothing killed within this enchanted cavern truly dies." His brother's voice rose to a wail as he fully considered his fate. "I have been left by those vile cutthroats to rest in pieces!"

At this admonition, the woodcutter once again felt that great constriction in his throat. This truly was a horrible fate, the kind Ali Baba might wish upon no man, even his brother.

"I cannot leave you like this!" the woodcutter cried in sympathy. "Please tell me what must be done!"

With that, the head gave out a great sigh. "Indeed I cannot live like this. But I would like to be reassembled before I die."

Ali Baba stepped quickly out of the way as a foot and leg hopped on past him toward the pile of gold. His brother's request seemed most reasonable, considering the circumstances.

"Very well," Ali Baba replied. Still he realized, as a woodcutter, he had far more experience with chopping things apart than with putting them together. Therefore he asked: "Do you have any idea how I might accomplish this?"

The head nodded at the hands and feet that were gathering around the base of his golden pile. "I am afraid my torso is quite without any form of locomotion. If you would fetch it to go with the rest of me, I shall be grateful for the remainder of my days, which, my present situation granted, might be a very limited proposition." Kassim paused to sigh again.

His torso? Ali Baba inquired as to the exact present location of said torso, and was informed that it had been discarded in a corner of the outer room.

The woodcutter returned then to the outer chamber, and, now that he had been fully informed as to the nature of the strange noises emanating from dark corners, located Kassim's last missing part in no time. The way it flopped about in the shadows, it reminded the woodcutter of nothing so much as the world's largest dung beetle. Of course, as Ali Baba approached the thing, it looked more like the blood-soaked remains of a human form. This was, he reflected, not the most pleasant of tasks, and, come to consider it, what had his brother ever done for him?

Ali Baba took a deep breath in an attempt to quiet his fevered imagination. Bloody torso or giant dung beetle, it made no difference. As he had carried his family obligations this far, he might as well complete his task.

He therefore cast his glance about the room, until it fell upon a cluster of wicker baskets in one of the cavern's many recesses. He

chose a particularly large one, and, removing its lid, discovered
that it contained nothing but precious stones larger than goose
eggs. He tipped the basket over so that the many stones might roll
free, and then, being careful not to breathe in the vicinity of the
body part, rolled the torso into that space which the gems had
occupied.

He then carried the wicker basket back into the golden chamber
and, with great efficiency, loaded the various pieces of his brother
therein.

"Careful!" his brother called as Ali Baba dropped the head in
with the rest of the body. Kassim had always been the type to
criticize.

As Ali Baba was about to lift the basket and carry it from the
confines of this hill, he had a further and rather disturbing thought.
"But what happens, O Kassim, when we depart this cavern?" the
woodcutter asked with some doubt. "Will I kill you if I take you
hence?"

"Do you call this living?" was the head's forlorn reply. "If I
must die, let me do it somewhere else than here."

So did Ali Baba honor his brother's request, half carrying, half
dragging the now weighty wicker from the treasure room back into
the antechamber.

"You may wonder," Kassim mentioned casually as his parts
were being moved from room to room, "how I came to this pass."

Wonder? Ali Baba realized he had been too shocked by this
recent turn of events to wonder about much of anything. Still, he
would no doubt marvel at the manner in which his brother would
place the responsibility for his current condition squarely upon the
woodcutter's shoulders.

"It was my fault," Kassim admitted, to the woodcutter's
surprise. "I could not remember the magic words."

Ali Baba stopped dragging as he faced the boulder. "Simplicity
itself," he replied. At least this was one area where his brother
needed him enough to listen.

"Simplicity itself?" Kassim replied from within the basket. "I
don't remember *those* words at all. No wonder I was at a loss. I
thought the incantation had something to do with grain or some
such."

"No, no," Ali Baba answered. "Those are not the words!"
Apparently his brother Kassim was not prepared to listen, after all.
But before the woodcutter could make a further explanation, the
boulder began to roll of its own accord.

"Those are not the words and the boulder is moving?" Kassim asked skeptically. "It is not nice to fool a man who has recently been chopped into six pieces."

"I did not speak the magic words," Ali Baba replied flatly.

Ali Baba's tone robbed his brother's voice of skepticism. "But why did the rock—"

"Somebody else must have spoken them. Someone on the outside, desiring to come in."

The rock stopped rolling.

"Well, dear brother, at least we tried," Kassim said with a certain resignation. "Perhaps our two heads may have long conversations if they leave us both on top of the gold."

On top of the gold? Alas!

Ali Baba once again felt that constriction of the throat, as he suddenly had a vision of his life in pieces.

♦

Chapter the Sixth,
in which we learn
that one good thief deserves another.

Ali Baba looked at last within the space formerly occupied by the boulder. He was not in the least surprised to see it now occupied by black-clad thieves. What was surprising was that the thieves did not seem angry in the least. Instead, they appeared rather pleased by this current course of events.

"Aha!" said their leader in the most boisterous of tones. "See what we have found patiently awaiting our return. It is Number Forty, is it not?" The first thief took a step toward the woodcutter. "Or at least that is what we used to call you when last you graced our ignoble band."

Ali Baba was not sure what type of a response might be appropriate to such a greeting: a bow, a friendly hello, or a desperate plea to spare his life. His consternation, he was sure, came largely from not knowing the exact nature of event that might make this sort of thief this cheerful.

"We're very good at finding things," Thief Number One admitted grandly. "We are even better at taking things. That is why we are thieves. One should always know one's strengths." He waved at some of his fellows. "Dispose of the gold in the usual place."

Four of the thieves, each carrying a sack of moderate girth and weight, passed by Ali Baba on their way to the golden chamber. Their current profits seemed somewhat smaller than the last time the woodcutter had encountered this band. Still, he imagined that sort of variation of income came with their business.

The leader took another step toward Ali Baba. "We were very disappointed that you didn't come along with us. It is very good for you that you have decided to return to our group. Otherwise we would have to seek you out and murder you in some imaginative yet incredibly painful manner. That would be, of course, after we found you again in whatever place, however unlikely, that you might have foolishly chosen to hide. But, as I recall mentioning before, we are very good at finding things.'' Even as the other man approached him, Ali Baba became extremely aware of the amount of time expended by the first thief in toying with the hilt of his sword. ''And it is so difficult to find good thieves these days. As the wise thief says, those who do not squander do not seek.''

''Now, though, you are back where you belong.'' The chieftain was now so near that Ali Baba could smell the other man's breath upon his face. The woodcutter wondered if the food had spoiled before or after the thief had ingested it.

''Please do not quake,'' the thief continued. ''Your life is not forfeit. At least, not at the present moment.'' His smiling face was mere inches away from the woodcutter's own countenance. ''Oh, of course I might lop off a limb or two to teach an important lesson to my men. But we never waste a good thief.''

The leader of the brigands raised a hand, and was greeted by total silence. Not that Ali Baba had noticed any of them to be talking previously. But when the hand was raised, the others also ceased to breathe.

''Can someone tell me this man's current station within our ranks?'' the leader asked gently.

''Number Thirty-Nine, O chieftain!'' came the ragged call from about half the surrounding number.

''I never knew thieves were bright enough to count!'' came another voice close at hand.

''Oho!'' the first among thieves announced. ''Perhaps, as little as I like it, we may have to do some cutting upon our new recruit, after all. But then, a woodcutter should be more than familiar with cutting.''

But the very polite and even more frightened Ali Baba had not uttered a single word. So unnerved was he, in fact, that it took him a moment to determine the exact source of the other voice.

''So,'' that extremely unwelcome voice chided again, ''still letting your sword do the talking rather than your wit? Why, of course, it is as obvious as that very large nose that graces your countenance! Could the reason be that you have no wit?''

With that remark, the leader's complexion went from a deep olive to an even more unattractive purple. ''Cut? Did I say, however reluctantly, that we would cut? I meant cuts, in the plural, and dozens of them at that! They will be small ones at first, but rest assured they shall grow in severity and pain!''

But Ali Baba was no longer paying great attention to the extent of those threats against his person, for he realized, with horror, that the critical voice was emanating from his brother in the basket!

"Cuts?" his brother's voice scoffed with the most derisive of laughs. "As I said, here is a mind totally lacking in imagination. It is obvious that a man of your limited intellect can think of nothing new, but cannot you unearth some idea new enough that it does not seem to decay upon your lips?"

"How dare you?" the first thief demanded of the woodcutter as he drew his sword. "My reluctance for bloodshed is disappearing completely."

"But," uttered Ali Baba, the presence of a sharp scimitar finally prompting him to find his own voice, "it was not I who spoke!"

"It is true, O captain!" another of the thieves pointed out. "The voice is of a different timbre altogether, and this man's lips do not—"

The thief paused abruptly as he found his leader's sword thrust with his innards. The first among thieves lifted a booted foot and pushed the now silent underling off his weapon, then wiped the scimitar upon his robes. Ali Baba noted that blood didn't show at all on the black fabric. This detail did nothing to put the woodcutter's mind at ease.

"As much as I hate impudence," the leader explained in the softest of tones, "I hate it even more when people interrupt. You have been promoted to Number Thirty-eight. Many thieves have to wait months for such an increase in status." He paused to consider his statement. "Well, perhaps more properly weeks"— he glanced at the brigands around him —"or maybe days. At the least, hours. In any event, you should be very proud that you received advancement within our ranks, and I hope the thought gives you comfort during your prolonged and hideous death."

"But effendi!" Ali Baba called in the sort of voice he generally reserved for high officials and his wife's family. "I have not spoken a word. The sharp tongue is that of my brother!"

"And it is not the only thing about here which is sharp," Kassim added from his basket home. "You cannot imagine how uncomfortable it is to have bone shards poking in your ear."

The leader of the thieves took a step away as he at last realized the truth of Ali Baba's words. He pointed his newly cleaned sword at the basket. "You have brought an accomplice!"

"It is wise of you to step away," Kassim stated in a low voice. "All sane men beware the vengeance of the wicker basket!"

"You mock me!" The leader of the thieves was becoming far more agitated than Ali Baba had ever seen before. "I am not mocked! I am—I am—" He waved his sword about, searching for the word.

"Gently chided?" one of the thieves suggested.

The chief's sword came down abruptly upon he who had spoken last. "No, that is not it, either. Do I hear any other suggestions?" Besides the sound of a body falling to earth, there was now nothing but silence. The first thief turned back to Ali Baba. "You are now Number Thirty-seven. And your friend in the basket is Number Thirty-eight."

"In my present state," Kassim remarked, "I could be Numbers Thirty-eight through Forty-Three."

The bandit chieftain glared at the wicker. "Does your friend so dearly wish to feel my sword?"

"You've already done that," was Kassim's dismissive reply.

" I have?" The chief's eyes flashed with the thought of that blood he so dearly wished to spill. "Well, perhaps then I will have to do some cutting!"

"That old thing?" A sound came from within the wicker that could only be a yawn. "You've done that, too!"

"*What?*" The first thief once again wiped off his sword. Apparently, he desired that it be clean for every use. "Enough of this foolishness. I will kill you immediately!"

"That's been done as well!" Kassim complained loudly. "Can't you come up with *anything* new?"

The scimitar's point quivered mere inches from the wicker. "The man who talks to me has already been cut and killed?" The chief of thieves frowned. "Who could our mystery victim be?"

In this instance, it was Kassim's time to sound surprised. "You do not remember? You are even more witless than I imagined."

"Well, you have to understand," Thief Number One began apologetically, "in the course of a day I kill so many—witless?" His voice rose. "You dare to call me witless? I shall do worse than kill you! I shall—I shall separate your head from your body!"

"Decapitated?" Kassim replied in a voice that implied that he was barely even interested anymore. "Too late. You've done it already. But why do I bother to mention that again?"

"I have?" The brigand paused to look down at his scimitar. "Perhaps I have been getting too excessive with my everyday assassinations. I know! I shall prop your severed head up somewhere and—''

"Leave it there as mute warning for any others who might cross our band?" Kassim finished the other's sentence. "Already been done. Have you thought of retiring and allowing someone to run your band who does not have cobwebs upon the brain?"

"Retire? Cobwebs? Brain?" The leader gave an odd little laugh and made meaningless feints in the air with his scimitar as if the spirit of thievery had left him completely. He took a deep breath and looked back at the woodcutter. "I know what is amiss. Our band is not at its full complement! Events never proceed at the proper pace unless there are exactly forty thieves!"

He sheathed his scimitar. "We can lose no more of our number! No matter what the basket says, he is one of us!" He pointed a finger at the wicker by the woodcutter's side. "But, as soon as we recruit Thief Number Forty-one, beware!"

In this instance, Ali Baba noticed, it was the first among thieves who was quivering.

"Find horses for them," the bandit chieftain ordered. "It is time to be off!"

A pair of thieves rushed forward to handle the wicker as a half dozen of the others rushed outside—no doubt, Ali Baba surmised, to gather the mounts.

"If you would follow me?" The chieftain, once again filled with unctuous good cheer, waved to Ali Baba. The woodcutter could see no other course of action. Kassim, however, was not going to easily accept this new twist upon his already strange destiny.

"How can I be a thief?" he demanded as his basket was hoisted into the air. "I am cut into six pieces. I'll have to check my torso, but I don't even think I'm breathing."

"That is no objection," their leader paused to say. "He is still talking. The first rule of a good thief is: If you can talk, you can steal."

"We have very low entry requirements," whispered one of the men who was handling the basket.

"Of course," cautioned the other man with the basket, "the benefits of the job aren't that extensive, either."

With that, the two men hurried to follow their leader, who had boldly stridden out into the sunlight beyond the cave. Ali Baba did his best to join them quickly, not so much for fear of the chieftain's reprisals as not to be in the wrong place when someone mentioned "Close, Sesame!"

And, true to his premonition, the woodcutter was barely free of the rock before those two fateful words were again uttered. He noticed that all around him took an involuntary step backward as the great rock rumbled back into its place to guard the cavern beyond.

The bandit leader chortled, no doubt sensing a future filled with high adventure. "Men! Grab our newest recruit. He will not get away so easily this time. Tie him to a horse!"

With that, Ali Baba found himself grabbed roughly and dragged over to one of the steeds, a fine, dark stallion with a hint of white between his nostrils.

"And what of our other addition?" inquired one of the men with the basket.

The chieftain stopped his hand before it could again draw the scimitar. He mumbled something deep in his beard, and stamped his boot heel deep into the earth. At the very least, the task of keeping his band forty strong seemed a great burden.

Emboldened by their leader's uncharacteristic caution, the man who had last spoken continued. "It is very difficult for a wicker basket to ride anything."

The chieftain's hand once again started for his weapon. He bit his knuckles instead.

"And you might recall," quickly added the bold speaker, "that on our recent raid we ran into certain—difficulties." He stumbled over the last word, realizing perhaps from the current expression upon the face of his chieftain that he might be able even now to go to a point where there was no choice but the scimitar. "I only meant to mention that we are somewhat short on horses. At the moment, of course. I am sure it is the most temporary of problems."

"Very well," their leader replied after his underling had finally finished. He waved his bloody knuckles in dismissal. "Tie them both to the horse!"

The lesser thieves went about their work quickly and diligently, so that Ali Baba and the wicker basket containing Kassim were trussed together atop the horse's saddle. So firmly was he tied, in fact, that the woodcutter could move neither foot nor finger.

"We have done as you have bidden, O great chieftain!" the thieves called out when their work was complete.

That was precisely what their leader wanted to hear. He quickly mounted his own stallion and lifted his right hand above his head.

"We are off, to strike fear into the hearts of the honest! Thieves! After me!"

With that, thirty-six thieves galloped quickly away, leaving behind one horse, one man, and one basket.

Ali Baba did not care for the present situation. He had once again not followed the bandit leader's direction, and that particular chieftain seemed to sport the sort of temperament which one did not wish to cross upon frequent occasion. On the other hand, the woodcutter had a further problem which he proceeded to speak aloud. "How do you get a horse to move when you are so thoroughly and entirely trussed?"

"I believe," replied his brother from within the basket, "that I have a free hand."

◆

Chapter the Seventh,
in which Kassim attempts
to pull himself together.

So it was that Kassim managed to move one of his hands in such a way as to sufficiently push aside the lid of the basket, so that his hand might crawl through, much as a small rodent might emerge from a hole he has gnawed in a sack. Then did that hand have to feel about the knots that held his brother captive, and unravel them largely by touch, for the view of Kassim's head was largely obstructed by the wicker.

As difficult as this process sounds as I relate it here today, know that, in actuality, the process was ten times more formidable than that. So it was, by the time Ali Baba and Kassim were free of their fetters, the band of thieves was some hours distant. It was therefore far too late to follow the other men of that disreputable group. Both brothers also agreed that it would be an equal folly to wait here at the cavern for the bandits' return, for there was no knowing how long it might take for that to transpire, or indeed, to predict the mood of the bandits upon their rearrival.

At last, the two agreed that there was nothing to do but return to their homes and pray they would hear no more of thieves or outrageous riches ever again. Of course, life is never as simple as that.

So it was that they shared the horse as they returned to their homes in the city, the rope, though removed from Ali Baba, still wrapped around the wicker in such a way as to keep the basket secure. And, as they traveled, Kassim reflected upon his fate.

"I should die at any time now," he said. And then, some time later: "Really, if you think upon it, I have been cut into six pieces. Certainly that is enough difficulty so that I might expire." There then elapsed some moments of silence, after which Kassim mentioned: "I should be drawing my last breath at any moment now. Not, that I think on it, that I am actually breathing."

And further did his ruminations go in a similar vein, to such an extent that it would do no good to repeat them here, for, truth be known, even a patient man such as Ali Baba began to find them tedious.

But, even within a great field of tedium, a meticulous man can find a kernel of truth. So was it that the woodcutter's thoughts dwelled upon the magical nature of the cavern that they had so recently quit; that same cavern where his brother had met what should have been his demise.

Perhaps one carried the magic with one, no matter where one went. Indeed, Ali Baba remembered how he had used "Open, Sesame!" to unlock his gate. It was as if, once he had seen the magic work upon the gateway to that cave, he was able to carry that spell with him back to the city, where it lost none of its potency. Could that same sort of magical potency be given to his brother as well? Once granted this spell of life, perhaps the six portions of Kassim were destined to remain separate but lively for all eternity.

Ali Baba therefore interrupted his brother's mumblings with this conjecture, but his brother did not appear to be overly cheered by the thought.

"Forever doomed to be six parts, dumped in a basket?" he wailed. "What have I done with my poor life to deserve such as this?"

Ali Baba had a few ideas on this account as well, concerning his brother's relation to the notorious One Thumb, and the errands Kassim would perform under the cloak of deepest night. Then, of course, there was his brother's folly in completely forgetting the magic words that would free him from the cavern.

But Ali Baba decided that his brother had had enough trouble for one day, and should not have to hear a recounting of his sins at present. Besides, if Kassim was going to spend the rest of his existence in a basket, there would be no way he could depart should Ali Baba decide to complain to him at length at some future time. In certain ways, the woodcutter thought, pleasant thoughts could come from the greatest hardships.

There was, however, a further matter that Ali Baba decided he should discuss with his brother more immediately, before such a situation should arise again. And that was the matter of causing insult to those people who were eager to use large swords.

His brother was not sympathetic. "What can they do to me that they have not already done? Dice me?"

"I was thinking rather," the woodcutter chided in the most gentle and brotherly of fashions, "of what they would do to *me*."

"I did not consider that possibility."

His brother, Ali Baba thought, never did.

"I will have to hold my tongue," his brother continued to the woodcutter's surprise. "Well, not literally, of course. My tongue is still more or less where it should be. Not that anything else is. Still, should I be truly angry, who knows what I might be capable of?" Kassim laughed ruefully. "Being cut up into six pieces and furthermore carried around in a wicker basket does change my perspective upon many things."

Ali Baba was silent for a long moment. This was a remarkable admission upon Kassim's part.

"What will my wife think?" murmured Kassim as he continued in this uncharacteristic vein. "All my parts still remain. She might be somewhat upset, however, with their present arrangement."

At least, the woodcutter ruminated, his own wife would not have the worst of things to be woeful about for a change. So it was that the two brothers continued on in silence while their horse proceeded toward the city, as day turned to evening, and evening to a star-filled night.

They reached Ali Baba's gate in those early morning hours when nothing is awake save those small animals of the night and the occasional dog who wishes to tell the world about those small animals. The woodcutter therefore did not wish to again disturb his wife, and so went about opening his gate in the alternate fashion that he had so recently learned.

Ali Baba therefore said in a voice both quiet and clear: "Open, Sesame!"

"Wait a moment," his brother protested. "I'm losing my lid!"

Ali Baba glanced behind to see that his brother did indeed speak the truth. Therefore, not only did the gate before him unlock and open in response to the magic words, but the lid of the wicker basket jerked about as if it would fly off the basket completely. The woodcutter realized that, in future, these magic words would have to be spoken very carefully.

Yet, after a brief struggle, in which it appeared that both lid and Kassim's hands would go flying away, the various portions of Ali Baba's brother prevailed, and the wicker basket was still once more. Ali Baba therefore urged the horse forward into his courtyard through the now open gate.

Despite the hour, his wife and maidservant awaited him inside.

"Oh, woe!" his wife greeted him. "So great was my worry about your safety that I could get no rest. And dear, noble Marjanah has elected to wait up with me for your return."

Ali Baba nodded, for in this he knew the true nature of things. When his wife was in one of her moods, no one slept in the household. But most assuredly, his wife would rejoice when he told her of the fate he so narrowly avoided at the hands of the fearsome brigands.

He opened his mouth to speak, but received no opportunity to do so.

"Oh, woe!" his wife added as she saw there was no second man upon the horse. "My husband returns alone in the middle of the night!"

"No, no," the woodcutter reassured her, for he wished to conclude this business as quickly and quietly as possible. "Kassim is with me."

"Oh, woe!" was his wife's immediate reply. "My husband returns with Kassim in the middle of the night! But where is your ne'er-do-well sibling?"

Ali Baba glanced back at the basket. "Well, I did not state that I had brought back a whole Kassim—"

His wife instantly grasped the meaning of his words. "Oh, woe! My husband returns with Kassim in pieces in the middle of the night!"

"That's not to say that he's dead, exactly—" Ali Baba once again attempted to begin an explanation.

"Oh, woe!" his wife rapidly remarked. "My husband returns with Kassim not quite dead even though he is in pieces in the middle of the night!"

Ali Baba stopped himself before he might make any further attempts at explanation, for, with every few words he produced, his wife would cry out at greater length and volume than she had even the time before. Should she continue to bewail in such a voice, she would wake up not only the immediate neighborhood but this entire quarter of the city. He therefore dismounted his horse, and stated calmly: "If you would help me to remove this basket, we might take the remains of Kassim—"

"Oh, woe!" she again interrupted. "My husband has ruined a perfectly good basket filled with the pieces of the not-quite-dead Kassim in the middle—"

But with that, the clever and kind-spirited Marjanah stepped forward to intervene. "I shall take that basket, master," she said in that voice as sweet as spring nectar, "and we shall find a suitable place for the unfortunate Kassim." So it was once again Ali Baba's clever slave saved the night. For, as anyone who has ever heard a tale teller knows, without the intervention of clever slaves we should all die of our own stupidity.

Ali Baba breathed a sigh of great relief. With Marjanah taking charge of his enchanted brother, mayhaps he might at last be able to obtain some much needed rest. Even his wife seemed less woeful as their servant bustled the wicker basket toward their insubstantial dwelling place.

A new voice stopped the woodcutter before he could travel another pace.

"O most noble brother-in-law, what news of my Kassim?"

Ali Baba decided he would have to manage this quickly, before his wife could produce another "Oh, woe." He therefore clapped his hands so that Marjanah would bring the basket, calling: "You shall have your answer in a moment."

"But where is my Kassim?" his wife inquired.

"I am here," Kassim's voice emanated from the basket, "more or less." Marjanah lifted up the basket so that Kassim's wife might better examine it.

The wife frowned. "I remember you as being somewhat taller."

Kassim then quickly described his fate, including a version of Ali Baba's theory on why he was still alive.

"Most interesting," replied his wife, who seemed somewhat taken aback by the course of events. "You will forgive me, O husband, if I inquire if there are any parts missing."

"To my knowledge," Kassim replied boldly, "I am all in here. Every bit of me."

His wife bit her lower lip. Ali Baba wished his own wife might become such a lip-biter!

"This could be interesting," Kassim's wife mused. "It might provide some much needed variety." She accepted the basket from Marjanah and departed with the strangest of smiles.

If only Ali Baba's wife might show a little bit of that enthusiasm!

But there could be no more conjecture on what should and what should not, for now that the basket was out of his hands, Ali Baba felt his strength drain away as well, and so immediately retired to sleep the sleep of the truly exhausted.

But his eyes were to be opened much too soon by his usually sympathetic maidservant.

"Master!" Marjanah called from the doorway to his sleeping chamber. "There is something you must know!"

Even as the woodcutter awoke, he resolved that he would not be cross with his servant. After escaping from a band of murderous bandits and rescuing what was left of his brother, any other news he might receive would be welcome.

"What is it, child?" he therefore called in a calm and reasonable tone as he squinted in the early morning sunshine.

"When I was upon my morning errands," Marjanah replied with a seriousness that belied her tender years, "I came upon a man dressed in black, much like you have described the thieves you encountered."

Ali Baba felt the first pangs of doubt, before remembering what he had resolved. There were undoubtedly many men in black who traversed the streets of this city every day. "It is nothing to worry about," he therefore replied.

But Marjanah's worry would not be stopped that easily. "He was asking many questions," she further asserted.

This time, the pangs of doubt were gone almost as soon as they arrived. How, Ali Baba reasoned, could people make sense of the world unless they sometimes asked questions? How easy life could be when you were serious about your resolutions.

"It is nothing to worry about," he said agian.

"He was," she added, "asking after anyone who had been recently cut into six pieces."

It was then that Ali Baba realized there were some resolutions that were impossible to keep.

♦

*Chapter the Eighth,
in which Ali Baba learns
that things are not always as they appear,
or don't appear.*

That most recent revelation was far from the woodcutter's only worry. Before he could even properly consider the information that Marjanah had imparted to him, there came a loud knocking upon his ramshackle gate.

Had the black-robed thieves found him this quickly? Ali Baba jumped from his repose and rushed about his inadequate dwelling for some means to defend himself, at last deciding upon his trusted axe as the best weapon available.

The knocking came again, perhaps even more pronounced than before. No matter how hard he leaned against his side of the gate, he could not remove the quaver from his voice. "Who is it that requests entrance?"

"This is One Thumb!" came the gruff reply. "And *I* ask the questions!"

One Thumb? That was the nefarious employer of his brother, Kassim. But what would one of such bad reputation want with a humble woodcutter? Had Kassim already spoken with his employer before this recent unpleasantness? Had Kassim and One Thumb exchanged words, and could one of those words have been "gold"?

Ali Baba decided it would be for the best if he were to exercise continued caution. The quaver was still there as he spoke again:

"What is it that I may do for you?"

"That's a question!" was One Thumb's enraged response. "I ask the questions! Lackeys! Break down the gate!"

Ali Baba barely had time to leap aside before his ill-constructed gate had been reduced to splinters. Two men wearing ostentatious robes encrusted with gems stepped over those wooden fragments where once a gate had been, their scimitars drawn and their eyes hidden deep beneath their shadowed caftans.

"There!" one of the two called as he spotted Ali Baba. "The questioner!"

Two swords pointed to him as the men quickly approached. There was no way the woodcutter could defend himself against such men as these! Ali Baba immediately dropped the axe, only to find himself pinned against that fence he shared with his brother's household.

"Ah," announced another voice from the direction of what had once been a gate, "I see that our questioner has been reprimanded. A simple reminder, my friend. The next step after reprimand is removal."

The woodcutter looked beyond the swords to regard the one known as One Thumb.

Now, Ali Baba had seen Kassim's employer upon occasion in the past, at times when that authority would attend a festive gathering at his brother's house, or discreet other occasions when it behooved One Thumb's organization to uses Kassim's dwelling for the questioning and eventual removal of certain unfortunate individuals. Still was it a shock to view this man now at close quarters, especially after Ali Baba had spent so much recent time among thieves who were lean-muscled riders of the wild. In comparison to those individuals, who resembled nothing so much as dark reeds in the wind, this man now before the woodcutter looked as if he might have devoured the entire city and still had room for a sweet cake. Ali Baba knew from his brother's talk that One Thumb was not a man of moderation in any circumstance, but his girth was even further emphasized by his habit of always wearing robes of spotless white.

"Now we shall see who asks the questions!" the enormous individual rumbled. Ali Baba's one-legged chicken hopped away in fright as One Thumb lumbered across the insignificant expanse of the woodcutter's property.

"Now!" One Thumb demanded of the woodcutter. "Kassim!"

Ali Baba considered for one reckless instant that he might inquire precisely what One Thumb wished to know about his brother. The problem with this approach was that, in order to proceed with any inquiry, the woodcutter would have had to frame a question. And One Thumb had already made it extremely clear how he felt upon that issue.

Ali Baba, therefore, said nothing.

"He does not speak," One Thumb remarked in a voice of total calm. "Perhaps he is not the spineless piece of offal that his brother so often described.'' He smiled at the woodcutter. ''We are not always as others describe us. I know how bad feelings can run in families. I had many of my own toward my parents and siblings, before I killed them all!'' His smile vanished; the moment of camaraderie had come to an abrupt end. ''But you have not answered me.''

Ali Baba had been unaware there had been a question. Perhaps, he thought, if he simply made up a question of his own and gave that an answer, he could at least partially satisfy One Thumb.

''Yes, Kassim is my brother,'' he began.

''I do not wish to hear what I know already!'' One Thumb demanded. He shook a hand free from his blindingly white robes. The hand was the size of a small dog. It was also thumbless.

''Specifics!'' the large man instructed.

Specifics? thought Ali Baba. But, from what Kassim's employer had already mentioned, they had to be specifics with which One Thumb was not already familiar. And wouldn't this large man know far more about his brother's recent life than Ali Baba could even guess?

The men in ostentatious robes nudged their scimitars forward so that their points pressed against the woodcutter's well-worn attire.

''Quickly!'' One Thumb demanded.

Ali Baba knew he must say something beyond One Thumb's knowledge or face instant removal. But what wouldn't One Thumb know?

''When I was seven and he was five, my brother and I would collect small toads—''

The swordsmen stepped away. Had the woodcutter made the proper choice of topic?

''Wrong!'' The great hand of One Thumb smashed across Ali Baba's face.

The woodcutter blinked at the points of light dancing before his face. He hoped that this most recent action on One Thumb's part would at the least help calm the large man for the immediate future.

''Now look what you have done!'' The tone of One Thumb's voice seemed rather the opposite of calm. The large man thrust his white sleeve beneath Ali Baba's nose. When the woodcutter managed to focus upon the fabric, he could see that it was pristine no more. The dazzling white was speckled with reddish brown. No doubt it was blood. Ali Baba put a hand to his nose. No doubt it was Ali Baba's blood.

"New robes!" One Thumb announced.

A third man clad in overly bejeweled finery rushed in from the street, carrying a new set of pristine white garments.

The other two men returned to menace Ali Baba with their swords while One Thumb changed his outer robes. When he had inspected his new garments to assure they were entirely without mark or flaw, he returned his attention to the woodcutter.

"No one," he explained between clenched teeth, "bleeds upon me without permission!" He brushed an invisible dust mote from his sleeve. "I had no such difficulty in dealing with Kassim's wife. When I asked her for her husband's whereabouts, she very promptly told me that only you could explain!"

Ali Baba frowned. Was this, then, the question? About Kassim's whereabouts? Or was it about Kassim's wife? Or did it have something to do with bleeding without permission? That recent blow to the head seemed to have confounded his clarity of thought.

"What shall we do now?" The large man looked meaningfully at the two men with drawn scimitars. "Since you bleed so easily, perhaps we should encourage you to bleed a bit more."

At that, the third overdressed man approached nervously and whispered in One Thumb's ear. The white-robed leader frowned as he glanced back at Ali Baba. "It appears that I have used up my last change of robes." He shook his head ruefully. "It *has* been a busy day, has it not? Very well, O lowly brother of Kassim. Your life is spared until I complete my laundry. Then my questions, one way or another, shall be answered in full!"

Questions? Ali Baba still had not heard any question. He had, however, decided that this current lack of questions was a point that did not currently need to be addressed. In fact, he could think of no point sufficiently worth discussing when that point was backed by a pair of men with swords. Perhaps, Ali Baba reasoned, these men would volunteer whatever information they deemed necessary before they departed.

But One Thumb removed himself from Ali Baba's inconsequential home before he could impart any further instructions, and his bejeweled yet silent guardsmen quickly followed.

Ali Baba closed his eyes and moaned. This day was beginning in an even less pleasant fashion than the pair of days before.

"Is there something I can do for my master?"

He opened his eyes to see the concerned and pleasant countenance of the slave Marjanah staring up at him. But even her young and charming face could not lift spirits as oppressed as his.

Ali Baba attempted to summarize his dilemma in the most reasonable fashion possible: "I must hide from the leader of a fierce group of bandits, who truly wishes to do me harm. However, as you no doubt can see, I no longer have a gate to hide behind!" Truly he felt as miserable as his wife often sounded.

Even in the presence of such dispiriting information, still did Marjanah retain her smile. "Ah, O kind master, have you considered that there is more than one way to hide? And further than that, there is more than one way to make a gate?"

But Ali Baba's thoughts were still befuddled from his recent encounter with a four-fingered hand. "I am afraid I do not catch your meaning."

"Then I shall demonstrate," the still-smiling Marjanah announced, "While you make a replacement gate out of those pieces of wood we can find around the yard."

So he should make a new gate? That much of Marjanah's reasoning he could understand. If there was one item his household did not lack for, it was wood. A surplus of that item was, in fact, the primary benefit of being a woodcutter. Ali Baba rubbed his still-stinging face. The surplus of that item might, in greater fact, be the only benefit. He pushed himself away from the wall, and began to study those scraps that were littered close by his feet.

"Very good," Marjanah agreed. "While you are fashioning a replacement gate, I shall busy myself around that space where the former gate once stood. Should some individuals pass by with whom you do not wish to converse, I shall do my best to distract and dissuade them from entry." With that, she bowed most properly. "It is always a privilege to obey such a wise master."

She went about her business, and Ali Baba decided he should go about his. His was certainly happy that, no matter what else might occur, Marjanah was always agreeable about following orders, even those orders that the woodcutter could not precisely remember issuing.

So it was that Ali Baba walked around the yard and house, collecting those larger twigs and logs that he might be able to tie together into some semblance of a gate. Then did he further carry these many items to that small work space he had devised behind the kitchen, so that he might toil in as private an area as his pitifully small holdings might allow. And, as he pursued this task, he found his spirits lightening, for working with wood was both

his life's pursuit and his greatest joy, and he wished fervently that
he could spend the rest of his existence socializing with trees and
bushes rather than bandit leaders and brothel keepers.

But such a wish was as unobtainable as a trouble-free day for
the woodcutter, for soon did Marjanah's voice interrupt his
concentration upon his work.

"Pardon me, sirrah," spoke his slave in the most pleasant and
gentle of tones, "but you are unable to pass that way."

"Do you mean that entry here is not permitted?" a second, far
gruffer voice replied, and the sound of that voice almost stilled the
heartbeat of the woodcutter. Surely, it was the voice of the leader
of the bandits! And further, that villain meant to enter the
woodcutter's insignificant courtyard, and there were none but a
young maiden to bar his way!

But Marjanah's voice betrayed none of that same fear. Instead,
she laughed, as if Thief Number One had simply spoken the
greatest of witticisms.

"O wise sir, surely you make fun of a young and unschooled
servant. You cannot pass this way, for, were you to take but a
single additional step, you would walk directly into the gate of my
household."

"Gate?" Thief Number One declared in astonishment. "I see
no gate!"

Marjanah's laughter was the pure sound of bells. "Of course
you see no gate there! It has recently been removed in order that
it be repaired. But, surely, there is a gate before you." Ali Baba
heard the sound of a hand knocking against wood. "You of course
see this portion of the fence?"

The bandit chieftain grunted his assent.

"And this as well?" Marjanah knocked again.

Again, the chieftain grunted.

"These are the walls to either side of the gate. Truly, for these
walls to have a purpose, there must be a gate between them, even
if you cannot see that gate!"

"What?" the first thief called in a voice heavy with disbelief.
"Dear child, this is nonsense! If I were not a kindly old man out
for an afternoon stroll, but instead, for example, I was the chieftain
of the most cutthroat band of thieves ever to ride, I might take
exception to your statement and walk straight inside."

But Marjanah was not to be fazed by such veiled threats.
"Before you consider such an act, which you, as a kindly old man,

never would, let me pose a question. Which is greater: a simple piece of wood, or tradition?''

"Why," the other answered, "for an old man, as I most assuredly am, it would be tradition, most certainly."

"Then you should pause to hear my tale," Marjanah continued. "From the time I first came here as a small child, and for a score of years before that, a gate has stood upon that site. What would you call that double score of years?"

"So long a space of time?" the thief said, although his voice betrayed an amount of uncertainty. "That certainly—sounds like tradition."

"Well, then," Marjanah responded cheerfully, "tradition says there is a gate!"

There was a prolonged moment of silence. When the bandit's voice next spoke, it was but to murmur something to himself for another period of time.

But that voice took on a guileful edge as he spoke again. "Dear child, you say this gate is being repaired? Might the man repairing it be a woodcutter?"

The rope fell from between Ali Baba's numb fingers. He could no longer work upon his gate. How would Thief Number One know that Ali Baba was a woodcutter? Perhaps only from his inauspicious clothing, and the two times that the thieves had captured him while he was carrying his woodcutting tools, and no doubt from the great amount of talking Kassim would have managed before he was cut into pieces.

Besides these eventualities, Ali Baba could see no reason why the bandit chieftain would be looking for a woodcutter. But what could Marjanah answer to the evil man's question but the truth?

As if in reply to his thought, the woodcutter's servant's response wafted back to his hiding place. "Most assuredly, wise sir, it is being repaired by a man who repairs gates."

"Yes," the chieftain responded in a voice of considerable force, "but is this man who repairs gates a woodcutter?"

Marjanah's voice, in reply, was the very spirit of innocence. "Would you cut wood to repair gates?"

"What?" the thief answered with some distraction. "Well, most certainly."

"Then I imagine he is that as well," was the servant's reasoned response.

The man in black sighed so deeply that even Ali Baba could hear it from his hiding place. "But is he a woodcutter," the thief further insisted, "who travels to dark and distant corners of the forest, and returns in the middle of the night with donkeys laden with mysterious sacks?"

"Why would he want to repair a gate in dark and distant corners of the forest?" Marjanah replied lightly.

She was quiet then, once again politely waiting for the other to speak. But the thief seemed only to mutter darkly to himself. Therefore, after a fitting period of time had elapsed, Marjanah seemed to feel it proper to ask a question of her own:

"Do you have a specific reason for asking of these things?"

"Oh, no," the first thief insisted, the force of his voice replaced by gentle mischief. "Simply idle curiosity. Call it an old man's whim."

There was a moment's silence before the old man spoke again:

"Have you ever considered a career as a thief? Oh, I know you are a woman and all, but, were we to supply you with sufficiently bulky robes, no one need notice."

The chieftain coughed. "Pardon me. I forgot myself for a moment. I am naught but an elderly gentleman, whiling away my remaining years by making discreet inquiries of all I see."

"Most certainly," the slave replied with her usual unflagging humor. "And it has been most diverting to have a conversation with someone so old and wise."

"Yes. Well. I suppose if I cannot pass through the gate, I might as well amble along until I can find someone else of whom to make discreet inquiries. Which reminds me. You would not happen to know of someone who has recently been divided into six pieces?"

Ali Baba heard the sharp sound of Marjanah clapping her hands. "Six pieces? Oh, I know! It must be a riddle! You elderly are so clever with your riddles! Perhaps the six pieces are the ages of man, from the crawling infant to the bent elderly—no disrespect, O venerable sir."

"Well, it wasn't a riddle, really—" the chieftain attempted to interject.

"Not that kind of riddle?" Marjanah replied in that sort of bright voice that no man would dare to interrupt. "Perhaps the six are the four elements—air, earth, water, and fire—along with the gentle west wind, and the east wind that blows us storms from sea—"

Still did the chieftain attempt to regain control of the conversation. "Actually, forgive me for even mentioning those six—"

"Are the six the legs of an insect?" Marjanah added with a little whoop of joy, as if this time she was sure she knew the answer. "Perhaps a diligent ant, struggling with a weight ten times as great as itself—"

"I really must be moving along now," the bandit leader interrupted even more forcefully. "So pleasant to chat."

"Such a shame," replied Marjanah, her voice betraying the slightest bit of polite disappointment. "The next time I see you, I will surely have discovered the answer to your riddle!"

"No doubt," the chieftain answered wearily. "There is one bright spot in all of this. I trust that you spend very little time in particularly dark corners of the forest."

"Come back and see our new gate!" was Marjanah's only reply.

The bandit chieftain's dark muttering faded with the distance. Still did the woodcutter wait a suitable time before he peeked out from behind his hiding place.

"Most excellent Marjanah," he addressed his servant. "Could that man with whom you so recently spoke be who I thought he was?"

Marjanah nodded merrily. "Black robes, vicious scowl—he matched your description of the bandit leader in every particular."

"So we must be prepared for his return, no doubt beneath the cloak of night," reasoned the greatly relieved Ali Baba. "I shall finish the gate with all dispatch."

But the woodcutter's relief would, as usual, be of extremely short duration, for another's voice called into the conversation.

"Before you return to your labors," his brother called from the fence, "there are certain debts that must be discussed."

Ali Baba turned his gaze to see that Kassim's wife had perched his brother's basket directly atop the fence between their properties. Not that Kassim's wife paid overmuch attention to her charge. Once again, she did not watch her husband, but seemed only to desire to gaze upon Ali Baba.

But the woodcutter would not allow this woman's alluring gaze, not her long dark hair, nor her full, moist lips, nor the way her bosom quivered every time she took a breath; he would not allow any of that to stand in the way of his clear judgment. And furthermore, despite what hardships his brother had suffered, Ali Baba discovered a trace of annoyance in his brother's attitude. "I must complete my fence, or any discussion of debts will have to be conducted with a dead man."

Kassim's tone became indignant. "You dare to take such an

attitude with me, a member of your own family, after all the upheaval I have suffered?''

Well, the woodcutter thought, it was true that without the information Ali Baba had provided, Kassim might still be a whole man. Could that be the reason that Kassim's wife now stared at Ali Baba in so fixed a manner? He swore again that he would not let that gaze be his undoing. Still, he had not realized before now that her deep brown eyes also held tiny flecks of green.

"Perhaps I do bear some responsibility," the woodcutter therefore admitted. "I do apologize for any difficulty the two of you might have had in resuming normal relations."

"Oh," Kassim's wife remarked in a low voice, "I would not concern yourself overmuch with that."

"While we had some difficulty locating certain pieces," Kassim added gruffly, "we have persevered."

"And more than that," his wife said as her smile broadened, "you cannot imagine the positions—"

"But that novelty is past," his brother added. "It is far beyond time that you made amends!"

Amends? Again the woodcutter felt anger stir within him. Amends for what? For his brother forgetting the magic words and being trapped in the cave? But Ali Baba's speech faltered once more when he looked to Kassim and his wife, a problem inspired in part by the difficulty of looking at a wicker basket eye-to-eye.

"And you should be quick about your decision as well," Kassim's wife further chided. "Do not forget that I must soon get back to our houseguest."

"Houseguest?" were the two syllables that Ali Baba elected to utter.

"Most certainly," replied the wife with the sort of condescending smile that those who have wealth and expansive property reserve for those who have none. "We often entertain houseguests in one of our many extensive gardens."

"My wife is the most considerate of hostesses," the man in the basket proudly added, "so that the generosity of Kassim might be talked about in both bazaars and palaces!"

"This newest guest," his wife continued in a voice even more pleased than before, "is a charming old man dressed all in black whose pleasure is to amble about the neighborhood making discreet inquiries."

Ali Baba found that he had no remarks on that information whatsoever, except for a thought that building a gate might now be considered inessential.

◆

Chapter the Ninth,
in which that which comes apart may come together,
or not, according to circumstance.

Fortunate was Ali Baba that he still had the slave Marjanah standing by his side.

"That houseguest?" she said in the most dismissive of tones. "Oh, yes. We have already entertained him at some length. In fact, I was surprised how difficult it was to get the gentleman to depart."

"You have?" Kassim's wife replied, her smile of superiority crumbling to a frown. "You were? He did?"

But his slave's quick wit had helped Ali Baba to find his voice as well. "Marjanah," he therefore instructed, "tell her the rest of it."

"There is more?" Kassim's wife asked in alarm.

Marjanah therefore continued with a series of questions, in the manner of all great instructors. "Have you given any thought to the matter of this man's dark clothes? And further, has he made any inquiries concerning individuals that have been divided into six pieces?"

"Wait a moment!" came Kassim's wicker-muffled call. "Even one trapped in a basket can see where this line of inquiry may lead! Are you implying that our visitor is one of those thieves we have so recently escaped?"

"What," Ali Baba further asked, "might be worse than this old gentleman merely being one of those thieves?"

"You mean that he is their leader?" Kassim squawked as if his body were being ripped asunder one more time. "And my thoughtless wife has allowed this foul bandit access to our most private gardens? Reach into this basket, woman, and pull out my arm so that I may beat you!"

His wife looked askance at her wicker-clad husband and master. "In front of the neighbors?"

63

This question caused even Kassim to pause. "Perhaps I forget myself. The way I am divided, that is a distinct possibility. But what shall we do if this man knows of our whereabouts?"

"I have not said a single thing about my husband being divided into six pieces," his wife said in a voice that implied she was hurt by any suggestion to the contrary. "Certain things, after all, should stay in the family."

"Forgive me, O master," Marjanah said most sweetly, "but might I suggest the most humble of alternatives!"

"Please do!" Ali Baba agreed enthusiastically. "In me, your humble words will always find a ready ear!"

"Very well," Marjanah replied. "It has recently occurred to me, and no doubt would occur to all of you after a moment's thought, that your problem centers on a man who is divided into six parts. But what if those six parts were once again made into one?"

"Reverse what has happened to my husband?" asked Kassim's wife, astonished at the very thought. "Would that it could be so! But no one in our household knows anything of magic!"

"Forgive my most modest of suggestions," continued Marjanah, "but the only magic I am thinking of is a needle and thread."

"A needle and thread?" Kassim restated in disbelief.

"And we shall sew him back together?" His wife laughed and clapped her hands. "While we proceed with these repairs, mayhaps we can make a few improvements!"

"Have a care, wife!" her husband warned. "Or I will indeed have you remove one of my arms so you might beat yourself profusely! And a leg, so that we might add a few kicks as well!"

"You must forgive my husband," his wife continued. "He is not truly himself. Otherwise, he would see that this young woman's idea has true merit."

But Kassim was still unconvinced. "To sew me up? With a sharp needle? Can you imagine how much that might hurt?"

"You have been divided into six pieces," his wife answered incredulously. "Truly, that must have caused you even greater pain!"

"Enough to last a dozen lifetimes." Kassim shuddered. "Perhaps you can sew up somebody else, instead!"

Once again, Marjanah's wit came to the rescue. "I know of a blind tailor whose touch is as sure as the tread of a cat. I am sure he could sew those parts together with a great sensitivity."

"Sensitivity?" Kassim wailed, no more convinced. "Oh, at the very least, it is going to tickle!"

"Very well," Marjanah replied meekly, as if her only desire were to obey, "therefore, when next the bandit leader confronts you, he will simply have to deal with the pieces."

"Oh, there is that." Kassim did his best to laugh. "Well, what is a little pain?"

"Pardon?" Kassim's wife frowned and turned away from the fence to have a young serving woman whisper something in her ear. When she returned her gaze to Ali Baba, she appeared even more distraught than she had previously. "My servants have informed me that we have left our guest waiting too long in the garden. He has announced that, while he awaits our hospitality, he shall wander about our grounds seeking out interesting curiosities."

The slave leaned forward and whispered something further in the woman's ear.

"He said," she related with a growing alarm, "that he is particularly interested in living individuals who have been cut into pieces."

Ali Baba's panic at this most recent information was temporarily interrupted by the voice of his wife as she emerged from their inadequate dwelling place.

"Oh, woe!" came her familiar yet piercing cry. "Why did you not tell me that you were speaking with our family?"

But the woodcutter had no ears at present for his wife's remarks. Instead, he spoke to the spouse of his brother. "How soon may we expect his arrival?"

She frowned as she considered. "Well, it should be a moment. From what my slave has told me, he has begun to stroll in a completely different direction from that spot where we now stand. From his position within our estate, I would estimate that, to arrive here, he would have to traverse at least three formal gardens."

"Ah!" Kassim exclaimed. "So that is where you had put our guest, in the very best quarter of our palatial grounds. The beast did not deserve to even gaze upon such refinement! Yet, do not forget that to reach the gardens, he must pass the large and quietly peaceful reflecting pools."

"Oh, yes," his wife agreed at the reminder, "at least four of those, depending whether or not he traverses the aviary."

"And may I be so presumptuous," their slave added much in

the manner of Marjanah, "I would also mention the seven outbuildings he would have to pass through?"

"Yes," Kassim's wife concurred, "and that only if he took the most direct route. But, besides those and the topiary, the bathhouse and of course our modest yet well-stocked trout stream and game forest, he could arrive here at any time."

"Oh, woe!" Ali Baba's wife interrupted, doing her best to regain her usual mastery of any conversation. "Our family talks of their hospitality and you do not care to show them any of ours?"

Considering the severity of the current situation, even the usually patient Ali Baba found that he could not concentrate upon his wife's complaints. "Not now, my beloved," he therefore stated gently.

"So it begins." His wife nodded her glum countenance all too knowingly. "It is thus that communication falters between husband and wife. Can the downfall of the marriage be far behind?"

It was up to Kassim's wife to speak louder than the wife of Ali Baba. "We must get my husband repaired with all dispatch. Where might this blind man that your slave speaks of be found?"

But new objections were to emanate from within the wicker. "I am not going to be touched by a blind man, much less sewn!"

"Nonsense!" his wife replied. "Do you expect someone who can *see* to do this sort of work?"

Kassim laughed ruefully. "Do you not expect even a blind man to have some difficulty with this task?"

"It is a relevant point." His wife rewarded the basket with a smile. "I think it would be far better for our purposes that you were to pretend to be dead during the reconstruction."

"Dead?" Kassim yelped as if the very idea caused him pain. "But my body parts are still warm. What if this tailor should strike a nerve or tickle the skin?"

"Then we will state that you are very recently dead," his wife commented in the most soothing of tones. "And no matter what might transpire, we shall give the blind man a sufficient quantity of gold so that his lips will be as unspeaking as his eyes are unseeing."

But Kassim would not be silenced so easily. "Gold? Where are we to get that kind of gold?"

His wife's eyes returned to Ali Baba. "We do not have to look any further than your brother's generosity."

Before the woodcutter could properly consider this offering of his funds for his brother's continued well-being, another voice joined the conversation.

"Gold? Did I hear someone mention gold?"

Alas! It was the old man who was in reality the leader of the thieves! He had crossed those three gardens, four reflecting pools, aviary, topiary, trout stream, game forest, and seven outbuildings with remarkable speed. Both wives and Kassim cried out in surprise.

"I did not mean to startle you," the man in black stated with a smile that might have been kindly under other circumstances. "I am only looking for the unusual. My, that is a large basket that you have there. It is truly amazing, it is not, what you might carry in a basket of such girth and height and construction?" With that, he took a bold step toward the basket so that he could get a closer look at what might lurk therein.

Each of the family members glanced to the others as if silently asking what they might say next to rescue themselves from certain discovery. But the woodcutter knew there was only one answer.

"Truly, there is but one thing to do," Ali Baba said as he averted his face in such a way that the bandit leader might not recognize him. "There is but one person who can make sense of all this, and that person is Marjanah!"

"But you have not told me," the thief called in obvious enjoyment as he took yet another step, "why you refer to gold."

His enjoyment evaporated as rapidly as the morning dew when Marjanah stepped forward to meet him. "O venerable sir, much as I hate to contradict someone as old and wise as yourself, I am afraid that your equally venerable ears are suffering from age. When you thought you heard the auspicious mention of *gold*, the actual word used was the much more unfortunate mention of *cold*."

"Cold?" the bandit replied with an expression of dismay.

"A very severe illness," Marjanah continued simply, as if that answer were the only one possible. "A truly uncommon cold. We have, of course, followed the old family remedy, and somehow fitted the afflicted one into yonder basket."

Kassim sneezed obligingly.

The thief halted, deciding perhaps that he did not immediately need a closer look within the wicker.

"But you are a man of venerable age and great learning!" Marjanah stated enthusiastically, as if this thought had only now entered her pretty young head. "You must have a knowledge of many rare diseases! Surely, if we were to show you the afflicted one, you might easily recognize the large, bleeding pustules upon his body and furthermore identify the peculiar, gangrenous smell coming from his every pore!''

With that, the thief frowned and looked up at the sun. "Why, see what time it has gotten to be! Although I am sure I could give you good advice on such matters, I fear I must be leaving immediately. Even kindly old men must occasionally keep appointments!''

"Are you certain?'' Kassim's wife responded with the slightest of smiles. "We were about to prepare a fine repast.''

"And wonderful hospitality I am sure it would be,'' the thief called over his shoulder as he trotted toward the nearest of the outbuildings. "Most certainly, I shall enjoy it at another time!''

And with that, the bandit chieftain disappeared from view.

"Most excellent Marjanah!'' Ali Baba exclaimed as soon as he was certain the bandit was beyond the range of sound as well as sight. "You have saved us again!''

"I only wish to serve,'' was the slave's humble reply.

"Oh, woe!'' the woodcutter's wife chimed in. "That we cannot all perform our tasks so gracefully!''

"But I still fear we have not seen the last of our bandit leader,'' Ali Baba cautioned. "We must take my brother and get him resewn at our first opportunity!''

Recent events had been of such severity that even Kassim no longer objected. Therefore, after a brief discussion, it was decided that Ali Baba should carry the basket to the blind tailor, for he was often seen about town making his deliveries, and so was unlikely to arouse suspicion. By the time this was finally determined, it was further resolved by the group that a sufficient time had elapsed for the bandit chief to make good his escape, and further time would only allow the ruffian to have second thoughts and might return to plague them again. Therefore, if Ali Baba and Kassim were to leave, the best time was this moment.

Marjanah and Kassim's wife therefore waved farewell, while the woodcutter's spouse graced them with a final "Oh, woe!'' and Ali Baba carried the wicker basket out through the space where once his gate had stood. Marjanah had given him very detailed directions to the tailor's shop, which was in actuality only some distance down the same street on which the woodcutter and his brother dwelled. So it was that Ali Baba carried his burden, which he had previously cautioned to be silent, past Kassim's home. But they had barely gone a dozen places beyond his wealthy brother's large guardhouse before they were set upon by four men dressed all in black!

The basket was wrested quickly from Ali Baba as two other men pinned his arms, and turned him roughly about to face the bandit chieftain!

"I told you there was no escape from our band," Thief Number One remarked with the most open of smiles. "Now that your meddling woman servant is no longer about, you are ours for the rest of your lives." He paused to smile knowingly at the other thieves. "Not, of course, that that will be a period of great duration."

◆

Chapter the Tenth,
in which we learn
what it takes to be a thief.

This time, Ali Baba was sure he was truly doomed, pinned by two of the dark-robed, heavily bearded men. He would never see his meager home or inadequate family again!

The bandit's even more sinister leader paced back and forth across the suddenly very empty and totally quiet street. No one, it seemed, whether man or beast, might wish to be in the company of these men by choice. Nor did it help Ali Baba's mood that the chief of thieves was using this opportunity to gloat at great length.

"Ha ha ha," the first thief uttered as he pushed his face close to that of Ali Baba. "And furthermore ha, and ha again! This should prove to you, without fear of contradiction, that no one escapes from the grasp of the forty thieves. To steal is to live, to live is to steal!" He spun to face Kassim. "And you in the basket. Cutting you into six pieces was only the beginning of your new existence!"

And with that, even Kassim began to wail. "I have found a new reason, then, to curse my undying being. Now I shall be forced, day after day, to listen to you!"

"And trust me," said the chieftain, who apparently took that last remark as an odd sort of compliment, "you will be by my side constantly!" He chortled. "Once again we shall have forty thieves. And, when we reach our full complement, no power upon this earth shall be able to stop us!"

He pointed to each of his three subordinates in turn. "Guard our newest recruits well. I shall summon the rest of the thieves. And then we will ride!" With that, he turned and ran down an alleyway behind Kassim's estate.

Was this, then, the last Ali Baba would see of his home, his city, his woodcutting livelihood? Even a mind as humble as his rebelled at such a thought. Surely, there had to be some way he and Kassim could make good their escape. Ali Baba shifted his weight slightly, but found each of his arms in a pair of iron grips.

"Please do not struggle overmuch," the thief holding Ali Baba's left arm said with a surprising gentleness. "You are in enough difficulty at present without having to add to it."

"Yes," said the thief at Ali Baba's right, "no one has ever escaped twice from the thieves before."

"At least," the brigand who held the basket joined in, "no one who has remained alive."

"Not that our chieftain would have you killed," the first of the three added in a somewhat reassuring tone, "at least not directly."

"No," the second further added, "more likely he will send you on an errand, say, down the side of a sheer cliff, or straight into the mouth of a shark, from which there is no return."

"Then nothing shall happen to us at the hands of your leader?" Ali Baba asked, not sure if this fact was enough to foster a sense of relief.

"Nothing could be further from actuality," the first among the three said in a more vehement tone. "I hear that you two may veritably receive"—and he paused briefly before he could finish the sentence—"a demotion."

The other two bandits gasped in what might have been terror. The thickness of their beards made it difficult for Ali Baba to discern their true emotions. And yet, poor woodcutter that he was, he had to have these matters presented clearly before him. "Is this 'demotion,' then, that terrible a fate?"

"The only thing after demotion," said the last of the three before inserting another one of those unpleasant pauses, "is death."

"I have a proposition," the gentle first thief suggested. "What say we thieves release our burdens for the moment? But know this, our newest recruits: Our resolve is no less great than before. I also feel that I would be remiss if I did not mention that, as a member of our fearsome band, my swift knife hand is only exceeded by the speed of my amazingly sharp sword, which is as a snail's pace to the alacrity of my poison-tipped arrows." He coughed gently as he released his grip upon Ali Baba's arm. "You should be well served to heed this point of information."

And heed he did. Even though the pressure was gone from his either side, the woodcutter felt no freer than he had before. Still, if he was fated to join this band no matter what his will, perhaps he could put the best face possible upon it.

He stepped over by the basket that contained his brother, which the third thief had lowered to the ground.

"I suppose a life as a thief will at the least be a change of pace," Ali Baba ventured. "Perhaps we shall see some of the countryside."

The three thieves gathered together and glanced at one another. None of the three appeared very enthusiastic concerning the woodcutter's observation.

"What can you see?" the first of the three responded. "You will always be in the middle of a mass of moving horses."

But Ali Baba would not be discouraged. "Then perhaps I might hear new sounds, like the voice of exotic birds and the susurration of the distant ocean."

"What will you hear?" the third chimed in. "Only the roar of the victorious and the screams of the victims. You will certainly be given no instruction."

Yet was the woodcutter stubborn in pursuing his goal, much as he would not be finished with a log until he had fully split the knothole. "But surely in my travels there will be some new experience—"

"What might you experience?" the second questioned. "There will be nothing but sun and heat and dust."

"But," the woodcutter began again, and even he could hear the desperation growing in his voice, "don't you know—"

"What will you know?" the second further asked. "You will certainly never know where you are, for you will always be surrounded by thieves."

"But what about the rest—" Ali Baba attempted again.

"When will you rest?" the first commented in summation. "It is always gallop, gallop, gallop, steal, steal, steal."

This did not seem like the most positive of futures. And yet, being of a generally positive demeanor, and further perhaps looking for any straw in a windstorm, Ali Baba was not yet defeated in his search for consolation. "Perhaps we can learn something, then, from your forceful leader."

All three shook their heads again.

The first began: "A more vile man has never existed."

But Ali Baba would not easily accept so negative a comment. "Surely, there must be something positive you may say about your chieftain."

All thieves paused in thought.

"He is not a patient man."

"He is not a moderate man."

"He is not a humane man."

"Nor generous," the third added after some further deliberation.

"There are indeed," the first of the three again summarized, "many things he is not."

At this, even the lighthearted woodcutter was close to admitting a total defeat. "Then he has no positive qualities whatsoever? He is lower in the celestial chain than even those creatures who digest the offal of the earth?"

The first leaned forward to tug a warning at Ali Baba's sleeve. "Do not say such a thing so loudly! Our chieftain easily takes offense." He rubbed his lower beard with some agitation. "Sometimes he kills the listeners as well. He is extremely good with a sword."

"Good with a sword?" the woodcutter replied. "That is positive, at least in a way."

The thieves thought some more before the second one mentioned: "His knowledge of torture is enormous."

With that encouragement, the third one added: "And, furthermore, his lust for gold is insatiable."

"See?" The first among them grinned. "We have not given our leader sufficient credit. There are any number of positives associated with our chieftain."

There followed a moment of silence. For, after such a topic, what else might be said? Ali Baba became increasingly uncomfortable as the silence lengthened, for he realized he was among men who spent their free time pillaging and looting, and therefore would prefer if their thoughts did not wander overmuch, especially in such close proximity to his insubstantial home and, more specifically, to that newly dug trench within his kitchen.

Rather than endure this silence, the woodcutter decided he would try another road to friendship, and introduce himself.

"My name is Ali Baba."

"You will be Number Thirty-Nine," said the first among the bandits. "We do not use names."

"Then none of you have names?" the woodcutter asked in some surprise.

"Oh, yes," the first contradicted, "we certainly have names. We just don't use them—at least, not around our chieftain."

"Thief Number One has certain peculiarities," the second of

the three added. "His insistence upon numbers is chief among them."

"It has to do with his requirement that there always be forty thieves," the last thief stated. "That is a mystic number for him."

"It is a shame," the second pointed out, "that he finds that number so difficult to reach."

"A shame?" Ali Baba asked.

"For all of us," the three thieves said together.

The woodcutter was unsure if it would be in his best interest to request further information.

"But you have asked us for our names," the first of the three said quickly, as if he could not wait to alter the subject. "I have been with the band for a great enough time to become Number Thirty." He glanced quickly up and down the street before adding: "In an earlier time, men knew me as Aladdin."

So the thieves would introduce themselves in turn? This willingness to converse made Ali Baba, if not comfortable, at least no longer as ready to scream in stark fear. As the thieves spoke further, Ali Baba allowed himself to study each of them in turn, and, despite their similarity of robe and beard, he could see certain characteristics of each which would mark them as individuals. So it was that the one known as Aladdin, or Number Thirty, was taller than the other two, and broader of shoulder, as if he had had to work himself up within the world outside before he entered the world of thieves.

The second one of the three then stepped forward, and introduced himself in turn. "I am now known as Number Twenty-Eight within our circle." He lowered his voice for the next statement. "But for all my tender years before, I was called Achmed."

This man was by far the youngest of the three, his tall gangly figure not fully filled out to manhood. His beard disguised his age, but upon close appraisal, Ali Baba would guess that Number Twenty-eight was not that much more greatly advanced in years than his sweet Marjanah.

"It is left to me to conclude these introductions," said the third member of the thieves. "I am known as Number Twelve, for I have been a thief for a score of seasons, but in the distant past, when I dwelled within a palace, I was called Harun al Raschid."

This last of the three was also the eldest, with great amounts of gray mixed within his beard. He furthermore spoke more forcefully than his younger cohorts, as if he were indeed used to the life of rulers and others who dwelled in palaces, and would not bend so easily to the will of the bandit leader.

Ali Baba found himself most curious about those names they had before they were given numbers. While Achmed was a common name, Ali Baba had heard stories concerning men named Harun al Raschid and Aladdin. Could these be the same men as had served in those stories? As unlikely as the events of the past couple of days had been, this seemed to be straining the very bounds of creditability. Further, the woodcutter could think of no uncomplicated way to gather this information from the thieves. It had been difficult enough to gain their names. What pleading might it take to get them to tell their life stories?

For the moment, then, Ali Baba decided to travel down the road of politeness. "We are most pleased to make your acquaintance." Before he could indulge in further courteous conversation, however, he was interrupted by the usual disembodied voice.

"We? Might I remind you that no one has introduced *me* to anyone?" Kassim cried from beneath his wicker lid. "They chop you up, put you in a basket, and everybody ignores you! Isn't that always the way?"

"Yes, most certainly," the man once called Aladdin remarked politely. "We have been ignoring Number Forty."

But the woodcutter's brother would not be so easily mollified. "Kassim to you! A man of great importance in this city. A man with powerful and influential friends!"

Ali Baba realized his brother must be referring to his employer, the large and unpleasant One Thumb. "There is one powerful friend whom you have chosen not to speak with at present," he reminded his brother gently.

"Well, there is that," the brother in the basket said in a somewhat softer tone. "It is only a temporary setback, I assure you. When one is in my present state, one is reticent to make excessive explanations."

For example, Ali Baba thought but did not speak, his brother was avoiding an explanation of what Kassim had been doing in the presence of a great quantity of gold without first alerting One Thumb.

"I think, Number Forty, that you protest to excess," said the thief once named Achmed but now referred to as Number Twenty-eight. "Even in six pieces, you have certain advantages."

"Name me one," replied the unconvinced voice of Kassim, "and I shall rest quietly in my confinement."

"Well, as I recall, you do have a beard," was Achmed's answer.

"I most certainly do." Kassim grunted. "At present, it continues to tickle the inside of my knee in the most uncomfortable of fashions!"

"Ah," Achmed said with a smile that revealed his true boyish nature. "You are therefore closer to the ideal thief than your beardless brother."

Kassim remained unconvinced. "I am an ideal, even though I am in six discrete parts?"

"There are no rules whatsoever about remaining in one piece. But there are definite rules about beards." Achmed tugged upon his own.

Harun, or Number Twelve, regarded the woodcutter's face with some concern. "If you have been attempting to grow a beard, it does not appear to be going well."

"Then again," said Achmed, "if you have not been attempting to grow a beard, the situation will be far worse."

"Either way, I do not expect it to go well," Thief Number Thirty, formerly known as Aladdin, said in as grim a manner as Ali Baba had ever heard. "Grow your beard quickly. Should our chieftain have a few minutes for quiet contemplation and observation of his underlings before the hair upon your chin has reached its full potential"—he pulled at his own beard as a means of demonstration—"you will have to be most careful."

"Luckily for most of us," Number Twenty-eight said in a somewhat lighter tone, "our chieftain has very few moments for quiet contemplation."

Ali Baba found that he could not speak, for he was overwhelmed by a painful awareness of the inadequacies of his hair follicles.

The three thieves did not seem to notice. "It is most true of all our lives," the thief once called Aladdin said instead. "If there were moments of repose and quiet contemplation, some of us might make good our escape."

"As we have said," asserted the man in black who had once lived in a palace, "we were not always thieves. We all have past lives before our present situation."

Thief Number Thirty's eyes opened with excitement at this very topic of conversation. He nodded his head with enthusiasm. "And all of us have stories from those pasts; stories of some merit."

"Oh," Achmed called out in some alarm, "he is about to start the adventure of the lamp again!"

"It is a worthy tale!" rejoined Thief Number Thirty, who was also known as Aladdin.

"And ours are less so?" remonstrated Thief Number Twelve, Harun al Raschid the Palace Dweller. "We should remember who has seniority among those present."

Lamp? Ali Baba thought to himself again. Could his unlikely conjecture of some moments before actually bear some truth?

But before there could be any stories from any quarter there came a great pounding of hooves, a distant rumble at first, but growing in force from heartbeat to heartbeat.

"The thieves come!" Achmed called.

"There will be no more time for stories!" Harun added regretfully. "There will be no time for conversation of any kind!"

"It will be ride, ride, ride, steal, steal, steal!" Aladdin commented with a certain air of defeat.

As the rumbling increased, a great quantity of dust and noise emanated from the alley by his brother's house. At first the woodcutter thought it was odd that the thieves should choose to travel down an alley. Of course, Ali Baba considered, in keeping with the scale of all things concerned with Kassim's dwelling, the alley was wide enough for three horsemen to ride abreast.

"It has been good to talk to you," the thief who once was Aladdin called to him. "Pray that we might do it again at some time in our lives, however brief those lives may be."

But those were the last words any of the newfound companions spoke, for at that instant Thief Number One burst from the alley on the back of his night-black stallion, followed by the remaining dark-robed thieves.

"Aha!" the bandit chieftain shouted exultantly. "Now we will go about our business! And no one will be able to stop us, for we will be a full forty strong!" He waved at Thieves Number Thirty, Twelve, and Twenty-eight. "We will again tie our newest members to their horses. But this time the three of you will escort them out of town!"

The thieves appeared to have come up in the world, for this time both Ali Baba and the basket containing Kassim received horses of their own. The woodcutter found himself thrust into the saddle of one mount by Achmed and Aladdin, while Harun carried the basket to strap upon the other steed. Other bandits threw great quantities of rope at those three to secure the newcomers. There was so much rope, in point of fact, that the three had some considerable difficulty handling the excess.

"Could you get that rope from around my leg?" Achmed asked of Aladdin as he shook the coils from his knee.

"Which of the thieves are you?" the chieftain then asked of Achmed.

The young thief came to attention, all thoughts of the annoying rope temporarily forgotten. "Number Twenty-eight, sir."

Their leader smiled, at peace with his world. "There is such a security in numbers."

"Come," Thief Number One called as he raised his hand for the others to follow. "We will pillage the richest quarter of this city. Surely, every corner of every palatial household shall be filled with gold!"

"If you might wait a minute," Harun attempted to call over the ever-increasing stamping of horses' hooves, "and allow me to get my hand free from this rope?"

"Someone has tied knots all the way through this rope," Aladdin shouted against the din. "It shall take us a moment to extricate—"

"Thieves!" the bandit chieftain shouted as he urged his horse to a gallop. "It is time to ride!" Thief Number One shouted in the most bloodcurdling of fashions, and his ululating cry was picked up by the other horsemen, so that their fearsome screams seemed to propel their horses to a full gallop.

And with that, the other thieves rode off, leaving the five of them behind.

"Oh, dear," Harun said as the street returned to silence. He managed at last to free his hand from the tricky series of knots.

"It was bound to happen sooner or later," Achmed remarked as he threw down the coils of rope that had been weighing down his body.

Aladdin stepped past the mess of tangled hemp he had been trying to make sense of. "It is a shame that it had to happen to us."

"I do not understand!" Kassim called from his basket. "What has happened here?"

"Thief Number One," Aladdin explained, "in his haste for wealth, has left us behind."

"Perhaps this is a boon?" Achmed asked uncertainly.

"Or certain death," Harun suggested.

"How foolish of me," Achmed agreed with far more conviction. "It must certainly be certain death."

"He always acts in this manner," Aladdin added with an incontestable fatalism of tone.

"It happened as he spoke that word 'gold,'" Achmed said with a desolate thoughtfulness.

"Logic escapes him the minute the word is mentioned," Harun furthered the grim explanation.

"Still," Aladdin noted, "look upon the positive aspects of our situation, as I am sure the woodcutter would say. This certainly takes a certain weight off our shoulders."

"You mean when he cuts off our heads?" Achmed asked, his voice calming considerably as soon as he had asked the question. "Yes, that is quite comforting, in a certain way. What could possibly be worse than that sudden and painful death?"

It was at that precise moment that One Thumb emerged from the alley.

◆

Chapter the Eleventh,
in which we learn what is not hair today
will truly be gone tomorrow.

Ali Baba looked back to the thieves. "You mean your leader would kill us that readily?"

With that, Aladdin shrugged his substantial shoulders. "It would depend upon the availability of replacement thieves."

"Of course," Achmed added, "our leader is not that particular about his recruits for our band. Take a good look at the three of us. Even more to the point, take a good look at the two of you."

Any venture toward further conversation was interrupted by the shouts of One Thumb and his cohorts as they rushed toward Ali Baba and the others.

"There you are," declared the massive man in white, "attempting no doubt to depart without informing us of your whereabouts. It will go very badly for you! There is but one way in which you might be able to escape my awesome vengeance. You will tell us the whereabouts of Kassim at this instant. I am tired of getting no answers!"

"Was there a question in there?" Achmed asked.

One Thumb chose not to respond beyond affording the youngest of the thieves a sharp glance. Instead, he motioned one of his bejewled henchmen forward.

"Hassan," he instructed his underling. "See what is in the basket!"

But before this Hassan could take a single step toward achieving his goal, the three thieves stepped forward in such a line that the basket was hidden behind their dark robes.

"You realize that the basket is not your property," Harun said with some authority.

His speech only made One Thumb laugh in a particularly vile fashion. "I take what I want!"

Aladdin saw fit to return the smile, accompanied by these

words: "That only works if the other person is willing to give the item in question."

One Thumb's expression transformed from one of derision to one of pure fury. "Then you refuse me! I will show you what happens to those who refuse One Thumb! And besides that," he offered almost as an afterthought, "I am the only one here who is allowed to ask the questions!"

"Who said anything about refusing?" Achmed asked in a voice so smooth that even the claws of death itself might slide away. "It appears that we are still engaged in the defining of terms."

As quickly as the anger had appeared on One Thumb's face, that rapidly did his expression transform itself into one of total confusion. While his mouth worked for some moments, his brain seemed incapable of supplying any accompanying sound.

"It seems to me that 'to give' is another way to say 'to present,'" Achmed said as he began to explicate his point. He stepped aside to reveal the wicker prize. "Now look at this poor basket. See how the lid is bent, and the handles are worn. The wicker is even frayed in two—no, three—places. This object is far too shabby to even be considered as a present. You are right to be offended at the very mention of such an exchange. But all is not lost in our negotiation, for I can think of a number of other objects immediately to hand that would make far better gifts." He reached forward and pulled the scimitar from Hassan's scabbard with remarkable speed. "May I?" he added after he already held the sword in his hand. "A fine example of a perfect gift would be this jewel-encrusted sword."

Hassan's shout at the loss of his sword revealed a certain degree of incoherent anger. He then became so upset as to utter the first question Ali Baba had ever actually heard from any member of One Thumb's entourage. "You then plan to give my master his own jewel-encrusted sword?"

Achmed shook his head with a sad smile, as if that particular action were as far from his intention as a slave is from a sultan. "Oh, no," the young thief further expounded. "I said nothing about giving him the sword. Or those other two swords, now in the steady yet practiced hands of my confederates."

But One Thumb had witnessed quite enough of Achmed's subterfuge. "Men!" he therefore cried in far from the most pleasant tones. "Cut them down like undomesticated dogs!"

But there was no cutting to be done this day, for while Achmed

had held everyone's attention, the two other thieves had stripped
One Thumb's cohorts of their respective scimitars.

"What?" The fury bubbling within One Thumb rose to a full
boil. "You dare, you forest looters!"

"We do not dare, we do," was Achmed's reply. "Do you find
this surprising? You have simply never before met thieves of the
first echelon."

"Show me the leader among you," was One Thumb's inappropriate reply, "and I shall strangle him using only my naked
hands!"

"Alas, we are all equals within our present company," Achmed
replied with such pleasantness that Ali Baba began to suspect the
thief might be some relation to Marjanah. "Our leader has left us
here temporarily. No doubt, though, he will return with the rest of
the thieves."

One Thumb once again issued that unpleasant bray that might
be taken for a laugh. "What are a few thieves, more or less,
compared to the might of One Thumb!"

"Even should there be a full complement of forty of them?"
Achmed asked gently.

"For-forty thieves?" One Thumb sputtered in a manner that
made him appear even less pleasant than before. "*Those* forty
thieves?" He waved vaguely at the men in black. "You may keep
the swords. I am happy to give a present to so famous a band of
men. In the meantime, I am afraid that I have a great many
appointments elsewhere."

So even One Thumb turned away? And after the brothel keeper
had actually been so disconcerted that he had asked a question (a
situation that the woodcutter imagined did not happen with
particular frequency)? Ali Baba was quite impressed with both the
acumen and the reputation of the band to whom he now belonged.

But, before he departed, One Thumb lifted a forefinger into the
air. "Tell your master, though, that I do not forget," he said with
a voice heavy in portent. "And, when the time is right, we shall
meet again, and he shall be sorry he ever played that game with the
chickens!"

Chickens? Then again, the woodcutter considered, perhaps the
thieves' reputation was not as great as all that. Ali Baba once again
perceived that strange feeling that he had entered the room
halfway through a storyteller's tale.

Aladdin, who despite protestations to the contrary, seemed to
lead this small group of thieves, found his voice to cry: "No one

meets the forty thieves unless we want to meet *them*!'' In a somewhat softer voice, he added as he glanced at Ali Baba: ''And sometimes we even forget about that.''

Ali Baba was not comforted by the thief's shared confidence. Amidst all this confusion, he had once again begun to yearn for the squalid yet simple pleasures of his home, still so close at hand but perhaps now forever out of his reach. He was about to be taken away from everything he knew and loved. For the shortest of moments, the woodcutter almost wished he had never taken that enormous quantity of gold. But that feeling passed rapidly as well. Life could be long, a man's destiny was unsure, but it did not hurt to have untold wealth buried beneath your kitchen. Yes, it was a thought worthy of utterance by the wise. And, no matter what perils he might face at the hands of these thieves, he would return to that gold again. Not to mention his inadequate household and meager family. And then, only then, would he find true peace.

He looked to these three thieves who now held them so casually captive. These men had revealed bits of their life stories to their prisoners, and in so doing had become individuals rather than a part of that murderously thieving bearded mass. Ali Baba realized, before that mass of thieves even returned, that he could never fight or reason with the group of them. But if he could speak to them singly, as one man to another—how they had come to join the group, perhaps, and how they or others had tried to leave—he might find some way to win his freedom. Simply because one log is rotted does not mean one has to forsake the forest. So it was that he would persevere until he could find his home.

He thought he would begin his search for information with this talkative youngster before him.

''Tell me, Achmed, pardon me, Number Twenty-eight,'' Ali Baba quickly amended as he saw the thief's frown, ''but how did one as well-spoken as you descend into a life of stealing?''

''It was not quite a descent,'' the young thief replied with a laugh. ''Quite frankly, I began my life in a position perhaps even inferior to that of a thief. More specifically, I was a slave for a wealthy household. It was in such position that I learned to have a practiced tongue, for slaves have to be clever, or their masters would be helpless without them.''

And, indeed, Ali Baba knew the wisdom of this statement, for it was common knowledge to all men. ''But how,'' he asked of the youngest among the three, ''did you manage to find yourself in this present state?''

"I was captured with my companion, the illustrious Sinbad."

Here, again, was a name famous with the storytellers. Perhaps this group of thieves had more to them than they might care to admit. On this occasion, Ali Baba chose to pursue the subject in greater detail. Therefore, he asked:

"Was it the illustrious Sinbad the Sailor?"

But Thief Number Twenty-eight shook his head. "No. Actually, it was the somewhat less illustrious Sinbad the Porter."

There, thought Ali Baba. That was what happened when a poor woodcutter jumped to such conclusions. Aladdin's lamp was probably something he used to read by at night.

"Still," Achmed continued, no doubt in response to the appearance of distress upon the woodcutter's countenance, "he is quite famous in his own way."

"For porting?" Kassim asked in disbelief.

"Actually, he has gotten beyond that," was Achmed's explanation. "He was promised a very important position by my actual master, but in order for that to occur, we would have to return to Baghdad. Not that that matters anymore. Baghdad might as well exist in another place and time, for now we are part of the forty thieves."

"And a part of the forty thieves we shall remain," Harun added in a voice with the weight and timbre of a sage, "until our dying day, which, through using my powers of observation, I deduce to be in the not-all-too-distant future."

"Such is our lot with the temper of our master," Aladdin agreed.

"Such is our fate thanks to the perils of thievery," Achmed added.

"And, even more than that," Harun concluded with as sober a face as the woodcutter had ever seen beneath a bushy black beard, "such is our destiny facing the deadly mystery of the cavern."

Temper, Perils, Mystery, and Death? More than he did not wish to leave his home, more than he wanted not to be forcefully inducted into the forty thieves, Ali Baba wished they would stop dwelling on these particular topics. Still, he had not heard of this deadly mystery business before. Could the thieves be talking about that same gold-filled cavern that cursed his brother to a perhaps eternal life in six parts?

"And this is the situation that my thoughtless brother has forced me into!" Kassim complained with great fervor, perhaps to compensate for the fact that no one could see his face hidden in the basket. "Have I told you yet how he led me into this sorry state?"

Then Kassim would reveal all? Ali Baba could not believe that even his brother could speak thus, without thought of the poverty-inducing consequences. If Kassim told such a story, no doubt the thieves would recall they were missing a great deal of gold, and further, where that gold had quite likely gone. And since the place that the gold might rest was only a few paces down the street, what was to prevent them from reclaiming their ill-gotten riches, which Ali Baba was certain they would just as gladly ill-get all over again?

Even the most levelheaded of men might panic. So it was with the usually quiet and industrious Ali Baba, as he spoke before any could urge his brother to further explain.

"Are you sure you wish to hear the ravings of my brother?" the woodcutter said with what he hoped sounded like a carefree laugh. "He has not quite been himself of late."

As usual, Kassim was swift to take offense. "How dare you say that of your own brother?" But living in six separate pieces within a basket can, no doubt, do wonders toward the increase of one's humility. So it was that, after a moment's pause, he added, "Well, if we were to use the most precise of language, I imagine I would be many selves, wouldn't I? Still would I like to tell my story. Or, considering my present state, should it be stories?"

His brother continued to mutter like this for quite some time, so that the others about paid him less attention with every passing remark. At this point, the humble woodcutter might have gone so far as to feel some guilt over the way he had manipulated his sibling, but there was no guilt great enough to cause Ali Baba to reveal the secrets of his kitchen. Thus it is that gold will get you to forget even the obligations of family.

"But I was going to tell you how I gained the lantern," ventured the thief once named Aladdin, no doubt to bring the subject away from Kassim's semi-coherent mumblings. "And how it once gave me great happiness, before I came to lose it again."

Ali Baba squatted near the ground, and prepared to listen. If he was going to be held captive for the rest of his life, the least he could be was entertained.

"In my early life," Aladdin began, "I was not so different than you see me now, for I was the son of a poor tailor—"

"A tailor!" Kassim wailed. "Now I shall never be reassembled!"

"You are correct," Achmed said to Ali Baba. "Your brother is most definitely undone."

"It is quite understandable," Harun said reasonably. "The shock alone could not help but be enormous. And what of future consequences? How could you continue to live if you knew you could wake up some morning and find your pieces missing?"

"Pieces missing?" Achmed inquired. "If they have been removed now, they are surely from his brain."

"I pray you," Kassim beseeched those around him, "transport me to the shop of the blind man down the street."

"He probably does not realize," Achmed said with great gentleness, "that he is making no sense."

"Perhaps," Harun mentioned sagely, "he is reliving his childhood."

The two thieves nodded most solemnly, as if that indeed were Kassim's dilemma.

"But come, Number Thirty, and finish your tale," Achmed called to Aladdin, "and perhaps this time we can hear it from beginning to end."

"Very well," Aladdin said with the slightest of smiles. "Now, when I was young, I was not the most obedient of boys, and I chafed at having to learn my father's profession."

"Cannot we move swiftly to the lantern?" Achmed interjected. "If there was one thing I learned upon my long voyage, it is this: In times of adventure and danger, travel straight to the story's heart."

But all assembled heard another sound before Aladdin could utter a further word, the fearsome noise of galloping horses.

Around the corner the horses came in a tight pack, and upon their backs were the men in black. Ali Baba's mouth felt dry, and his knees weak, as the bandits rapidly rode up to them, fearsome shouts upon their lips and great clouds of dust around their horses.

"Ah!" the bandit chieftain called to those he had left behind. "It is good that you waited for us, for it would have meant your lives if you had not." He paused to smile graciously. "I of course realized that you could not tend to our newest recruits so swiftly, and would further be a burden to us in our rapid movement, so decided it was best that we left you behind." He waved at his fellow riders. "Now you will be privileged to see our great success. Show them our plunder!"

One of the other thieves held up a small bag that clinked dully.

Not that Ali Baba was especially well versed in these matters, but still, in terms of plunder, it appeared a little pitiful.

"That is all?" the bandit chieftain demanded, as if only now realizing the severity of the situation.

"You were with us, O master," said the man who held the bag. "You saw how few valuables those people had, and these even included the difficult ones that necessitated the removal of fingers to obtain."

"How dare you criticize my methods?" The bandit chief drew his sword. "I will pluck out—no, no, I must remember my thief count. You were only trying to supply me with information. Bad information!" Thief Number One came close again to cutting, but thought better of it before he had sliced more than the man's outer robes and perhaps a bit of skin. The leader rapidly resheathed his blade before he could have any third thoughts. He paused and looked imploringly at the sky.

"It is not the way that it used to be for my fearsome band. I do not understand the difficulty." And from the fevered look of the chieftain's dark face, Ali Baba could tell that he was a man truly obsessed. "All things should be fortuitous when we are forty strong." His frown grew as he looked back to his men. "Unless, perhaps, we do not have the correct forty thieves!"

Then the bandit leader would blame his minions for the inadequacy of their plunder? Ali Baba remembered again how quick and merciless their leader was with his sword, and the woodcutter was grateful he was standing at least half a dozen sword lengths from said chieftain.

His gratefulness evaporated when he saw the way Thief Number One regarded him.

"Aha!" the bandit leader cried with the excitement of one who has discovered that problem which truly plagued him. "It comes clear to me in this instant!

"Do I see a member of our party without a beard?"

♦

Chapter the Twelfth,
in which counsel is given
and hair is achieved.

The woodcutter prepared himself for the sudden but no-less-unpleasant pain of violent death.

But no such agony was forthcoming. Instead, there was naught but an embarrassed silence.

"Oh, pardon me," the bandit chieftain explained with a pained smile. "It must have been my mistake." He glanced quickly among the other brigands, as though looking for a culprit. "No, my thieves are all fully bearded!"

All? thought Ali Baba with some consternation. Did that mean his beardlessness had driven him out of their ranks? It was the only sane alternative. And yet he would think that the most typical rejection by this group would be punctuated by the end of the sword, but since the chieftain had apologized, his hands had not even wandered close to his scimitar.

Whatever had happened, it no longer appeared that Ali Baba was in danger of imminent death. Would the thieves then be content that they numbered only thirty-nine, and let him return to his woodcutting ways?

He moved his hand to stroke his chin in thought, and cried out in sudden alarm. There was something attached to the lower portion of his face!

Ali Baba fought back the urge to strike at whatever strange furred animal had managed to latch onto his person. In the present company, he did not want to call any more attention to himself than was necessary. But what could be hanging from his face, and why could he not feel the pressure of its claws? Had he become so frightened by recent occurrences that all feeling had left his upper extremities?

However, and this was stranger still, none of the bandits about him were looking at him as if he had a large and obvious something attached to his face. Perhaps, when you were a brigand, whatever you decided to do with your personal appearance would be considered your private business. The woodcutter therefore determined that he would follow the lead of all those about him and act as if it were the most natural thing in the world for him to casually reach forward with both his hands and feel up the length of that creature that hung down his front.

It certainly was a furry thing, with thick hair that curled about every which way, but, no matter how deeply the woodcutter felt within the furry mass, he could not feel the creature's form. Still, throughout the course of his initial exploration, the woodcutter had not yet gotten bitten, and this bit of happenstance led him to a further act of bravado. He would have this thing off him so that he could look it squarely in the eye! Therefore did he grab the fur in both his hands and yank upon it, swiftly and without prior warning.

The cry that Ali Baba had previously issued, when he had first found this hair beneath his chin, was as to nothing in comparison to the scream that now emanated from between his lips. Somehow, this vast coarse and curly mass was fully attached to his chin and cheeks.

This could lead to but one conclusion. The thing in his hands was, indeed, a beard. Furthermore, it was his beard. In the space of the single blink of an eye, Ali Baba had somehow managed to gain that which he could not grow in all the years of his adult life. It was truly amazing, the woodcutter thought, what the human form could accomplish when motivated by fear.

"There is but one solution to our present situation," the leader called to his brigand troops. "We shall have a counsel!"

"What is a counsel?" Ali Baba asked of no one in particular.

"Why do you have to ask?" answered an older man who the woodcutter realized was Number Twelve, once known as Harun al Raschid. "Ah. You are one of our new recruits. It is most prudent that you have managed to grow a beard. It did, however, take me a minute to recognize you with your new facial hair."

Ali Baba fully agreed that it would be difficult to discern his true identity, for, surrounded by so many with virtually identical beards and clothing, he, too, found it nearly impossible to recognize those among the thieves whom he had so recently learned to know as individuals.

"But you asked after these counsels," Number Twelve continued in the way of the elderly and wise. "That is the time that our leader invites suggestions and even modest criticism from his underlings with the understanding that such suggestions will not result in sudden death, or, in point of fact, even serious maiming.''

Number Twelve leaned closer and said in an even lower voice, ''Still, it is best not to speak—ever. I did not grow to be one of the oldest among the thieves by taking foolish chances. There may not be any purposeful swordplay during the course of what is about to transpire, but it is amazing how often after these counsels certain outspoken thieves meet with unfortunate accidents.''

''Unfortunate accidents?'' Ali Baba was struck by this man's honesty. ''Is life among the thieves, then, always so perilous?''

''It does wear upon you, more and more with every passing day.'' The older thief sighed with that. ''I was not always like this,'' he said, and the pain of his change was evident in his every word. ''Once I was light of heart, and told clever stories about the foibles of men and beasts.''

The woodcutter could not imagine that this dire man had ever had a happy thought in his lifetime. Would Ali Baba's time among these thieves change him as profoundly?

Another of the thieves had produced a small gong, and beat upon it with the flat of a dagger. ''It is time for the counsel!'' he called, although he had some trouble with the *s* sound, whistling more than speaking it, since he was missing most of his teeth.

''That is Number Two,'' the man whose name was once Harun explained. ''Be careful to show him deference.''

''Counsel time!'' Number Two called.

Ali Baba thought he understood. ''He is so high among the thieves because he dispenses wisdom?''

''Few thieves dispense wisdom,'' Harun said bleakly. ''But there is another of our chieftain's many rules: If your number is less than ten, you may have someone killed in your place. For this reason, it is best not to anger—it is even better not to even talk with—the lower-numbered thieves.''

''Time for the counsel!'' Number Two remarked to accompany his gonging.

Ali Baba turned away from his grim advisor. Every moment among this ignoble band brought him a new unpleasantness. But, despite the older man's warnings to avoid undue conversation, there were still many questions the woodcutter would like to have answered.

''Counsel commencing immediately!'' the second thief added.

Ali Baba determined to ask one such question aloud: ''Then

your chieftain has no way to discipline those among the upper echelons?''

"Ready yourselves for the counsel!'' Number Two called as he redoubled his gonging.

Instead of an answer to Ali Baba's inquiry, Number Twelve pointed to their chieftain.

"That is far too much banging!'' Thief Number One declared as he glared angrily at the fellow with the gong.

Thief Number Two allowed both gong and dagger to fall from his numb fingers as he looked upon his leader in utmost horror.

"Another tooth?'' was his simple yet terrified question.

"Another tooth!'' the chieftain commanded.

"Hand me a rock,'' his underling replied with an air of resignation, "and it shall be done!''

Their chieftain nodded pleasantly, pleased with the way the men obeyed his authority. "The counsel begins!''

No one spoke immediately, disquieted, perhaps, with the sound of the man attempting to dislodge his own bicuspid.

"How much gold have we gained?'' Thief Number One asked as he turned to another of their band, a thin man with a prominent nose.

"That was my traveling companion,'' someone whispered in Ali Baba's ear. He glanced over to see it was Achmed, also known as Number Twenty-eight, who pointed to the thief their leader had singled out.

The thief with the prominent nose who was once Achmed's traveling companion picked up the small sack of gold and took but an instant to glance inside.

"One hundred and twenty-seven dinars,'' was his immediate answer.

All traces of a smile left the bandit chieftain's face. "That is all? At this rate, we will be bankrupt from expenses alone. There will have to be some changes made!'' He looked out at his assembled thieves. "I need some suggestions that will gain us some gold, and I need them now!''

Thief Number One spent a moment to scratch deeply at the whiskers upon his chin. "Who have we not heard from of late?'' The scratching hand shot out to point at one of their band. "Number Twenty-two!''

All faces turned to one smallish thief who was standing toward the left of the group.

"Um,'' Thief Number Twenty-two began as he shifted his weight from one foot to the other. "Er. Let's see. That is—''

"Your opportunity has expired!" The leader of the thieves snapped his fingers, and men in black to either side of Number Twenty-two grabbed him and began to drag him away. Certain other thieves drew their swords and followed.

"When we have a counsel, you are allowed to speak," Harun said close by the ear of Ali Baba. "The one thing you are not allowed to do is not speak."

"Careful there," Thief Number One called to the others. "Do not kill him completely. We need to maintain our ideal numbers, at least for the time being."

The chieftain frowned at the others. "But we have made no progress toward gold. Someone must be able to make a suggestion, before I lose my patience." He pointed straight at Ali Baba. "You! Number Thirty-nine! You are so good at growing a beard, surely you must have some worthwhile recommendations."

Ali Baba's throat felt as though it had encountered a sandstorm rising from his stomach. He had to come up with an immediate suggestion, or he would end up as almost dead as Number Twenty-two. But what did he, a poor woodcutter, know about the accumulation of gold? The only time he had witnessed any great deal of money, save for that in the cave, was in the marketplace, and that was only at a great distance, among those wealthier merchants who never stooped to deal with poor woodcutters.

Wealthy merchants, too lofty for poor woodcutters? Of, course, for gold there was always the marketplace!

"This is a city," Ali Baba said as quickly as he was able. "There are caravans arriving every day."

Thief Number One did not react with any particular emotion to this news. "We are busy thieves. We do not enjoy waiting."

"Often there are more than one," Ali Baba added hastily, even though he was not certain this was the case. "On a good day, you can find dozens!"

At this, the bandit leader smiled. "Dozens of caravans, laden with gold? That sounds like a job for the forty thieves!" He pulled his scimitar from his belt and brandished it in the air. "The counsel is finished. Lead us, Number Thirty-nine, and we shall plunder!"

What else might a humble woodcutter do? Ali Baba turned about and ran toward the marketplace. He trusted there would be a caravan in the vicinity. If not, well, perhaps becoming almost dead was not quite as bad as Ali Baba might imagine.

Still, he really imagined it was even worse.

◆

Chapter the Thirteenth,
in which we see that the future is sometimes planned, and sometimes simply occurs.

The thieves approached the marketplace from the west. Ali Baba ran on before them on foot, followed by thirty-odd mounted horsemen, and his brother's basket strapped upon another horse's saddle. With every step he took, he began to doubt the wisdom of his advice to the leader of the band. What if there was nothing resembling a caravan at the marketplace before them? What if there were no more in that group of stalls but the buyers and sellers of vegetables? The woodcutter had already seen bandits lose fingers and teeth for the slightest affronts to their chieftain. What might Ali Baba lose if he could not produce that gold which Thief Number One so feverishly desired?

He turned the final corner that led to the market square, and saw, at the eastern approach, a group of men slowly advancing astride camels; a large enough group, no matter what their true purpose, to serve as a caravan. Ali Baba would always have a difficult time expressing how overwhelmingly happy this sight had made him, except perhaps to recall that this was the first time he ever felt the slightest desire to kiss a camel.

"Look!" he called to those who followed. "The very thing that I foretold!"

And with that, thieves and horses galloped past him, so that the air was filled with great clouds of dust and thundering hooves, shrieks of triumph and screams of fear.

By the time the dust had cleared, the caravan, if caravan it truly was, had been defeated. At the very least, all those men who had previously ridden camels were now prostrate upon the ground, begging for their very lives as the gloating thieves stood above them.

"We have triumphed!" one thief announced, pointing his scimitar at the prone travelers.

"We have booty!" another called, holding up two large sacks heavy with some quantity or other.

"Mostly, we have vegetables!" a third added, reaching into another of those sacks and pulling out something large and green.

"What are you saying?" cried their leader, who still surveyed their triumph from atop his horse. "Is there no gold?"

"No, there is a certain quantity of gold," replied one of the thieves left holding the sacks as he looked within his bag. "But there is no denying we have also captured a large quantity of tubular vegetables."

Their chieftain frowned at this. "Are you certain?"

The thief who pulled forth the large bulbous object glanced down where it still sat in his hand. "It must be a vegetable."

"How can you tell?" asked one of his fellows, obviously ill versed in the ways of agriculture.

"For one thing," the first one replied reasonably, "it has no legs."

A number of thieves nodded at the wisdom of this.

"A tubular vegetable?" their leader demanded. "Is that all you can find?"

"Well," said that thief who had first explored his bag, "There *are* green ones and orange ones."

"What good are vegetables?" their leader remarked as his face began to turn a most unpleasant color.

Ali Baba, who felt more than distantly responsible for this present turn of events, and who further continued to fret about the potential sudden loss of his own extremities, perceived that it was time to do a little justification of what now lay before them.

"We might always eat them," he therefore mentioned.

"Who among us can cook?" one of the other fellows in black asked. "We are all thieves!"

"But enough of vegetables!" their chieftain demanded. "What of the gold?"

"Oh, there is a certain amount of gold," the fellow with the prominent nose remarked as he held up an exceedingly small pouch. "Seventeen dinars."

"That is all?" Thief Number One remarked, a quaver in his voice that might put certain earthquakes to shame.

"Have mercy upon us, O fearsome thieves!" called the leader of the caravan, although his face was still pressed into the dirt. "We did indeed once transport great quantities of gold and jewels, until thieves in the desert stole them all. Time after time, we lost our valuables in such a way that there was no longer any gold to be used for commerce, and we were forced to barter in vegetables. Alas, we can no longer transport what we do not have!''

''That is it, then?'' The chieftain spoke in little more than a whisper. ''We have been *too* successful?'' For the first time, Ali Baba thought he saw fear upon the face of Thief Number One. ''How, then, can we possibly pursue our livelihood?''

The woodcutter had never seen the bandit leader so distraught. He was quite certain he would be losing some fairly major body part in short order.

But instead of ordering Ali Baba to cut himself indiscriminately, Thief Number One turned his ire back to the men upon the ground.

''Come, my thieves!'' he called to his villainous minions. ''Examine these wretches more closely, to see any secret places they might have within their clothes or bodies.''

A modest amount of ripping away of clothes and prodding with swords quickly produced a handful of coins and rings and even a semiprecious stone or two.

''That is all?'' Thief Number One called in disbelief. ''There is a grim fact that we must face, O my thieves.'' His scimitar pointed toward the man who had called for mercy. ''Perhaps this son of an unmarried dog is right, and we have already collected almost all the gold that exists in this realm.''

This seemed such a serious topic to their leader that Ali Baba's transgression was apparently forgotten. In fact, with the consternation and argument now taking place among the thieves, even the woodcutter seemed to be forgotten.

''Time for a counsel!'' Thief Number One exclaimed.

''A counsel!'' the other thieves murmured in agreement.

And, as he thought upon it, why wouldn't the woodcutter be forgotten? Now that he had a beard, Ali Baba realized, he was an equal among thieves, and no one appeared to be paying him any attention whatsoever.

''A thief without booty is a man without purpose!'' Thief Number One announced. Many of his brigands nodded their heads in surly agreement.

Ali Baba now stood at his local marketplace, only a few blocks from his home. A few casual steps away, and he would never have to worry about losing body parts again. This nightmare could be over forever.

"I have a thought," the man who was Achmed's friend suggested.

"Speak, O greatest of my thieves at handling a dinar," their leader encouraged.

"What if we gave some of it back?" the other thief asked.

Ali Baba took a pair of steps away from the center of this commotion. No one appeared to take notice.

"You *are* talking about the gold?" the brigand chief replied darkly. "There are certain thoughts that one should not even mention in counsel! It is almost time for certain thieves to have an accident!"

"Hear me out!" the other man said with an undoubtedly foolhardy boldness. "We wouldn't give it back for very long. We rather lend it to them, so that it might multiply in the presence of their other riches. And, at the moment they join it to their other wealth, no matter how cleverly hidden, we will strike!"

Then the woodcutter might possibly escape? His thoughts turned briefly to the rescue of Kassim. But, the woodcutter reasoned, his brother could no longer lead a normal life in his present condition. Perhaps, indeed, he would think less about his misery if he led a life of adventure.

Thief Number One had paused to think about this most recent proposal. "Then you are saying, Number Twenty-seven, that we would not really give these riches back to these fools."

"No, no, not permanently, by any means," Achmed's friend, Number Twenty-seven, replied with great assurance. "We would indeed give only for so long as it took before we could steal it back!"

"Therefore, we manage to retain all the gold within our kingdom, and still ply our trade with some regularity," mused Thief Number One, quite pleased with the possibilities. "I foresee but a single difficulty. It cannot even be hinted that we are giving back gold to honest citizens. Think what such a rumor would do to our reputation among cutthroats and ne'er-do-wells!"

Ali Baba pushed himself gently to the back of the cluster of thieves.

"Oh, there should be no such rumors, nothing so simple as that," Number Twenty-seven explained. "From the very first, all shall realize that this is, of course, a part of a greater plan."

"A greater plan?" their leader asked in fascination.

"The Greater Caravan Redistribution Program," the other thief explained. "Yes, we give these travelers a little gold. Then we swoop down upon them and redistribute that gold, plus whatever other goods they may carry, to ourselves."

The chieftain appeared to have a final doubt. "We wouldn't have to go back into the cave, would we?"

"Certainly not," Number Twenty-seven replied. "We need only work with the gold in hand."

"Sheer genius," the chieftain declared. "May no accident occur to this fine thief for a hundred years!" He paused to chew upon a ragged and filthy fingernail. "But how do we proceed? Still, I think there is yet gold to be had in the immediate vicinity."

All the thieves were before Ali Baba now. No one would even think to stop him if he ran back to his household. Once under the protection of the fast-talking Marjanah, he might be forever beyond the grasp of this ignoble band!

So Ali Baba ran. And, to his amazement, he heard no pursuit. Up one street and down another he sped, until he had reached his inadequate gate, which, in his absence, had been reconstructed, and was now closed and no doubt bolted.

He banged upon the wood, which was of a more sturdy construction (and therefore far less inadequate) than the gate he had erected here before.

"Marjanah," he called, "open this gate immediately!"

And the gate opened.

"Who are you?" Marjanah demanded.

"Where are your eyes, girl?" Ali Baba demanded. "It is I, your master!"

But this answer did not please the young woman. "Though my master has many talents, growing a beard is not one of them."

The gate slammed shut again, and Ali Baba could hear the distinct sound of a bolt being thrown back into place.

This was as disastrous, Ali Baba thought, as a sandstorm followed by a flood. His new appearance had temporarily confounded his slave. But if he did not quickly remove himself from the street, others of his appearance might again make his life extremely difficult. But how was he to leave this street if this gate was locked before him?

It was then that Ali Baba remembered there was more than one way to open a way that had been closed to him.

"Open, Sesame!" he declared.

The gate opened.

Marjanah glared at him from the other side. "How did you do that? As if I had any doubt about your true nature!" In her hand,

Marjanah brandished a very familiar hatchet. "We know the ways of thieves!"

The gate slammed with a resounding crash.

This was to be the woodcutter's fate, then. Marjanah could not know him, for she had never seen him with a beard. Fickle, then, was the hand of Destiny! This beard, which had saved his life but a moment before, had now left him homeless.

How, indeed, could his day become any worse?

"Ah!" came the all-too-familiar voice of Thief Number One. "One of our number has found a likely hiding place for gold!"

♦

Chapter the Fourteenth,
in which things most decidedly and definitely become worse.

Ali Baba spun away from the door. "Gold?" he said in a voice of great incredulity. "Why would there be gold in such a humble dwelling as this?"

Thief Number One smiled pleasantly at this falsehood, while the thieves ranked behind him laughed most pleasantly.

"It is true," the bandit chieftain remarked, "this looks like the least likely spot where one might find riches. But as the wise man says, even jewels may be covered by a coating of bat guano."

Ali Baba had visions of many lost extremities, not to mention certain areas beneath his kitchen which would soon be emptied of their newfound treasure.

"We are very happy you are so concerned as to help us to increase our riches," the bandit leader continued smoothly. "It was unfortunate that you neglected to tell us where you wished to lead us. Lucky are we that your brother in the basket also knew the way."

"Yes, it was my brother who was responsible for my present condition." Kassim's smug voice originated from that wicker basket that was now placed by the chieftain's right side. "But, say, did you know that there was a blind tailor in this neighborhood?"

The leader of the thieves seemed to hold very little interest in blind tailors at the moment. He instead continued to address Ali Baba. "Your most recent actions place your loyalty somewhat in question." He paused to allow the return of his wicked smile. "However, all questions shall be removed once we receive a sufficient quantity of gold."

"Yes!" Kassim's voice came somewhat feverishly from within his basket. "I know exactly where the gold is! Put me back together, and I promise to show you vast quantities of gold!"

But that most recent threat from Thief Number One did naught but give the woodcutter a certain grim resolve. He would not give up the gold. If he were soon to be dead, at least he would not be dead and poor.

But resolutions mean nothing if they are not followed by action. Ali Baba knew he would have to devise some hurried explanations or he would experience a very hollow kitchen floor.

"You can see from this pitiful gate," he said as he beat his hand against the assembled scrap wood, "that what lies beyond must be totally insignificant."

"Very well, we shall inspect this situation further." The chieftain pointed to another of their number. "Number Twenty-eight. Climb to the top of that fence. What do you see?"

The thief who was once called Achmed did as he was instructed, clambering up the rough-hewn fence as surely as he might climb a ladder. He surveyed the yard beyond for a moment before he replied, "There is naught here within view but a bucket with a large hole and a one-legged chicken."

"That bad?" Thief Number One asked in surprise. "No one who had any money whatsoever would make do with such possessions as these. Perhaps Thief Number Thirty-nine speaks the truth."

"A thief speaking the truth?" one of their number, a man of even darker complexion than those about him, remarked in awe. He paused to regard Ali Baba with a certain speculation upon his countenance.

"He is new to our ranks," answered the thief who had once been known as Aladdin. "We must give him time to learn our ways."

"As you say." And with that, the darker thief turned away.

"Wait!" Achmed called from his position upon the fence. "There is more! I now see a young woman with a hatchet."

"That is all?" their chieftain asked after a moment's pause.

"Well," Achmed replied after another silence, "she is actually a very attractive woman."

"I tell you," Kassim called out excitedly, as if in fear of losing the other's attention, "he is hiding the gold!"

But with that remark, resolve redoubled within Ali Baba; a resolve that had become even stronger than his feelings toward his extended family.

"Did it ever occur to you," the woodcutter therefore said to the assembled thieves, "that this man might be sending you on a pointless search of my property to protect something of his own?"

He looked meaningfully down the avenue toward the much more elaborate and fortified gate that adorned the household of Kassim.

A smile returned to the face of the bandit leader. "These are the first words I have heard that might hold a grain of truth."

"There is more!" Achmed called from his lookout. "Her hatchet is rapidly approaching my face." He leapt backward to the ground as something hit the fence with a loud thump.

"So she is not only beautiful but a woman with spirit?" mused their leader. "I tell you, there are more riches in the world than gold."

"But gold is what you want!" Kassim interjected in that same overexcited tone, aware perhaps that his case was already lost. "Sew me up, and your hands shall be full of it!"

"Who are you going to believe," Ali Baba remarked coolly, for he believed he now had the upper hand, " a full-bearded thief or a head in a basket?"

"You make a persuasive point," the brigand chieftain agreed. "There is but one way to determine truth or falsehood." He clapped his hands as he turned to the others. "Thieves! Open both these households!"

Half a dozen of the bandits stepped forward to the inadequate gate of Ali Baba, while the rest of the despicable band trotted up the street to Kassim's abode.

It amazes me yet, but what happened next occurred in as little time as it might take me to complete only a simple sentence. Ali Baba's deficient gate was removed with a simple push by a half dozen hands, while Kassim's entryway resisted for a few seconds longer, necessitating the judicious use of axes and clubs.

The many thieves immediately disappeared within their respective destinations. Ali Baba thought about following those bandits who had entered his own abode, but was discouraged by the scimitar that Thief Number One currently held against his rib cage. Kassim, for his part, made a series of high, incoherent noises, as if only now was he feeling the true pain of being divided into six portions.

"There is no need for either of you to move," the bandit chieftain reassured them with far too gleeful a demeanor. "Whatever you wish to see again within these households shall, I assure you both, be brought out before you in no time whatsoever."

Kassim raved and ranted, repeatedly asking why the leader of the thieves would treat him so, and furthermore, if whatever small riches he might hold were to be taken, the least the thieves could do is resew Kassim by way of recompense. Ali Baba remembered the great resolve he had felt only a moment before, then looked down at the sword poking his robes and remembered where that resolve had gone.

But the woodcutter did not have long to reminisce, for already thieves were emerging from the ruined gate of Kassim's household, carting forth large and ostentatious objects made of gold and precious stones of the sort that Kassim and his wife generally favored.

"This is but a fraction of the riches we have found inside!" the first of the thieves said with great enthusiasm. "Reflecting pools set with pearls! Formal gardens with golden pathways! Gem-encrusted statues! Treasure-laden outbuildings! The place is riddled with riches!"

"So you would show us gold?" the leader said approvingly to Kassim.

Kassim could but reply with a clearing of his throat: "Well, there is, of course, *that* gold." Considering the present state of his head, Ali Baba was surprised that his brother had a throat to clear.

And still did thieves emerge from the brothel worker's estate, carrying objects of ever greater size and value. This whole procession gave the first thief some pause. "I have been inside that household. Now that you make mention of these things, and I see many of them brought before me, I recall this location." He paused to shiver in a way that did not appear to be voluntary. "There was a certain female slave that perplexed me so greatly when I visited the home next door, my mind shies away from the entire sequence of events."

The last of the thieves emerged from Kassim's residence, pulling with them Kassim's exceedingly beautiful wife and five of her maidservants.

"And aren't you the pretty one?" Thief Number One remarked of Kassim's wife with his very best leer. "I shall see that you get the most special of treatments."

Kassim's wife, poor, frightened creature that she was, did her best to smile through these very worst of circumstances and to say, bravely, "Then let it be known that I expect no less than the very best."

The bandit chieftain roared at that. "The best you shall have! But what of the treasures of the other household?"

A pair of thieves emerged from Ali Baba's poor residence, but, to the woodcutter's great relief, they carried nothing between them.

"There is nothing within but wood," the first of them announced. "And much of that is of an exceedingly inferior variety."

Were Ali Baba not so worried about the fate of his household and the gold therein, he might have taken offense at mere thieves criticizing his woodcutting prowess.

"We considered taking some of the nicer pieces," the second thief admitted, "but all our extra sacks are already filled with vegetables."

"Our search of the house was not entirely without success, however," the first of the two added with a grin that Ali Baba did not care for in the slightest.

The woodcutter found that he could no longer breathe. Now that they had had their little jest, would they then bring out his gold?

But instead of what poor Ali Baba expected, the remaining four bandits came out in pairs, each pair escorting one of the household's two women.

"You!" Marjanah called defiantly when her gaze fell upon the leader of the thieves.

"You!" the leader of the thieves cried in shock as his gaze in turn fell upon her.

"This is the young woman I had previously mentioned," Achmed said as he guided Marjanah by her left elbow. "Is she not of a special quality?"

"She is, indeed, a very attractive young creature," the chieftain said with some distaste. "However, should we decide to sell her, we may have to cut out her tongue."

"Sell her?" was Achmed's somewhat startled reply.

"Well, not immediately," Thief Number One allowed. "A maiden as lovely as this is destined first for the Palace of Beautiful Women."

At that, all the bandits cheered. Ali Baba found his breathing impaired all over again. The Palace of Beautiful Women sounded as though it might not be the most wholesome of places. What had he done? His gold might still be safe, but the two most favored women in the world had been placed in mortal jeopardy!

"Oh, woe!" his wife cried as she was brought forward. "We are to be taken away by horrible bandits!"

"See?" the bandit chieftain said to Marjanah. "This is more the sort of respectful fear we expect of our captives!"

"Oh, woe!" Ali Baba's wife further remarked as she fell to her knees. "We shall never see our pitifully humble home again!"

The chieftain looked on with approval. "Groveling, the tearing of hair, and the rending of garments, all these are elements of the proper misery."

"Oh, woe!" she continued, her voice rising as she gained confidence. "Never again shall I sleep under my leaky and inadequate roof."

"Of course," the leader added as his smile became the slightest bit severe, "there is a limit to even the best of things."

But Ali Baba's wife had not yet reached a limit of her own. "Oh, woe! Never again shall I attempt to somehow carry water from place to place in a bucket that sports a large hole!"

"O chieftain!" one of the subsidiary thieves interrupted, to his leader's greatly evident relief. "We will have to leave some of the vegetables behind. We have not enough rope for both the foodstuffs and the women."

"Very well," the chieftain said loudly, doing his best to ignore the woman's ever-increasing wail. "Have it done quickly. I am eager to be on my way. We have a great distance"—he grimaced at the thought—"to travel before we reach the Palace of Beautiful Women, and of course—" He paused again, and when next he spoke, his voice was softer, and seemed tinged with dread. "The enchanted cavern."

"Oh, woe!" Ali Baba's wife continued with even greater exuberance. Even the woodcutter had to admit that this was one of her best wailing performances ever. "Never to see again the city of my birth, to visit the same lice-infested watering hole, to throw the evening slops over the back fence!"

The chieftain paused in his preparation. "That is quite enough!" he demanded.

But Ali Baba knew from experience that nothing might stop her now. "Oh, woe!" she further caterwauled. "Never again will I have to suffer the sweet indignity of owning a chicken with but one leg!"

"I will do horrible damage to you with a sword!" the leader threatened as he suggestively grabbed the hilt of his scimitar.

"Oh, woe!" she replied. "He will do horrible damage to me with—"

The chieftain removed his fist from his sword so that he might better wring his hands. "That is it! Leave her behind. The rope will be better used for the vegetables. After all, we have to eat!"

"Oh, woe!" the woodcutter's wife moaned. "They are leaving me behind and using the rope for—"

"Throw her back inside her courtyard and shut what is left of the gate behind her," the leader screamed as he raised his fists to his temples. "I can bear no more!"

"Oh, woe!" Ali Baba's wife continued. "I am to be thrown back into the courtyard—"

A pair of thieves quickly did what their master bade them before the woman could wail further.

At least, then, Ali Baba thought, his wife would be spared. It was good that these thieves did not know the woman in the same way the woodcutter did, or they would realize that her fretful wailing was one of her most endearing traits. Now, though, she would live, and someone at least could spend the great quantity of hidden gold. It was a pity, though, that he would never be able to partake in that pleasure.

But, while Ali Baba would suffer in silence, Marjanah would not. "Do you think yourself so high and powerful, then," she said of the leader of this fearsome band, "that you control the life of individuals at your whim?"

"I command more than life, wretch of a woman!" the bandit chief replied regally. "I also command death!"

"Yes," Marjanah replied with the slightest of smiles, "it does take such a great command of philosophy to hold a sword. Or perhaps you would be more comfortable conversing further on the nature of gates?"

The bandit chieftain did but stare at her for a long moment, although his face during this period turned to a number of colors other than that which was the most natural.

The woodcutter could see where this confrontation would lead. First, he was deprived of his wife's company, and, a moment hence, he would be deprived of Marjanah's existence. Ali Baba could no longer help himself, and thus let out a noise of quiet desperation.

But with that, the young slave turned to him with a look of surprise and wonder.

"Master?" Marjanah asked. "Is it, then, really and truly you?"

"Yes, it is, my dear girl," Ali Baba said with a smile, for she had startled him from his desperation. "What led you at last to recognize me?"

She replied as follows: "I have served you through hard times and even harder times.'' That was indeed a good description of his life. ''I would know your whimper anywhere.''

''We have no more time for names or past lives!'' the chieftain called, now that he had again collected his thoughts. ''We are all thieves, forevermore! Tie the women together, so that we can lead them behind the horses!'' At that, the bandit leader laughed at his mastery over the helpless females. ''No one can stand against our strength!''

But even now, the slave of Ali Baba would not remain silent. She said instead, ''Your treatment of these women most assuredly shows me how strong you are!'' She showed him a defiant smile. ''Should you master us as easily as you master gates, then I truly believe that we are all free to go!''

Every remark Marjanah made seemed to make the chieftain more furious than he had been before. ''Your tongue may be removed soon rather than late!'' he said when he somehow managed to control his severe shaking. ''I am not exactly certain that, in your case, it would diminish your value!'' He waved dismissively at Achmed as he mounted his stallion. ''Place her at the end of the line so that I might have as little contact with her as possible!''

Achmed pulled the defiant slave girl away from the leader with surprising gentleness. Kassim made a final plea for a visit to a blind tailor as his basket was once again strapped to a horse, but his entreaties met with the same lack of result as had all of the woodcutter's previously held hopes and plans.

Ali Baba had to admit, for the first time in his life, that virtually everything was going truly, fully, entirely badly.

◆ ◆ ◆

BOOK THE SECOND:
being
ALADDIN'S STORY

♦

Chapter the Fifteenth,
in which an entirely different story
threatens to intrude.

The next few hours were but a blur to the woodcutter.

Another of the thieves came to him and gave him a horse. That much he remembered. He must have mounted that horse as well, for he found himself riding in the midst of the pack of black-clothed men, those same black robes that he himself wore. He heard nothing but the pounding hooves of horses, and the occasional hoarse shout that rose above the gallop.

Somewhere behind him were the town of his birth, the woman he had married, and the inadequate dwelling that now contained vast quantities of gold. He could not worry about any of these, for he would never see them again.

He had more concern for Marjanah, and, yes, he had to admit it, the wife of Kassim. They were to be taken to the Palace of Beautiful Women, by order of this ignoble band's despicable chieftain. And while the thief who had once been a woodcutter had no idea of the true nature of this place, still, when he considered the caliber of the men who would supply such a dwelling, Ali Baba could make some guesses as to the institution's true nature. Except for the fact that he remained in six pieces, Kassim, no doubt, would feel immediately at home in such a place. Ah, well, Ali Baba mused, perhaps there were blind tailors in the vicinity of the Palace of Beautiful Women as well.

But his ruminations were interrupted as the horses slowed.

"Have we reached our destination?" he asked of the thief once named Aladdin, who now rode upon the woodcutter's right-hand side.

"No, there is still a half day's ride before us," was the thief's reply. "We must have reached some sort of distraction."

"Pardon?" Ali Baba asked of that, for he could not grasp Aladdin's precise meaning.

Achmed, who rode upon the left-hand side of the woodcutter, chose to answer his confusion. "Our master, the chieftain of all the thieves, is an individual of a single mind. If he says that we will ride to such and such a place, we will ride there, no matter what the time or distance or difficulty of intervening terrain, until we arrive. There are but two exceptions to this rule. One occurs at those moments when our band unexpectedly meets with a caravan."

"There is always time to stop and steal," Aladdin agreed.

"Of course," Achmed added, "it hardly seems worth stopping for caravans these days, seeing the amount of monetary return. Perhaps this will be the first lot to experience our Caravan Redistribution Program.

"But we stop for more than caravans," Achmed continued. "The other contingency occurs when we face a situation of sufficient danger."

"A danger in which we might lose too many thieves," Aladdin further explained before Ali Baba could ask. "Oh, as I am sure you have noticed, we will often lose a thief or two in the course of a normal afternoon. But, should the situation threaten to cost us more than a dozen or so of our band, well, even our chieftain sometimes realizes that it does take time to replace thieves."

"Although not really that great a time," Achmed contradicted. "The requirements for entrance are really very basic." He leaned over and patted the top of the basket that rode atop the next horse over in the crowd. "And they are getting lower all the time."

"You wouldn't treat me so," Kassim replied with a certain amount of petulance, "if I had had a chance to be sewn back together!"

"But still," even Achmed admitted, "the more time that is spent in recruiting, the less time there is for gold."

"It is the force that drives all our actions," Aladdin added, and at least in this, the two seasoned thieves were in agreement. "Or, in this case, stops us in our drive."

The thief once called Harun now pulled his horse parallel to the others. "I see no caravan," was his only comment.

The calls came from ahead. "Sandstorm! Dismount! Take cover! A sandstorm is coming."

"We will have time to rest," Harun said to the others.

"We will have time to hide from the elements," Aladdin agreed.

"We will have time to get sand blown into our eyes and swept down our throats," Achmed further commented.

But the woodcutter could not immediately share the concern of the others. "Sandstorm?" Ali Baba asked in some confusion. "The sky above us seems not to contain a single cloud."

"No," Harun explained. "There is no question of what is to come. It is something that you shall learn, should you survive within our band for a great enough time, for there are those thieves among us who have certain extraordinary abilities."

"Well do I know that Thief Number Twelve speaks the truth," the bandit once called Achmed agreed. "As my master, who was once known as Sinbad, is remarkably good at estimating all things monetary, so is this other thief, a particularly dark-skinned fellow, amazingly adept at forecasting what will happen within the desert."

Ali Baba remembered the man with the deep complexion, and the intensity of his gaze when it fell upon the woodcutter. With a gaze of that sort, Ali Baba imagined this other man might know a great many things. He mentioned his concerns to his immediate companions.

"His actions are most peculiar," Aladdin agreed with a troubled frown, "and yet he seems somehow familiar. So much has changed in my life, it is sometimes difficult to place faces and events."

"When you are constantly looking at thirty-nine other men with black robes and long beards, everyone looks familiar," Achmed reassured his fellow.

"Perhaps you are correct," Aladdin replied as he turned his frowning face up to the sky. "And yet, this man, now that our new thief mentions it—" He paused, apparently with no further locale for his thoughts to travel. "If I but still retained my lamp!" He shook his fist at an uncaring sky. "But that is useless speculation. We must make ourselves ready for this change in the weather."

A lamp? So Ali Baba heard again an indication that one of these men might be the same as those revered by storytellers! For why would a man so regret the loss of a reading lamp? Unless such a lamp shone with a particularly clear light, he supposed. He frowned in much the manner of the thief now called Aladdin. Such speculation still produced no result. He looked instead back to the sky, and noticed the first tinges of black gathering at the horizon.

"This is why they have stopped us here," Harun commented as he rode on slightly in front of the others. "There is a gathering of boulders immediately ahead, which will give us some comfort from the elements.''

This was, the woodcutter realized, the first time this band had moved slowly enough so that he could actually remark upon his surroundings. They had now come to a place where the forests were behind them, and they were surrounded by the sort of grasses and low shrubs that indicated they were at the very edge of the desert. And, indeed, Ali Baba could now see the first of the thieves leading their horses down a low hill ahead, into the very collection of large rocks Harun had mentioned.

Ali Baba had seen such formations of rock before. ''Might there be some caves down there as well?''

''One never mentions caves when one is near to our chieftain,'' Achmed warned quietly. ''The first among thieves does not appreciate caves.''

''But,'' Ali Baba objected with a certain logic, ''he keeps all his riches within a cavern!''

''And that is the precise reason,'' Achmed agreed. ''One cave has soured our master against all others.''

Ali Baba remembered how the other thieves had said previously that he would never truly understand much of what motivated their band, for there would seldom be sufficient time for explanations. Upon reflection, that prediction seemed to be remarkably prescient.

''But come,'' Harun called from ahead. ''The storm is gathering force ahead.''

''Thief Number Twelve did not rise to his exalted position by taking unnecessary chances,'' Achmed called to Ali Baba as the youth hurried ahead in such a way as to indicate that, indeed, all might benefit from the older man's example.

And with that, Ali Baba heard the first distant hints of the wind.

The others moved quickly then, and Ali Baba did his best to follow, dismounting from his horse and helping with a great length of canvas which the others strung between two boulders as protection from the coming sand. Harun further instructed the woodcutter to take certain lengths of fabric, and wet them and tie them about his face to help protect his mouth and eyes from the sand.

When they had finished what preparation they could, including the laying of rugs and cushions upon the ground to increase their comfort, and the judicious placing of a pair of lamps that they might light when the sandstorm cut off all outside illumination,

Harun stepped from their newly constructed shelter to once again study the sky.

"It will still be a few minutes." He turned to look upon their horses, which had been tied behind the canvas enclosure to give them as much protection from the wind as was possible. "Come, let us take cover and converse for a few minutes while we await the worst of it."

Still was Ali Baba not content with his labors, for he was concerned for the welfare of Marjanah and the wife of Kassim.

"But what of the others?" he asked. "What of the women?"

"The others will fend as best they can," Achmed replied. "But do not worry for the women. They will be with our chieftain, who will have claimed the most protected corner of this place. As careless as the first among thieves can be with his men, never would he jeopardize someone destined for the Palace of Beautiful Women."

Thus reassured (if only he knew the true nature of that palace!), the woodcutter decided he would be best served by remaining within their protected enclosure. He could hear the wind now as a constant presence, a high, keening sound, as if composed of all the screams of any who had ever died by the power of the gale.

"But we have more to do than listen to the wind," Achmed said as he sat across from his fellows. "We have a pair of newcomers among us." He nodded both to Ali Baba and the basket which contained Kassim. "What better excuse to tell the stories of our lives?"

All three of the senior thieves agreed immediately to such a plan. There followed a brief period of haggling over which story was most worthy to be told first, with Harun obliquely alluding to many jests of great complexity, and Achmed making tantalizing reference to Sinbad and the many voyages. The thief once known as Aladdin seemed strangely silent during most of this exchange, and yet somehow it was determined that there would be a drawing of lengths of grass, to be overseen by the thief once called Aladdin. Whoever drew the longest blade of grass would be the one to tell his tale.

Quickly, and apparently to no one's surprise, the winner of this contest was Aladdin. Ali Baba glanced curiously at the others, as if there might have been some contrivance involved in this game of chance.

"He is stronger than either of us," Achmed said to the

woodcutter's unasked question, "and would even win should the fight be fair."

"Not that we might not object," Harun quickly added.

"Very quietly, however," Achmed added after a warning glance from the storyteller.

"This new thief among our ranks has asked questions that have unsettled me," the man once called Aladdin admitted as he sank down among the pillows, "so that I feel I must examine my life, to see how some part of my past might relate to my present condition, and perhaps my destiny."

"No man may forecast his own fate," Harun warned as he sat in a similar position.

"Although certain men may talk about it for all eternity," Achmed agreed as he, too, settled to the ground. "But to the story, before the sandstorm takes all our hearing."

Ali Baba decided he had best join them, and so gathered together sufficient of the pillows that remained to give him a comfortable position, as well as reserving a pair of large and fluffy cushions for the benefit of his brother, so that Kassim might have a proper perch for his basket to rest upon.

"Very well," Aladdin replied when he saw that all around him were properly settled. "And I charge you to listen carefully to my every word, for I somehow feel that this story may hold the answer to our very fates, including the possibility of escape from this ignoble band."

"Well, I'll give him this," Achmed said in quiet admiration and with the most moderate of whistles. "As a storyteller, he is great at beginnings."

And, with the wind ever rising behind him, Aladdin began his tale.

◆

Chapter the Sixteenth,
in which are revealed some complicated tales
and some even more tailored complications.

"Know ye that I was not always a lowly thief," said the thief who had once been called Aladdin, "but was, once upon a distant time, an equally lowly urchin of the streets, although between these two extremes, I found great fortune and lived for a time in a palace without equal."

"As did many of us," the one called Harun al Raschid was quick to add.

"If you listen to these stories for a great enough period of time," Achmed agreed, "you'll hear of many palaces without equal. It is truly amazing the sort of places that thieves have once lived."

"Yes," Aladdin replied with rather less patience than he had shown before, "but we are telling my story now, and I would thank you not to steal the center of attention."

"As any good thief would," Achmed commented. "Stealing is the reason we live."

"So our leader would have us believe," Aladdin persevered. "But I have not truly begun my tale."

"My palace was *too* without equal," Harun remarked with more than a little petulance.

"The palace was not important," Aladdin replied, "at least to the early part of my tale."

"Palaces are always of utmost importance," Harun answered with an intensity that Ali Baba had never seen before in the older bandit.

But intensity or no, Aladdin chose to ignore it. "As I was saying," he began instead, "I was a thoughtless lad of little more than a dozen years, who would spend his days in aimless pursuits as lads will, full of innocent games of sand wrestling and kick the fez."

"How many minarets did you have?" Harun asked with a pronounced sharpness.

"That is beside the point," the thief once called Aladdin remarked. "So it was that I ignored the entreaties of my hardworking father and long-suffering mother to find myself an occupation. So unenthusiastic was I that my family could find no one who would accept me as an apprentice, so my father took me into his own tailor shop, and attempted to introduce me to the rudiments of his sewing craft."

"Tailor?" Kassim's voice spoke up. So perhaps he had not dozed off, after all. "Did someone here say he was trained as a tailor?"

"Alas," Aladdin answered sadly, "the training did not take, for I was much more interested in continuing with my childhood games. So it was that I frittered away day after day, month after month, year after year, until my father took a sudden illness and died."

"That's very touching, I'm sure," Kassim said in the sort of voice he usually used in dismissing Ali Baba. The tone of his speech changed, however, with what he said next. "Certainly, though, you must have retained some tailoring skills."

"Well, I suppose I might be able to thread a needle under duress," Aladdin replied in a voice that indicated that sort of duress was very close at hand. "But with my father dead, my mother was forced to eke out a living doing the laundry of others, and even as her aged hands and eyes had to work from first light to the fall of night, only then could she afford to buy a crust of stale bread and a few elderly vegetables barely fit for the feeding of one's goats. And with that meager fare, she somehow managed to feed not only herself but her thoughtless son as well."

"Now that I have had time to consider the possibilities of my person being reconstructed," Kassim continued, perhaps to Aladdin, perhaps to no one in particular, "I am convinced it is the only way I shall have a future." Ali Baba realized that it was very difficult to discern the true nuances of a conversation when the one conversing had his head lost deep within a basket.

Aladdin, however, would no longer be deterred from telling his tale. "But no one can foretell the hand of Destiny. Or at least none that follow the path of righteousness. What, you may ask, do I mean by that remark?"

"You may have lost a palace," Harun responded to some other question altogether, "but I doubt that its minarets could compare in number or in splendor to that palace without match that I lost!''

"Very well," Aladdin proceeded, gazing not at any of those who had spoken but rather determinedly at a space some distance above our collective heads. "I shall answer no question, but forge straight ahead. So it was that my hardworking mother and her ne'er-do-well son received an unexpected visitor, who called himself my uncle, and my father's brother. And although my father had never mentioned that he had any brothers in his many years of marriage to my mother, and although, if you now look closely, you may see that I am of a Chinese heritage by the slant of my eye and the color of my skin, and the man who claimed to be our relation seemed to be of a darker hue entirely, as if he shared his heritage with the Moors, still did we not turn him away, for he showered gold, first upon me and then upon my mother, and provided us with many fine meals and further necessities of life that my mother had lacked for since the death of my father.

"So what if he looked nothing like my father, and in all other ways acted as if he were a total stranger to our lands and customs? With the amount of gold he was dispensing, he was entitled to the benefit of the doubt.

"But another wondrous thing occurred at this same remarkable time, as if you might wander through the greatest of deserts, and find not simply one flower blooming in the midst of the wasteland, but two.

"The three members of this new family had had one meal together when the uncle saw fit to reveal his identity, and a second meal where that uncle told that he had a further reason for seeking so far for his family, beyond his longing for a reunion. And this uncle said that he would reveal this reason at a third dinner, and therefore this final meal should be a repast surpassing both the others in magnitude and refinement. He therefore showered both Aladdin and his mother with such a quantity of gold that it made his earlier gifts seem like no more than motes of dust in the midst of a sandstorm.

"But I had mentioned the second miraculous occurrence which was even more wondrous to the lad than the sudden appearance of wealth! So it was that when the youth Aladdin took a portion of this third part of the stranger's generosity, and went to fetch certain articles for an even more sumptuous dinner than he, his mother, and the man who claimed to be his uncle had had previously, he was halted by a great commotion. And the young

Aladdin was soon to discover that this was far from an ordinary commotion.

" 'Beware!' called a trio of voices, far too loud to be so high in pitch. Three enormous eunuchs, as tall as one man squatting upon the shoulders of a second, and fully as broad in girth, marched past Aladdin through the city center, and announced that all men must go and shut themselves within their homes, for the fair Princess Badabadur wished to go for a stroll through the city square, and should any man gaze upon her without permission, that indiscretion would result in his instant death.

"In a panic that his life might end almost immediately after he had only recently experienced his very first truly balanced and complete meals, Aladdin rapidly sought some quarter where he might hide his face from the street. But, as Destiny would have it, that particular avenue that he now traversed was not a part of the public sector of stalls and shops, but was rather a residential quarter with private dwellings hidden behind high walls. Where could the lad go when there was nothing but stone barricades and barred gates to either side?

" 'Beware!' came the voices again. 'When we pass this way a second time, we shall see no other living soul, or their lives shall be forfeit!'

"Mayhaps, Aladdin thought, he could throw himself at one of those barred gates, or find a vine to climb over one of the fortress-high walls. But there seemed to be no vegetation to speak of except for the occasional low bush, and the gates that the lad took the time to examine featured many sharpened and unwelcoming stakes among the ornate metal grillework. There was no welcome for a street urchin anywhere in this quarter of the city.

" 'Beware!' called the voices, which once again grew closer. 'For our swords are drawn, and cut to the heart before a mortal man may make a sound!'

"Oh, that his life would end so unfairly! For the first time in his miserable existence, Aladdin wished he had pursued some more worthwhile goal in his life than the neighborhood championship of kick the fez.

" 'Beware!' came the ever-closer warning. 'For our ears are keen, and can hear the slightest breath of a man's desire!'

"Aladdin no longer looked for a wall or gate to hide behind. He searched wildly about for any objects whatsoever that might disguise his presence.

" 'Beware!' came those voices that now sounded as though they originated from about the closest street corner. 'For our eyes are clear and sharp, and can follow the movements of a gnat at fifty paces.'

"It was at that instant that the youth's gaze fell upon a recessed area immediately beyond the last gate in that particular row of dwellings. And in the recess were a trio of the low great bushes common to this street, and further were there three great earthenware vessels, of the sort used to house those less fragrant remains of the household until such time as the slaves could remove them to the river.

"Aladdin dove behind the collected bushes and vessels as the high voices called out again.

" 'Beware!' the voices called in unison. 'Do not think to hide from us, for no man may gaze upon the incredible beauty of Princess Badabadur and not call out in wonder and desire!'

"And with that, Aladdin heard the great footfalls of the eunuchs upon the dirt of the road. He clutched his hands above his knees and did his best not to make the slightest motion, even pausing in the taking of breath. And, as he became as silent as a stone, he heard the three tall eunuchs talk softly among themselves before they called out their next warning.

" 'All is clear so far upon our vigilant watch,' said the first of the three. From a narrow vantage point between two of the earthenware jars, Aladdin could see that this first one walked a bit ahead of the other two, as if that eunuch was in command. 'We are the obedient servants of our princess's every whim.'

" 'I wish the princess would have fewer of these whims,' complained the second of the three. 'My feet always hurt when we go on these marches.'

" 'Would that I only had to worry about my feet,' whined the third as that eunuch clutched at its stomach. 'I was unwise in what I ate at noontime.'

" 'It is time,' the first of the three said simply. All three joined to call, 'Beware! The Princess Badabadur walks among you!'

"As he hid from the eunuchs' vengeance, Aladdin found another reason not to breathe, for the earthen vessels close to his nose appeared to be near to overflowing, and from their pronounced odor, they must be destined for the river in a very short order.

"But all thoughts of odor—indeed, all thoughts that had ever flitted through the young man's consciousness—fled in a single instant with the next sight that reached Aladdin's eyes. For there was a girl who was dressed in robes the color of sunlight, and whose slightest smile might put the warmth of the sun to shame. She did not walk, rather she danced, and her dainty feet, clad in slippers laced with gold, barely seemed to touch the earth.

" 'This is a rather boring street,' she said with a sigh, and the sadness of her voice held the tone and beauty of the song of a nightingale. 'No shops or stalls or other items to divert my attention.' But all sadness in the world ended as she smiled again. 'Still, in all, there are very fine and sturdy walls to either side of this lane. And there are very ornate and fearsome gates within these walls, are there not? And look over yonder, at that fine collection of earthenware pottery and small bushes!'

"But that most recent utterance meant that this princess was gazing straight at the hiding place of Aladdin. That one so beautiful might almost gaze on this poor unworthy child of the streets was more than the youth could bear, and he flung aside all thoughts of large eunuchs with swift and sharpened swords. He found his mouth open, and a cry came unbidden to his lips, muffled only by the rapid insertion of his fist into that recently opened orifice.

"The three eunuchs paused, only a few paces beyond the space where the unlucky Aladdin now hid.

" 'Was that not the breath of a man's desire?' asked the eunuch who led the three.

" 'It sounded more like someone biting down upon his fist to stifle a moan,' said the second, who took this pause in their march to lean against a wall and massage his left foot.

" 'Pardon me,' the third remarked as that eunuch clutched his stomach with even more force than before. 'As I have said before, I should not have eaten those exotic cheeses for lunch.'

"Once having spoken, this third eunuch let forth with a remarkable flatulence that sounded like nothing so much as a bird being crushed by a clattering of timber.

" 'You do produce the most colorful of sounds,' their leader commented as the three once again resumed their protective march.

"So then these sexless soldiers would march forward, convinced there was naught here to warrant their attention? The youth could barely believe his good fortune. And yet Destiny would see that he not go completely unpunished, for Aladdin happened to be positioned directly in the rear of the retreating three, and so was privy to a new odor carried upon the wind that made the smell from the earthenware jars about him seem to be nothing but the scent of spring flowers.

"So overwhelmed was he by this more recent fragrance that the youth did not fully recover until the eunuchs and princess had wandered some distance out of sight. But, by that time, the great damage had been done. Aladdin knew he was finished with his childhood and all his childish games at last. He now had a purpose in life, for his heart was no longer his own. He knew he had to marry that princess, or he should surely die." Thief Number Thirty paused, a faraway look in his eyes.

"My former associate had a similar problem," the thief once called Achmed interjected. "Well, not too similar, actually, for it also involved the Queen of the Apes."

Aladdin blinked and stared at the younger thief with some consternation, as if mention of a queen of apes might totally destroy not only his fond dreams but his total concentration as well. And, indeed, that mention of animal royalty had piqued the woodcutter's interest despite his fascination with Aladdin's tale. Ali Baba realized that, should he survive within this band for great enough a time, there would be no end of stories.

"I will continue," Aladdin said with a certain brusqueness of tone, "for I feel that this story, unlike any mention of palaces or tailors or the Queen of the Apes, might be of importance to our future well-being."

"Tailors?" Kassim called with a suddenness that suggested he had recently roused himself from sleep. "I had almost forgotten. Think how much more rewarding your story might be if, as your tale unfolded, you were to practice with a needle and thread. What could be more fair that that?"

"Fair?" Aladdin replied in a voice rather more forceful than that which he had used before. "I shall be so fair as to spread your body parts so far and wide that they will never come together again!" He paused, and continued in a softer tone. "Forgive me. My life as a thief has given me a harsh and ungenerous edge. I know how much you have suffered, and no doubt suffer still. But please cease your interjections, or I shall toss your head outside the tent for the jackals to play with."

"Fairly said," Kassim replied in a rather more respectful tone. "My body parts will remain quietly in the basket."

But quiet was not to be a part of that day, for at that moment, the wind redoubled in force, shaking the canvas with such power that Ali Baba half imagined a giant might be kicking the fabric upon the other side.

"And I shall continue my story," Aladdin replied in a somewhat louder voice than before, "for we at last have come to the important part."

"The palace?" Harun suggested with a similar shout.

The storytelling thief shook his head wearily. "No," he called back. "The palace, while large, ostentatious even, and rather comfortable, now that I think of it, was nowhere near as important as what I have to say next."

"It seems to me," Harun managed to sniff while shouting, "that palaces are always important."

"Especially after you no longer have access to them!" Achmed added in a loud voice that was nevertheless almost lost to the wind.

Ali Baba saw the first evidence of sand swirling in around those corners where they had secured their canvas with rocks.

"Perhaps you should pause in your story until the wind dies!" Harun called. "Although who knows what worth such a tale is if it does not contain—" The end of his sentence was lost to the howling storm without. Ali Baba noticed that there was now quite a quantity of sand entering through the cracks in their shelter. He squinted as a bit of it flew into his eye.

Ali Baba pointed at the rippling fabric. "Are you sure this is secure?" he called to no one in particular.

"It had better be!" Achmed called back into his ear. "Or our lives may very well be forfeit!"

"Nonsense!" Aladdin rejoined in a voice strong enough so that it might still be barely heard above the wind. "We so seldom have an opportunity to tell our tales that it will take more than a single gale to stop my story!"

It was at that precise moment that the wind somehow gusted even stronger than before, bringing the canvas down upon their heads.

"It has been nice knowing you!" Achmed further called as the sand and the dark canvas blotted out the world around them.

It was at that even more precise moment that the earth gave way beneath Ali Baba's feet.

♦

Chapter the Seventeenth,
in which holes open within the ground,
and perhaps within the plot.

Any screams that he and his fellows might have uttered were completely lost beneath the wind. There was nothing but darkness, and the unwelcome sensation of falling.

Ali Baba found further cause to close his mouth when he discovered it was filling with sand. He landed with a jolt, but without immediately apparent harm, due no doubt in part to his new resting place being made up entirely of dirt and cushions.

So startled was he that Ali Baba did not realize the sound of the wind had greatly receded until he heard his brother's voice.

"What has happened to us?" Kassim called out in front. "I cannot see out of my basket!"

"In that," Achmed's voice replied, "you are for once the equal of us all."

"I seem to have lost my hand!" Kassim cried in rising panic. "No, perhaps my hand has lost the rest of me."

"We have fallen somewhere," Harun stated in that voice of authority which the elderly sometimes affect. "But I believe that all of our possessions have fallen with us."

"No, I appear to all be here somewhere," Kassim muttered, as if in agreement with the other thief. "Perhaps I have lost the top to my basket."

"If I might find a lamp," Harun observed, "and if the oil has not yet drained completely from it—" There was a pause as Ali Baba heard a prolonged mix of scraping, shuffling, and clanging.

Someone else yelped in the darkness.

"Sorry," Kassim's voice responded. "I was simply attempting to feel my way around."

"Ah!" Harun called in triumph. "I believe I have found the very thing. Now, if my tinder is still held within the folds of my robe—"

A moment later, there was a series of sparks. Ali Baba had to close his eyes for a moment to the brightness of the light. He blinked, attempting to bring the others into focus. Everyone seemed to be gathered together, although all appeared to be in some disarray.

"Where are—" Aladdin began, before yelping for a second time. "Would you get that thing away from me?"

"What thing?" Harun asked as he frowned into the gloom.

"This disembodied arm—rather, this portion of Thief Number Forty!" He pointed to Ali Baba. "You! You are his brother, are you not? See to putting him back together again!"

"He would," Kassim's head agreed from where it now peeked out of the basket, "if he had any shred of feeling for his family. And I don't mean simply collecting me together again, but also locating a reputable, if perhaps blind, tailor!"

The former woodcutter was quite taken aback by Aladdin's squeamishness. "Why do you have such difficulty?" he asked politely. "Are not you—beg pardon, are not we hardened thieves?"

"Thieves are not called upon to deal with body parts!" Aladdin said with a shiver. "Speak to me again when we are called the Forty Murderers!"

Ali Baba obediently arose from the place he had fallen and climbed across the piles of rugs and cushions.

"We seem to have fallen into a cave of some size," Harun said as he lifted his light and squinted about at their surroundings. "Our position in the sand, in combination with the storm, must have somehow dislodged an opening."

"Please stop squirming," Ali Baba instructed his brother as he retrieved the arm to be placed back in the basket.

"It is an easy thing for you to say," Kassim replied defensively. "But, when you have naught but an arm, squirming is your only form of locomotion."

"I will replace you upon your cushions," the humble Ali Baba said with great patience. He put the arm gently back among his brother's other parts, then lifted the wicker basket to give it a more solid position.

"Careful, there!" Kassim warned as his parts were jostled about with the carrying. "Traveling in such a fashion gives a whole new meaning to nausea."

"Do not talk of nausea!" Aladdin cried, and from the look upon his face, he seemed far too familiar with the word already.

"We seem to have all survived our ordeal," Achmed said pleasantly, then nodded to Aladdin. "Well, perhaps some of us more than others. And we are far more protected from the storm than before. Number Twelve! Can you see the limits of this place we have fallen to?"

Harun held the lamp over his head. "This place is vast, perhaps even the twin of the cavern where our chieftain has stored the gold."

There was a moment of silence following that remark. For the first time, Ali Baba heard a hint of the wind, but it now sounded remarkably distant.

"This dealing with lamps puts me of a mind to continue my story," Aladdin remarked. "Not to mention that the telling of tales might put certain recent events out of my thoughts!"

"By all means, continue," Achmed encouraged, "for, from the sounds of the storm still raging above us, we shall have a great quantity of time to fill."

"Then fill it I shall," Aladdin said with a resolute conviction. "My story continues as follows. After I had seen the most beautiful princess in the land, still was I able to collect myself sufficiently to buy provisions for this most important of dinners that my uncle had wished to present to my mother and myself. It was at that meal that I learned the first hints of my fate, and I was further set upon my true course of life.

"We had a sumptuous meal that evening, with a dozen courses followed by a dozen more, prepared by all the women of the neighborhood under the discerning eye of my dear mother.

"After the meal was finished, and we had paused a sufficient time to pursue the niceties of proper digestion, then did the man who was our benefactor turn to my mother and say: 'I have not yet done enough for this family. Therefore, I shall set up your most worthy son as a shopkeeper, specializing in whatever form of retail most suits his fancy, and I shall further stock his shop with the finest wares of anyone within this greatest of cities."

"Now, the lad's mother was overwhelmed at this news, for finally might her son have an occupation, and she would not have to return to her never-ending laundry at that moment when her husband's brother at last took his leave.

"In this way did the youth's uncle truly gain the mother's trust. But he was not done with his discourse, and the next thought he passed on to his family, while spoken in the same casual manner as most of his earlier conversation, seemed to be accompanied by an intensity of gaze that Aladdin had not witnessed in the man before.

" 'Then it is settled,' the uncle said. 'Unfortunately, tomorrow is Friday, and, as that is a day of worship, none of the shops or offices shall be open for us to complete our plans. Therefore shall I take the lad on the morrow to certain gardens that I know, for the successful shopkeeper should have a knowledge of beauty and refinement.'

"And the lad's mother agreed most readily to this as well, as she would no doubt have agreed to virtually anything the uncle might say. And so it was decided that this uncle would return at first light to the house, and thereupon would take the boy to further his education.

"So did the uncle meet the youth at dawn of the holy day, and did instruct him to accompany him briskly, for their walk was long. Now, there were many fine gardens within the city limits that would have been more than adequate for the instruction of the youth, if that were indeed the elder's true purpose. But they walked throughout the city, and then out of the western gate and onward for another hour besides, until they reached a point when the uncle said that the garden was nigh.

"But still did Aladdin not suspect that anything was amiss, for what did the lad know but the more esoteric rules of street games and how many different meals his mother could prepare using vegetables and stale bread? In this way had the elder chosen well, although he had truly picked the youth for other reasons entirely.

"But even a youth as unworldly as Aladdin might have a question or two. For although the uncle said they were near the garden, all the lad could see was a great plain stretching before them both, featureless save for those boulders strewn hither and yon, and the blackened remains of great shrubs and trees that had once dotted the plain, before a pestilence had taken the land and turned them all to withered foliage.

" 'Surely,' spoke the lad in all innocence, 'there is no garden here. Whither is our destination?'

"In response to his naive query, the lad received a playful cuff upon the ear, and was told by his uncle to gather up some of the dried vegetative detritus that littered the immediate area. This the lad quickly accomplished, at which point the older man asked the youth to stand some ten paces behind his back.

"When the lad had removed himself to a sufficient distance, then did his uncle remove a tinderbox from deep within his dark ut elegant robes. From this did the older man draw those things needful to start a fire, and set the dried brush ablaze. After this did he remove from his robes a container made of the finest tortoiseshell, and, drawing a minute amount of powder from within his box, sprinkled it above the fire while speaking certain words in a language unknown to the young Aladdin. A thick smoke rose from the fire where the powder had fallen, and the old man redoubled his unintelligible speech.

"Then did the lad notice that there was certain other activity about him, for the ground did tremble, and the boulders upon the plain did roll back and forth, and the dead trees did quiver so fiercely that they lost enormous branches. So great was the rumbling that even the sky seemed to tremble, and the ground itself let out with a great roar, half of anger, half of pain.

"And when the shaking stopped, there appeared in the once flat earth before Aladdin a hole, ten cubits wide by ten cubits long. And, at a depth of ten cubits within the hole, Aladdin saw a great marble slab. And, upon that slab attached a ring of copper, as wide around as the reach of a maiden's arms.

"'Surely,' said Aladdin to no one in particular, 'that is a magic spell.' The lad had never before seen a magic spell, and, now that he had witnessed one, was quite certain he would rather not witness one again.

"'Perhaps it is,' said the man who claimed to be his uncle. He smiled as he approached the lad, but the youth looked upon the elder in quite a different way than he had before. Perhaps this was why his father had never mentioned he had a brother, Aladdin thought with an immediate chill, for no one is proud of having a magician in the family.

"'Surely,' said Aladdin then, 'I have remembered an appointment back in the city which is most important and imminent.' So speaking, he gathered up the skirts of his robes and made to walk very rapidly back to the city of his birth.

"'But we have almost reached the garden,' was the old man's soothing reply. 'Surely, you do not wish to leave while we are so close.'

"'It has been a most enjoyable and invigorating walk,' Aladdin said in the most pleasant manner that he could muster, 'but, if I am not mistaken, I believe I hear my mother calling.'

"'You are going nowhere,' the uncle said, and as soon as he spoke, a hand shot out from among his robes more quickly than the young man's eyes could follow, and hit him upon the side of the head with such force that it made the world blur before the lad's eyes, and filled his vision with as many points of light as one might see cover the ocean at sunset. 'Except to open yonder door. Did not your mother teach you to obey your elders? We have come to visit a garden, and visit that garden you shall.'

"Aladdin shook his head, not so much to disagree with his uncle, but to attempt to clear his head, for he now knew the man to be not only a magician but a powerful magician, at least insofar as the manner in which he used his fists.

" 'What?' the uncle cried at what he perceived to be the youth's impertinence. 'You will not obey me even now?'

" 'I have not said so!' Aladdin replied most rapidly. 'I have to clear my head so that I may think about why my uncle might have cause to strike me so.'

"With that, his uncle affected a generous smile, and said the following:

" 'It is only for your own good, as are all things that your elders do.'

"These words calmed the youth, for this was the same explanation that he had always heard from his elders, and even though it made no more sense now than it did on all those other occasions he had heard it previously, still did he find a certain comfort in its familiarity.

" 'Now you shall follow my instructions,' his uncle further said, 'quite exactly, for it is important that youth always heed the wisdom of age. Climb down within that hole and pull upon the ring of copper so that you might move the marble slab aside.'

"The lad stared down at that great hunk of marble, which, if you have been paying close attention and know your figures, you have already determined was ten cubits wide and ten cubits long, and no man knew how many cubits deep. 'Surely, O uncle,' he said in a voice filled with doubt, 'that marble slab is far too large for a single youth to even budge it in the slightest.'

"Aladdin once again found the side of his face rocked by unseen but extremely powerful forces. If this continued, he wondered if his head should ever clear.

" 'Know that I only hit you repeatedly for your own betterment and future welfare,' his uncle said in a voice of surpassing gentleness. 'As I have told you, you must follow my instructions in every particular. Dearest boy, once you have done these things, you will be a boy no more, but the greatest among men.'

"So exhorted, Aladdin determined to listen to his uncle as best he could, despite that perpetual ringing in his ears.

" 'You have seen me open the earth before you, but let me tell you, I did this only for your own advantage. And below that marble slab is a treasure written only in your name, which can only be taken by yourself. No one but you may grab that copper ring, or lift that marble slab, or take a single step upon that staircase that waits beneath. But, if you follow my instructions quite exactly, we shall have so much riches between us that we might both live as kings.'

"The youth admitted that everything he had heard so far was very much to his liking, and so, with great resolve, he said, 'Then I will do this thing.'

" 'Most excellent!' agreed his uncle, who thereupon kissed the youth repeatedly upon his cheeks and fingers, an action the lad found only slightly less objectionable than the recent slaps. But, if he were to be richer than a king, he supposed he could forgive a little overexcitement upon the part of his uncle.

" 'Therefore,' his uncle said with an eagerness that was almost frightening in its intensity, 'leap down into that hole by the side of the slab, and take the copper ring in both your hands.'

" 'But the slab is so massive,' Aladdin mentioned as he took a step backward to avoid remaining within easy cuffing distance. 'Cannot you also jump within this hole so that you might add your strength to mine?'

"But, instead of striking out, the lad's uncle laughed at the folly of Aladdin's words. 'If I were to attempt to aid you in the lifting of the slab—indeed, if a hundred strong men of the great sultan's army were to attempt to aid you in the same—the slab would not move the slightest, but would act rather as if it were a piece of rock joined to other rock. Only you, alone, may move that heavy marble, and you may only do this in the following way: Grab the copper ring with both hands, and say aloud your name, then the name of your father, and the name of your father's father.'

"These instructions were easy enough to obey, so that the youth clambered down within the hole at last, and grabbed up the copper ring, which was surprisingly warm to his touch, and said, 'My name is Aladdin, whose father was named Mustapha, who was a tailor, and his father was a tailor named Ali.' And with that the slab sprung up and swung away, as if it had been pushed from underneath.

"Yes, tailoring was a family occupation held for generations that I no longer followed, and I thank those who currently reside in baskets for not remarking upon this at my most recent mention. But to continue with my tale, there was no sign of a living being beneath the slab. Instead, I saw a dozen marble stairs, and at the bottom of these steps a second door of bright red copper, filled with studs made of that same metal.

" 'Go down into that cave, my son,' his uncle instructed from where he stood above, 'and enter by the copper door, which will open of itself at your coming. You will then find yourself in a monstrous cavern, divided into three continuous halls. In the first hall, you will see four mighty bronze jars filled with liquid gold. In the second, you will find four silver jars filled with gold dust. In the third, you shall see four golden jars filled with minted gold pieces.'

"At this, the uncle wagged a finger at the lad below. 'It is of utmost importance that you pass all these objects by, and further hold your robe very close in about your waist lest it touch any of the jars. For, if you are to touch any of these urns with any part of your person or attire, you will instantly be changed into a block of obsidian.'

"He would be changed into a block of obsidian? Perhaps, the lad thought, he could still hear the voice of his mother calling. But, now that he had made his way down here, how was he to climb back out of this pit?

" 'At the end of the third hall,' the uncle continued, oblivious in his enthusiasm to the lad's discomfort, 'you will find another door, in all respects like the one at the bottom of the stairs, which will lead you into a magnificent orchard, with a score of trees all laden with fruit. Do not hesitate within that place, either. Walk straight across and you will come to a columned staircase with thirty steps, climbing up to a terrace. When you are on that terrace, you will see a niche facing you between those columns, and within that niche, resting upon a pedestal of bronze, you will further see a tiny copper lamp.

" 'Now, the lamp shall be still burning, so you must extinguish it, and pour whatever oil remains therein upon the floor at your feet, and then immediately hide that lamp within your robes. Then you must return to me by that same way in which you have entered. Though, upon your return, you may pause in the garden and eat of the fruit upon the trees if you so desire. But of course you should give me the lamp immediately once the two of us meet again.'

"With that, the uncle drew a ring from one of his fingers, and threw it down to Aladdin, with instructions that the lad should place it upon his thumb.

" 'This mystic bauble will guard you from all danger,' his uncle said in the most assuring of tones, 'and preserve you from every evil, defend you from all afflictions, safeguard you at each and every hazard, defend you from all misfortune, and maintain you against any liability. And did I mention that, when you return, you should give me this lamp immediately?'

"Aladdin placed the ring, which was of an ornate and foreign workmanship, upon his thumb, as he had been instructed. Somehow, the feel of the cool metal against his skin was indeed reassuring.

" 'After you complete this noble task,' his uncle further stated from above, 'you will no longer be considered a child, but shall have performed a labor worthy of manhood. And you should have no equals at that very moment when the lamp is finally in my possession. Only be very careful to lift your robe high and close to you when you pass through those other rooms; otherwise you and the lamp will be lost together.'

"With that, the older man waved at him with a great heartiness, and said, 'Depart in safety, my child. But perhaps I should jump down beside you for a final embrace.'

"So he should escape any more of his uncle's kisses, the youth departed upon his bold adventure immediately. He descended the dozen steps, and, as he approached the copper door, it swung open to let him pass. But there were no living beings apparent upon the other side of that door, either, but instead the three great rooms as his uncle had described. Lifting his robes high above his waist, Aladdin proceeded as the older man had directed, and so proceeded without harm through the farther door into the garden, and thence to the greater staircase, and the terrace which held the niche. There, upon the bronze pedestal that his uncle had also described, was the lamp burning with a pure crimson flame.

"The flame extinguished with a single breath from the youth, and he picked up the lamp and poured out what oil remained therein. He had some thoughts of the effect the oil would have upon his robes, but, to his surprise, the surface of the lamp was already dry, so that he quickly placed the small copper object quickly within the folds of his garment. Then did he descend from the terrace to the garden below.

"There did he take his first truly complete look at the fruit upon the trees of the orchard, for never in his short life had he seen fruit so large or perfectly formed. Then did he think about how long and hard had been the walk that day with his uncle, and he had not in all those many long hours stopped to take any refreshment whatsoever. Furthermore, his uncle had mentioned that this was the one spot he might pause within all this magic place, and that he might partake of this fruit.

"So did he reach up and pluck what at first appeared to be an apple, although, as his fingers first touched it, he was surprised at the remarkable firmness of the skin of this fruit. Indeed, it seemed upon closer inspection to be less of the consistency of fruit and more of the consistency of stone, beyond any machinations of finger or tooth, any only in form resembling the figs, oranges, grapes, melons (both green and orange), bananas, grapefruit, lemons, apples, pears, and other excellent fruits of China.

"He supposed these objects, then, to be made of colored glass, and although still rather hungry and disappointed that these would not satisfy his appetite, set about plucking some of the fruit-shaped baubles as presents for his mother and young comrades. So did he take fruit of every color, never suspecting that the red ones might be rubies, carbuncles, hyacinths, corals, or carnelians, nor the white ones diamonds, pearls, nacre, or moonstones, nor the green ones emeralds, beryls, jade, prase, or aquamarine, not to mention those many varieties of blue, violet, yellow, and various unknown colors and the fact that they might be sapphires, lapis, turquoise, amethysts, jaspers, topaz, amber, agates, opals, hematite, tourmaline, peridot, and chrysoprase.

"So enchanted was he by these stones that he selected many of each of the different colors, and went about stuffing them into his pockets and about his belt and within his sleeves and inside all the various parts of his robes where they might find a resting place, so that he soon looked like nothing so much as a beast of burden loaded for a trip to market. Somehow, though, he managed to propel himself forward, and lifted his lower robes sufficiently so that he passed by the dangerous urns in all of the three chambers again without ever touching them.

"Thus it was that he again passed through the copper door to those steps that led to his uncle. But his uncle, upon seeing him, did not appear immediately overjoyed at his nephew's return, but instead demanded 'Where is the lamp?'

" 'The lamp?' Aladdin replied. 'Oh, yes, the lamp. I could

swear I have it here somewhere. Perhaps it is that sharp-edged thing that is presently digging into the small of my back.'

"But his uncle did not wish to hear any explanations. 'What did I tell you about the lamp?' he demanded with a growing anger. 'I must have it immediately! Give it to me this instant!'

"'But dear uncle,' the lad replied with great reason, not to mention a certain joy that he had accomplished his task, 'how may I give it to you at this moment, when as you can see, my robes are stuffed to overflowing with these delightful glass marbles? Let me climb these stairs, and then give me further assistance to rise from the hole so that I can remove these marbles from my clothes and put them in a safe and level place so that they will not roll about and break. Then shall I be glad to give you the lamp, for it appears at present to be slipping down to my waist, and I fear it might scratch some sensitive area.'

"But his uncle was so hungry for the possession of this lamp that he was beyond reason. 'You will not give me the lamp? Son of a dog, give me the lamp or die!'

"Never had the youth heard the old man use such a terrible voice before, or address him with such harsh words. Aladdin remembered the slaps upon the side of his head. Then he remembered the way his uncle had made earth and sky move, and then a great hole to appear in the ground.

"Perhaps, the lad thought, he had not spoken in the most prudent of fashions. Perhaps, Aladdin thought, it would now be even more prudent to return to the interior of the cave until his uncle became somewhat calmer.

"This he did in what haste his overburdened form allowed, the copper door again opening for him and shutting firmly once he had reached the other side, both actions without the benefit of Aladdin's or any other human hand, which was just as well, since his balance at the moment did not meet with his usual standards.

"Even though he was deep underground, he heard the older man's voice with an amazing clarity, which did a great deal to help the youth determine the man's true nature, not to mention now making it far more easy for me to tell you a coherent story. And this is what the man who claimed to be the youth's uncle proceeded to do:

"'If I cannot have the lamp, then no one shall!' the man screamed as he again lit the fire and spread another quantity of powder atop it. As thick smoke once again rose, he said another group of unknown words, which caused the great marble slab to swing back into its original place, so that Aladdin might forever be entombed beneath.

" 'A curse be upon that stupid child!' the older man ranted above Aladdin's hiding place. 'It is a blessing that I no longer need pretend that I am a relation! Would that my magical arts, that foretold the location of the lamp, and that this Aladdin were the only one in all the world capable of the lamp's retrieval, could have also foretold that the lad would be obstinate and impossible. I might as well pack my spells and philters and return to Morocco!'

"Aha! thought Aladdin at last. As many of you now hearing my story may have suspected, this man was not my uncle at all, but a magician of great power who had traveled a substantial distance from the far land of Morocco, for but one reason, to find a way to obtain that lamp!"

"That is all very well and good," Harun interjected, "but it has very little to do with palaces."

"With this sort of audience," Aladdin said with a marked degree of acrimony, "it is little wonder that few tales get told within the ranks of the thieves!"

"Considering the length of your tale," Achmed said in a reassuring tone, "I think we have been very well behaved, at least for those who are among the lowest of the low."

"Well, listen again," Aladdin insisted, "for at this point, the man who was not my uncle but instead a vile magician from distant Morocco decided he could deal no more with this impetuous youth, and left me to die.

"Why would a man who was all-knowing leave at such a juncture, you might ask?" Aladdin asked instead. "I have thought much on this, and I believe this situation to be rather like the aged man who can make out the actions of birds upon the horizon but cannot fathom the marks on the parchment before him. The greater patterns were there for him to see, but the day-to-day actions of men were far beneath his notice.

"But Aladdin knew but one thing. Now that he had refused to immediately give up the lamp that the wizard desired so desperately, that wizard had sealed the cave again and left the lad there to die. This did not leave Aladdin happy. Rather did he wring his hands in great despair, crying, 'Oh, I shall never see my mother or my friends again! Nor will I be able to eat, for I shall have to spend my last hours staring dumbly at beautiful glass marbles!'

"But sometimes Destiny shall take a hand, and so it was upon this dark day, for as the youth wrung together his fists, so did he rub the ring that the wizard had given him for protection, and then forgotten in his rage. And when the ring was rubbed, a great veil of deep purple smoke did erupt therefrom, and, when the smoke cleared, a djinni did stand before him, with a skin like mahogany and eyes that glowed red like embers.

" 'I am the master of earth and wave,' the djinni did say, 'but slave of the ring and the wearer's slave. What will you have, master of the ring?'

"And the lad was greatly surprised by this turn of events, but determined that, in his present situation, he should leave no rock unrolled, and so asked of his supernatural visitor, 'Master of earth and air and wave, would you please get me out of this cave?'

"Before the youth could take another breath, the earth opened above him, and he was lifted as if by an invisible hand, and placed down upon the earth near that spot where the magician had stood to complete his spells!"

Ali Baba spoke quickly as Aladdin paused to take a breath. "Please pardon this intrusion," he said, "but is that not a ring you now wear upon your thumb?"

"That ring?" Aladdin looked down at his hand as if he had never seen the golden circlet before. "Nothing but a useless gewgaw, I am sure"—he paused to give the bauble a closer look—"although, now that I examine it, it does hold some similarity to a ring that I once possessed, that had a certain—secret about it. It looks rather like that ring that held a djinni of its own. Strange that I do not remember it."

"This reminds me of another spell," Achmed took the time to mention, "one cast upon a magician of my acquaintance."

"What is this talk of spells?" Aladdin objected. "That is all in my distant past. Now I am a thief!"

"As are we all," Harun agreed. "And may I mention that there has still been no mention of palaces? But, before you begin again, I notice a certain lessening of the wind above."

"I would not worry about that yet," another voice replied.

And that most recent remark gave Ali Baba cuisine for consideration. "Why do you worry so about the leader of the thieves? It seems to me that all of you wish to escape. Would not a sandstorm and a hidden cave afford you the perfect opportunity to act upon your wishes?"

The three senior thieves looked upon him with gazes of pity.

"The chieftain of the thieves will always find you," the three of them remarked in unity.

And now that Ali Baba thought upon it, this was truly the case. No matter how many times these thieves had left him behind, still did he somehow find himself again in their midst.

"And, when our band finds you again, your life will go from bad to worse," all three chanted together.

"But that situation shall not continue forever," said another voice.

"Who spoke then?" Aladdin demanded.

"Not I," Harun replied. "I was the one to suggest that we go above."

"I was doing my best to maintain a respectful silence," Kassim added, "so that I could ask you at a later time about tailoring."

"Hmm?" Achmed asked. "Oh, pardon me, but I must have dozed off recently."

"I would not return above yet," the other voice remarked. "This is but a lull in the storm."

This time, Ali Baba was quite sure, none of them had spoken.

"Who—" he began to form a question.

"Are you quite certain," the voice replied, "that you truly wish to know?"

◆

Chapter the Eighteenth,
in which the story develops
a certain ring of truth.

There was a moment of silence, after which Aladdin thought it prudent to change the subject.

"It does appear to be a little stuffy down here," he mentioned. "You know how caves can get."

"Now that you mention it," Achmed added, "I can do nothing but agree with you."

"Indeed, yes," Harun had cause to join in. "However, I do think that the closeness of our surroundings could be beneficially dissipated were we all to take a stroll, perhaps, in a tight-knit group, and with our scimitars drawn and ready."

"Threats are nothing against granite," the voice replied. "Furthermore, you do not know the proper way out of this place."

"There is truth to that," Kassim agreed with the mysterious presence. "Upon our arrival, we seemed to travel straight down."

"But come and relax," the voice entreated in the most generous of fashions, "for can you not still hear the storm rage above you?"

Ali Baba did note that the wind had begun once again to howl in the upper reaches of the cavern.

"And do not fear," the voice further instructed. "As long as you tell your tale, I shall see that no harm should come to you."

"At last," Achmed said in wonder, "Thief Thirty has found the perfect audience!"

"In that case, I shall continue," Aladdin replied, warming with remarkable swiftness to the mystery voice's suggestion. "So it was that the lad found himself once again upon the plain, with his city still visible in the distance, although so much time had passed that the sun was sinking toward evening. There was no sign whatsoever of the magician, and the djinni had likewise disappeared. But, certainly, there are many mysteries to life, the lad thought, and it is a sentiment I could restate today.

"Then did the lad return as quickly as his legs would manage to the home of his mother, although it was past midnight when he reached it at last.

"He found his mother awake upon his return, for she could not sleep, so worried was she when her son did not reappear at a reasonable time. She gave him cool water to drink, and all the food that was in the house to eat, telling him that she would hear his story when he was done. And the young Aladdin ate with a remarkable appetite, for he had been so close to death that he never thought he would see food again.

"When at last he had finished with his lengthy repast, he related the amazing events of the past day, much in the same way as I have related them to you now. Then did his mother rain curses upon the Moor as only a mother could. 'To think,' she said, 'that he almost took your life, and for what? Nothing but a pitiful copper lamp!'

"With that, the lad stood, and had an immense profusion of the great hard fruit fall from all portions of his belt and robes. 'And I have risked my life for these silly things!' he cried in bewilderment. 'I am no longer a child, to play with colored marbles!' So it was that the young Aladdin determined that this would be an experience to change his life.

"When the lad rose upon the following morning, he resolved anew to put aside all his childish games and act henceforth as a man. Before he should go out and make his fortune, however, he first desired a hearty breakfast. He informed his mother of such, and was rewarded by an expression of great upset and a rapid wringing of hands.

"'Oh, my dear, dear child,' his mother called in that distraught manner which she had perfected through years of hard effort, 'would that I could feed you this morning, but last night you were taken with such a hunger that you have eaten every scrap of food within the house. But wait a little while. I shall take in a few bundles of robes and, after an hour or two of scrubbing them at the river, will have earned a few pennies toward buying food for your repast.'

"Seeing his mother so, Ali Baba immediately wanted to make her happy. If his mother had not saved sufficient food, you may ask, why was he always the one to feel guilty? Let us say that this is always the way of mothers and sons, and be done with it.

"'No, no, dear Mother,' he therefore said. 'You have labored enough in your long life. Why not take this lamp and sell it at the marketplace? That will surely give us enough for a meal or two. And, once I have eaten and dressed, I shall take this great quantity of colored marbles and sell them among the less educated in the city. In that way, perhaps we can eat for a day or two, until I fully determine how I shall be a man and make my way in this world.'

"But fortune was kind, for by putting the lamp in his mother's hands, Aladdin had given it to the most fastidious of women in all of that part of the world. And his mother, looking upon this tarnished lamp, thought she could surely get a better price for it if it were to be polished before she took it to market. Thus did she take one of the many old rags that she usually wore as clothing, and, after applying a mixture of water and ash to that fabric, called upon that extreme strength she had gained through three-score years of hand washing, and worked to bring out the shine upon the copper.

"But no sooner had she rubbed once up and once down upon the lamp than a great deal of purple smoke issued from that instrument's mouth, and when the smoke cleared, there before them stood a djinni so tall that his head scraped the ceiling. And furthermore was this djinni the color of gold, and his eyes flashed bright blue like the summer sky. And in a great, booming voice that perhaps sounded even louder because of the confined space around the djinni, the magic creature said:

> "'*I am master of all, though I live in a cave,*
> *And you with the lamp may call me your slave.*
> *Command me, O mistress! Command me!*'

"Now, Aladdin's dear mother had even less experience with magic djinn than did her son. So did she stand there with large eyes and a tongue that seemed to fill her entire mouth and make speech impossible. But this condition would not endure for long, for Aladdin's mother soon fell forward in a dead swoon.

"However, Aladdin had been standing some little distance away as all this had occurred, and so quickly moved forward and grasped the lamp from his mother's fainting fingers. Should this particular spirit work like the great dark fellow he had met in the cave, his any wish should now be granted.

"'O slave of the lamp,' he therefore said. 'I am hungry, and have need of food for my mother and myself.'

"'Your wishes shall become reality,' the golden djinni replied as he held forward a large silver tray. And ranked upon that tray were a dozen gold dishes, and in each dish a different and exotic meat, well warmed and spiced. And behind those dishes were half a dozen loaves of the purest white, although upon their sides were drawn fantastic designs of men and animals, as well as depictions of stories from antiquity. And at the very rear of that enormous tray were two great flasks of fine wine, which had such an aroma that Aladdin was sure both were of the finest vintage, and two large goblets, both flasks and goblets fashioned from beaten gold and encrusted with small yet tasteful gems.

"The lad was well pleased with this presentation, and instructed the djinni to place it before him and his still-unconscious mother. This did the golden spirit do, after which it discreetly disappeared, as indeed should any good waiter.

"But such a mixture of sweet and savory smells did much to revive his mother, and she opened her eyes to look at the banquet that had appeared before her.

"'Our deepest desires are granted,' she said in wonder, 'for never have I seen such a meal. But how did we come to have such a fine meal on the very best of dinnerware?'

"Now did the lad pause for a minute, for he recalled what a fright the djinni's appearance had given to his mother, and he feared that, should his parent suspect that this feast came from a magical source, she should refuse to eat it, even though it appeared wholesome and nourishing in every respect. Yet it was, as with all obedient children, that he did not wish to precisely lie to the woman. Therefore, he determined that he must devise a compromise.

"'It appears to be a final gift from the man who would call himself my uncle,' said Aladdin, so that he was at least relating a certain version of the truth.

"But his mother seemed to like this explanation little better than she might appreciate what had actually occurred. 'That vile wretch?' she cried. 'We should spit upon his food, and throw it out into the street for the dogs!'

"This, again, was not precisely the response the lad was looking for. But the sumptuous meal before them, combined with the obvious look of hunger he witnessed upon his mother's pinched and haggard face, gave him faith that his reasoning would win her over.

"'Would it not be a far better revenge,' he therefore said, 'if we were to eat his fine repast while all the time cursing the magician's vile name?'

"His mother took one more look at the sumptuous repast and decided that, yes, eating this would be the best revenge of all. So it was that the two of them fell to feasting, for so long that their morning meal joined with evening meal.

"At last, when there was no way they could eat another bite, did they push the plates away, and Aladdin's mother saved what food they had not consumed for the morrow, and further locked the valuable dinnerware within the cupboard so that no one might steal it.

"And now that Aladdin had eaten so well, the lad considered, perhaps it would be a far better idea to wait until the morrow before determining in which way he would best find his place in the world.

"But his mother would not allow her son to yet enjoy that repose which he so richly deserved. 'It is time we had a talk,' she said in that tone which all children of mothers have learned to fear. 'Tell me truly, where precisely did this meal originate?' She wagged a finger of authority at the lad's nose to emphasize her next remark. 'And remember that a mother can always spot an untruth!'

"Aladdin relented then, and told his mother that the meal was produced by the golden djinni who lived in the lamp.

"'I do not trust such hellish things!' his mother exclaimed. 'Truly, you should rid yourself of that lamp, and the ring as well, for they must be instruments of the devil!'

"But Aladdin countered with the fact that these two items, and the spirits within, had brought them nothing but good, saying further that the spirit of the ring had actually saved Aladdin's life when he might have died within the cave. So it was that the lad resolved to retain these items, but never bother his mother about them again."

"While I hate to interrupt your tale again," Achmed stated abruptly, "may I point out that you have again mentioned a magic ring."

"Yes?" Aladdin replied with annoyance, as if he could not see how this pertained to him. "The ring is an important part of the tale."

"Much more important, apparently, then palaces!" Harun remarked with his usual sniff of impatience. "I am quite sure you have given us sufficient background. What say we jump ahead to the palace part?"

"Actually, I rather liked that part about caves," the mystery voice interjected. "I would not object if you went over that portion again."

"But that ring upon your finger!" Achmed again mentioned.

"Yes, I am sure that at some point it would make a more-than-substantial topic for conversation," Aladdin agreed. "As for now, I believe I should continue with my story, for this sandstorm will not continue forever."

Achmed opened his mouth to object, but Aladdin was well into his story before the younger thief could voice a single word.

"I shall be brief with this next part of my tale. Over the next several days, the youth slowly sold off the fine dinnerware that had accompanied the magical meal, and so he and his mother had more than enough to eat, while allowing the lad to pursue the neighborhood kick-the-fez championship one final time. Surely, though, he would come up with a greater plan for his future at any moment.

"So were his thoughts when he again heard the call of the three eunuchs. 'Beware, for the Princess Badabadur walks among you!' and then 'Beware, for should any man's eyes fall upon the princess, his life shall be forfeit!' And so forth and so on, much as Aladdin had heard these threats upon that earlier occasion.

"Ah, but once a man has tasted forbidden fruit, so forever will he return to the tree. So it was that Aladdin recalled that earlier incident with the eunuchs, and that thrilling glimpse he had had of the most beautiful princess in all of the world. He had lost his heart on that very day, but he was of so lowly a position, and she so exalted, what chance was there that they could ever look one upon the other, must less talk, or touch, or marry? This fatalistic thought, along with those occurrences concerning the duplicity of the magician, the danger of the cave, the wonders of the ring and lamp, and the everyday pressure of coping with his mother, had led the young man to place his thoughts of the princess to the very rear of his mind.

"But now he might have the opportunity of seeing her again, and, on this day, was upon a street of open stalls where there was far more to distract the eye than upon that previous occasion.

"'Beware!' called the eunuchs. 'For our scimitars are sharp!'

"Still, thought the lad, he should find some hiding place so that he might escape the swords of the princess's guards. He looked about him, intent upon asking the merchants where he might find a likely spot to hide. But all the merchants, and all their customers, and indeed all the merchandise had completely disappeared. "'Beware!' called the eunuchs. 'For our judgment is merciless!'

"Well, truly, the lad thought further, this disappearance was to his advantage, for now he might hide anywhere within this outdoor market, anywhere among the flimsy wooden stalls and threadbare throw rugs of the merchants, none of which would hide as much as a newborn babe.

"'Beware!' called the eunuchs. 'For we are just around the corner!'

"At this juncture Aladdin realized the true problem of the open-air stall, which is that it is an area surrounded by nothing but open air.

"He turned about, and there, marching into the marketplace, were the three eunuchs, with very sharp swords and very surprised expressions.

"'Do you see?' said one.

"'I certainly do,' said another.

"'Let us make that unanimous,' added the third.

"But all thoughts of the eunuchs left his head when he saw the princess, and further, the princess saw him.

"He could not move, except to smile. And, wonder upon wonders, the princess smiled in return.

"He thought to look back at the eunuchs. All three of them were smiling as well. He did not care as much for the eunuchs' smiles.

"'You have doomed yourself, young man!' one said.

"'Whatever male might see the princess,' added the second.

"'Who is not of her immediate family,' further explained the third.

"'Is sentenced to instant death!' all three of them joined in the most merry manner conceivable.

"'Oh, joy!' the third eunuch chortled. 'Do I get to cut him?'

"'You beheaded the last one,' the first of the three reminded him. 'Besides, let us be a little kind to this poor soul, and have not the last smell to enter his mortal nostrils be your eternal flatulence!'

"'I cannot help what I eat for dinner,' the third one replied defensively. 'Well, perhaps I could if I might resist pickled kumquats!'

"Aladdin let the three guards argue among themselves. He turned again to the princess as fair as the sun, and noticed that she seemed to still regard him in a most pleased of manners. He placed his hands over his heart to keep that organ from bursting forth from his chest.

"'Let us cut him together!' one of the three guards suggested. The other two indicated that would be a most novel and welcome compromise.

"Aladdin looked at the approaching eunuchs, all still smiling, all with very sharp swords.

"In another moment, he realized, he would not have to worry about his heart beating ever again."

◆

Chapter the Nineteenth,
in which our story continues
after an enchanted opening.

"The storm is over," the voice of mystery intoned.

"What?" Kassim complained. "You wish him to stop the story now?"

"I was but coming to the very heart of my tale!" Aladdin insisted. "The palaces would have shown up at any moment."

"You must forgive me," the voice replied. "I have, after all, only so much control over the weather. My powers are strictly regional."

This voice had not struck them down, or cursed them with boils, or done any of those sorts of things that one expected of mysterious entities. On the contrary, the voice seemed the very soul of politeness. It was with this in mind that the woodcutter screwed up his courage and asked, "You control the very weather? If I may be so bold as to ask, who or what are you?"

"I am here," the voice replied from directly overhead, "and I am here," the voice further remarked from some distance into the darkness, "and I am here," the voice continued to talk from a spot very near to Ali Baba's feet. "I am all around you."

Ali Baba was much impressed by this display. "You are omnipotent?"

The voice chuckled at that, and the noise seemed to surround them. "Not by any means. You are simply sitting inside me. I am, after all, an enchanted cavern."

The thieves gasped as one at the revelation. And all had certain thoughts, although Kassim was the first to voice them:

"You wouldn't possibly be any relation to certain other enchanted caverns?"

"All things are related in this world," the cavern replied. "Holes within the earth are no different."

"Then do you suggest," said Aladdin in wonder, "that you know of the cave that held the lamp and the gold?"

The voice was highly amused. "I suppose you might say that that cave was my brother."

"Where, then," Achmed asked, "is the gold within your chambers?"

"We all have our powers," the voice said somewhat reprovingly. "Some caves produce gold. This cave talks."

"You will have to pardon me," Achmed replied with a shrug. "It is my training as a thief."

"There is but one cave," Harun wisely interjected, "that is of our primary concern, one that is filled with gold, jewels, and riches untold, so that it resembles nothing so much as a palace underground. Well, perhaps that is naught but wishful thinking upon my part, but there is a further problem with this cavern, for, while it will always accept such riches, it will not always allow you to take the same without." The eldest thief paused to look at the wicker basket by his side. "And further, the cave has other peculiar whims."

"Such as refusing to let me die?" Kassim said, his voice betraying a bit of hurt. "I don't like to think of that as a whim, thank you. A cosmic joke, perhaps, but not a whim."

"'Ah, *that* cave." The voice allowed another rueful chuckle. "I know it as well as any, and you have good cause to be wary of that one. That great cavern is the father of us all, and feared by all those mystic caves, burrows, grottoes, tunnels, dens, nooks, and crannies in the land. However, know you this: Even the largest of caves is neither good nor evil. It is merely misunderstood."

This, at least, the woodcutter could comprehend. How could anyone understand a cave?

"But let us not dwell overlong upon other and cranky holes within the earth. I am eager to hear the continuation of your tale."

"But you say that the storm is over," Aladdin observed. "How can I tell you my tale when we must leave to rejoin our band?"

"It is the height of simplicity," the cavern replied. "Do you see the smooth rock at your feet?"

Aladdin looked down. There was a small rock, about the size of a man's knuckles, but generally undistinguished, being of a neutral gray with small bands of black around its middle, and smooth as though it had been washed by the sea.

Aladdin lifted it aloft. "Is this the one you mean?"

"The very same," the cavern agreed.

"Well, as you speak to me, so may you speak to this stone, for this rock is a part of me, and, as sure as I am an enchanted cave, this is an enchanted pebble."

"I have heard of stranger things," Harun remarked as he pulled upon his beard.

"You have?" Ali Baba asked in disbelief.

"Actually," Harun replied with a frown, "now that you mention it, I have not. When one is brought up within the courtly life, one is always polite, even to animate parts of the earth. But I have never heard of enchanted stones that can listen!"

"And also talk," the stone in Aladdin's hand remarked. "When you're a rock, you have to take whatever advantages you can get."

"It is a marvel!" Aladdin agreed.

"Is it really?" the stone replied doubtfully. "Think upon it. What good are talking and listening when you have absolutely no mobility?"

Still was the woodcutter astonished. Ali Baba had to admit that already his life among the thieves had opened his eyes to vistas that he had never dreamed of. Not, now that he thought upon it, that these vistas would be of any particular use, but at least they provided some variety from the constant riding, riding, riding.

"So," the cavern said with great camaraderie, "you need not stay within my confines for me to hear your tale. No, you may actually take a piece of me along with you, and tell your story as you go. What the stone hears, I shall hear as well."

"Then you will hear nothing but noise," Aladdin said, and as he spoke, Ali Baba saw the truth in this. "Once we ride, there will be no more time for tales, but only the pounding of horses' hooves."

"Oh, dear," replied the voice, "I had no idea it would be that bad. When you're a cave, you know, you have trouble dealing with much in the outside world." The cavern sighed, a sound much like the whistling wind. "Actually, as a cavern, you have difficulty dealing with anything that isn't cold and deep and dark. But I have much enjoyed the story you have told, and would like to listen to it at greater length."

At this, Aladdin nodded sadly. "And I would like to tell it. Would that it were not time for us to return to the surface."

As if someone above were listening to Aladdin's words, Ali Baba could hear a distant voice calling, "Thieves! The storm is over!"

There came a deep rumbling from the earth. "You have forced

me to a decision. I believe I have enough within me for a couple of sand squalls. That should delay any preparations that may be made above. But proceed quickly, for my energy is almost spent.''

The voices were closer now: ''Thieves! Thieves! Come forth! The storm is—*awk!*'' Any further cries were lost within a renewal of the wind.

''The squalls have begun,'' announced the cavern's voice, which already had begun to sound a trifle weary. ''Please tell your story with whatever speed you might muster.''

''Very well,'' the storytelling thief replied, and, from his tone, Ali Baba could tell he was greatly pleased with this turn of events. ''As you may recall, when we left my tale, my younger self, Aladdin, appeared to be at the mercy of three eunuchs who would have no greater pleasure than simultaneously skewering a young lad whose only offense was to be taken by Princess Badabadur's beauty.''

Aladdin clutched his hands before his chest. ''What was the lad to do? He wrung his hands together, certain he was dead.'' The thief began to wring his own hands in demonstration, then paused and frowned, as if such an action might seem somehow inappropriate. ''Therefore,'' he resumed, shaking his head to rid it of errant thoughts, ''what should the lad see emerging from between his open fingers but a strangely familiar purple smoke?

''With that, the eunuchs stopped their deadly advance, temporarily overcome by this strange happening.

''A moment later, and the smoke had cleared as quickly as it had come. The great djinni, the same color as obsidian, once again stood before the startled Aladdin and even more startled eunuchs. The spirit opened his eyes, and within them were reflected the fires of hell.

''The djinn smiled and spoke:

> '' '*I am the master of both more and of less;*
> *Though slave to the ring, I see you're in a mess.*
> *What will you, master, what will you?*'

''Oh, yes, the lad suddenly thought, so that was how this djinni thing worked again. Aladdin swore at the moment that he would get a better grip upon this magic, really he would, as soon as the shock of the whole thing wore off. In the meantime, however, the lad thought it best to remove himself some distance from the swords.

" 'Transport me, O slave of the ring,' he therefore said, 'back to my own home and the loving care of my own dear mother.'

"And with that, Aladdin saw the marketplace quickly fade from sight. And he caught one final glimpse of the three guards, with fearsome expressions that they had lost their quarry. But he also saw the princess, and in that last instant her mouth turned down in a frown. Could she be sad because he was gone?

"He blinked, and the marketplace had vanished, and he once again stood in the midst of his small but tidy home. His mother, after she had recovered from another faint, listened to this story with all attentiveness, but frowned when he mentioned the use of the ring.

" 'But, Mother!' Aladdin objected. 'The ring has again saved me from certain death!'

" 'Well, perhaps,' was her reply. 'But what were you doing in that marketplace, after all? And associating with *princesses*!' Her emphasis upon the last word made the lad know that his mother did not consider princesses to be at all a suitable class of companion for a son as fine as he.

"But the lad could keep his true feelings hidden no longer, especially in front of someone as dear as his mother. So did he tell her that he had lost his heart to this beautiful girl, and his mother, seeing her son in such obvious misery, relented at last, and remarked that perhaps certain princesses, if they were truly as wondrous as her son indicated, might barely make suitable marriage candidates.

"So it was that Aladdin convinced his mother to take his case before the father of the princess." He glanced at Harun. "At the palace."

"Always the best part of the story," Harun injected.

"So did the lad's mother prepare herself to go in front of the sultan," the storyteller continued, "dressing herself with finery that Aladdin obtained by selling yet more of the ostentatious dinnerware, and further bearing fantastic gifts that the mother pointedly did not ask the origins of.

"But, you may ask, would a woman as humble as Aladdin's mother actually be able to speak eloquently enough before the sultan so that Aladdin might be considered a suitor?"

"Alas," the voice of the cavern interrupted, "you will have to ask that question at some other time. Further control of the weather is beyond me. I am, quite simply, too spent to squall."

And, once again, the thieves heard the voices of the rest of their band calling from above.

"I am glad of the divertissement," the cavern further spoke. "It is difficult to get entertainment when you are a cave. Talk further about these things when you have the opportunity. In return for your stories, I shall show you certain things that you may use to your advantage." The voice made an odd honking noise that Ali Baba realized must be a yawn. "And keep that stone close to you, except that, in time of direst need, give it to he who has the youngest beard."

"The youngest beard?" Ali Baba asked, thinking truly it must be an odd way the magic cavern had to talk about their youngest thief, Achmed.

"That one who has just spoken," the cave further illuminated. "the one whose beard has been grown by magic."

"Me?" Ali Baba called in wonder.

"Trust me. The other cave likes you. It has allowed you to take its gold without twisting you into a pretzel. It would like to consider itself a good judge of character."

Ali Baba frowned, but said no more. He had told no one about the gold. How could a cave know such things? He supposed it went with being enchanted.

"But how do we leave?" Achmed asked of the cavern.

"You know your way out of here," the voice replied with a casual authority. "All you need is the magic word."

A magic word that dealt with caves? Of course! Ali Baba was the first to open his mouth and utter:

"Open, Sesame!"

And with that, a hole opened above them to show brilliant sunlight, and leading to that space above was a narrow but well-tended stair.

The thieves gathered up their belongings, Kassim included, and started for the exit. As they walked, the woodcutter noticed that there was a low but constant rumbling. It took Ali Baba a moment to discern the sound's true meaning. The cave was snoring softly.

"You know," Achmed said to Aladdin as they climbed the stairs, "if you have no more use for that ring, I should be glad to take it off your hands."

"The ring? Oh, yes, I do wear a ring, don't I?" But after that, Aladdin seemed to be much too intent on placing one foot in front of another to pursue the subject further.

But there was then no more time for conversation, as one by one the thieves emerged into the now blinding daylight.

"Ah!" came the voice of their chieftain. "Then we have not lost quite as many as we have thought!" He clapped his hands in approval, dislodging great quantities of sand from his robes, so covered that they appeared more white than black. "Good! I never like to recruit more than a dozen new thieves at a time."

One of those thieves pointed down those stairs where Ali Baba and his companions had emerged. "But they come from an opening in the earth! Should we not explore the crevice?"

Ali Baba squinted at his surroundings. Many of the sand-covered thieves seemed to have survived the storm, although he might not be able to make an exact account until he was able to see more clearly. However, it was not the thieves he was worried about.

"What of the women?" he asked in a hoarse voice.

The leader stiffened before him. "We do not talk about open holes in the ground in my group of thieves!" He clapped his hands. Two others ran forward. "Take him away somewhere and split him down the middle."

"But I only asked that question in case there might be riches below. My only concern was for the benefit of our band!"

"Very well. I shall be merciful. You may split him apart with his own sword."

He turned back to Ali Baba, who wished at that moment that he had never asked a question of another mortal, ever.

"The women, who are no concern of yours, are quite healthy," their chieftain said as he began to brush the sand from his robes. "They were with me." He redoubled his brushing, apparently feeling that no further explanation was necessary. A moment passed, and the leader turned to face the woodcutter again.

"But I have meant to talk to you," he said in a voice so smooth that the truth would slip and fall upon it. "I have both unfavorable information and excellent wisdom. Which would you like to hear first?"

Ali Baba felt as though he were on trial, and the only verdict would be painful death. Ali Baba had even allowed himself to relax for a moment during the telling of that story, and see what had come of it. Now he would have to watch his every action, for his life surely depended upon it.

The chieftain who liked to remove teeth and fingers for minor affronts was waiting. Which question would a thief ask first?

Certainly not about the good. Therefore, Ali Baba asked about the other, wary with every word:

"I think I would like to know the unfortunate information first."

"Spoken like a true degenerate!" the leader of thieves remarked. "You are learning to fit into our ignoble band with remarkable efficiency!" He smiled in a way that was not particularly pleasant. "The unfortunate news is that the two newest thieves have gained a promotion!"

Ali Baba stared at the chieftain. If this was the worst that would happen, perhaps he was concerned over naught. "Yes, certain of our numbers appear to have been lost, or suffocated, or dead with mysterious stab wounds during this most recent storm. Therefore, you are now Thief Number Thirty-three, and your brother in a basket is Thief Number Thirty-four!"

Well, that was not so bad, at least except for the part about those extremely suspicious deaths, but that was not Ali Baba's immediate concern, for Thief Number One was again watching him expectantly. The woodcutter realized he was expected to ask another question.

"And what, O leader," he asked with a somewhat lighter heart than before, "is the fortuitous wisdom that you wish to impart?"

Never had the woodcutter seen their leader's smile so broad and deep as when he gave this answer: "The fortuitous wisdom is that you will get to test your mettle in a life-and-death situation. Once we have lost our mystic number of forty, I always consider it less important to be overprotective of my new recruits. Essentially, at this point, what is another thief more or less?"

As if to punctuate that remark properly, there wafted back into their midst the screams of the man who had recently mentioned the cave before his sudden death.

"Very good," Thief Number One continued. "I am glad you have agreed."

He had? But then, Ali Baba could think of no nonlethal alternative.

The chieftain clapped his hands. "Issue him his sword."

Two men trotted forward, one with a scimitar in hand. At least they had taken the time to wipe off the blood. Ali Baba stared at the sharp instrument of death.

"Does he know which end is the hilt?" the man with the sword asked.

Ali Baba quickly reviewed all he knew about the sword, which was which end was the hilt. He grabbed that hilt as he had seen other men hold a scimitar. The sword jerked about in his hand. He never suspected a scimitar would be so heavy.

"Well, you will learn," said the man who had given up the sword, "or we will have to get another sword."

"Or perhaps another swordsman," was their chieftain's final word on the subject. "But you should not have to use it immediately. I think we can grant you a few hours to master it."

"Ho!" came a voice from the other side of the camp. "We have sighted a caravan! Approaching north-northeast!"

"Then again," Thief Number One further remarked, "perhaps you will need it immediately."

Chapter the Twentieth,
in which caravans are approached,
but little is exchanged.

"What sort of a caravan?" the chieftain called to the far side of the stones.

"Large!" came the answer.

At that, the leader's lips twitched in anticipation. "Camels?" he further asked.

"Hundreds!" was the reply.

Thief Number One hopped gleefully from foot to foot. "Yes, you will most definitely need that sword shortly. But you will need more than that, won't you?" The chief thief looked at Ali Baba as if they were sharing a secret. The woodcutter wished he could but guess what that secret might be.

"At last, it is truly time for you to prove yourself!" Thief Number One chortled. "Not that we want you to steal anything."

Ali Baba was uncertain how to react to this news. They didn't?

"At least not immediately," the leader continued in explanation. "You have a great honor before you. Yours will be the first experimental exploration of our generous Caravan Redistribution Program. Thus, you will be giving them gold, not taking it away. Surely, there is no problem with that?"

Ali Baba supposed that there wasn't. Maybe he wouldn't need the sword, after all. He tried to swallow, but all the moisture in his throat seemed to have dried up within the sand.

"Of course," the chieftain proceeded, "as soon as you see where they put your golden gift, you will go and take it away, along with any other gold and valuables that might have joined your offering." The main man in black coughed genteelly. "But then, as a thief, you should have no problem with that."

The woodcutter frowned. He supposed he shouldn't have. Why

couldn't he see the logic in the chieftain's words? He was probably far too fretful about the use of swords.

The chieftain then proceeded with a much more complicated description of what was to come: how he should approach the caravan with head down, and his gift held before him. His ineptness with a sword could even be used to his advantage. Who would distrust anyone who couldn't handle a sword? And when the unsuspecting merchants had accepted the gift and revealed their own treasures, Ali Baba, now known as Thief Thirty-Three, would give a signal, raising his voice for some reason, perhaps to loudly sing the merchants' praises. Once he had done that, the other thieves would manage the rest. With a plan so simple, there should be no problems whatsoever, should there?

"There is, of course, one thing you should know," the chieftain added in conclusion. "I do not look kindly upon failure."

Even within his limited experience among the thieves, this was one thing the woodcutter could agree with completely. Ali Baba lifted his sword up and attempted to stick it within his sash without stabbing himself.

"O brother!" Kassim called from his basket. "I may never see you again. Perhaps I have been too harsh with you. I shall let your wife know how you died."

This was the first time Ali Baba could ever remember his brother sparing him a kind word. Was the woodcutter's death, then, inevitable?

"You do not seem pleased to be going down to that caravan," the chieftain further remarked. Ali Baba realized he had not been hiding his emotions well. But then, if he was already a dead man, what did it matter?

"Do not worry," the chieftain reassured him. "We will not send you alone."

Then all the woodcutter's fears were for nothing? It would be a different matter entirely if he were to have a half a score of hardened thieves as his retinue.

"Thank you, O chieftain," Ali Baba remarked appreciatively.

But the first among thieves waved away the woodcutter's gratitude. "There is no reason to thank me. It is only what you deserve." He waved magnanimously at the basket at Ali Baba's side. "You may take your brother with you."

"I?" Kassim squawked from within his wicker. "But I have no way to help with the procurement of gold!"

"You are far too modest," their chieftain chided. "You have

two good hands to steal things and hold weapons, even if those hands aren't particularly attached to anything. And I can think of no better place to hide plunder than that basket!''

He chortled at his cleverness, and many of the other thieves laughed with him. ''But every new thief must prove himself within our band.'' He patted the basket generously. ''There are ways to overcome every handicap.''

''And one of the best ways to overcome them is death,'' Thief Number Two half said, half whistled in merriment.

''Ah, second among thieves,'' his superior said with the same charity of tone, ''do you still retain some of your teeth?''

The nearly toothless smile left the lips of the other as he nodded silently.

''Well, you will not for long,'' Thief Number One assured him.

Ali Baba did not know if he could bear to witness another bicuspid removal in his current emotional state. He felt compelled, therefore, to return the subject to its proper place. ''Pardon, O first among cutthroats, but would it not be better for us to complete our preparations before the caravan passes us by?''

''You dare?'' Thief Number One roared, his face shading toward the least attractive hue of purple that the woodcutter had ever seen. But the chieftain grabbed his beard with both hands, and somehow managed to quell the storm within him. ''No, no, it is not in our best interests for you to lose any fingers at present, when you already have such difficulty holding a sword. We want you to enter into your first test at your very best. We will be able to make as many adjustments to your attitude as we wish at a later date.''

''The caravan!'' came the voice of the lookout at the far end of camp. ''It has almost reached us!''

''You say it is time for our Redistribution Program,'' Ali Baba stated boldly, for if he were not shortly a dead man, surely he would be a maimed one. ''What shall I give to the caravan?''

''Give?'' the chieftain replied as if even now he was doubtful as to the true meaning of that word. ''Give. Well, yes. My, my. Give. I suppose we will have to take a look at what is available.''

He clapped his hands, and seven thieves scrambled to bring forth great sacks bulging with the former household goods of Kassim.

''Not all of it!'' the chieftain announced sharply. ''We need to look at but a little. We do not need to dole out the depository!''

Six of the thieves turned abruptly, so that all but one of the sacks were taken back to whatever secret and guarded area they had come from.

"Now—" The chieftain jumped as the thief with the sack leaned the open top forward. "No, do not empty out the contents of the sack! Something valuable might get lost in the sand. And it is all valuable! Every cup! Every coin!" He stopped for a moment to clutch his heart and control his breathing. "No, rather place it down carefully before me. I shall examine the contents in the most cautious of manners."

The thief with the sack, fearful, at least, for his teeth and fingers, lowered the sack as if it were composed of the most delicate of crystal. The leader of the thieves stepped forward and opened the top of the treasure satchel, his mouth set in an expression of grim persistence, and began to finger the articles inside, one by one, occasionally bringing one or another of them to the light above the pouch.

"No, no," he muttered, "too large, far too valuable." He searched for a while, interspersing the clanking within the bag with an occasional comment of "Never" or "An item like this would be irreplaceable" or "Over my desiccated corpse." But then he paused, his lips trembling as if he might have to say the word "give" again.

"Ah," he managed a moment later, "I think I have the very thing."

"Then you have found the gift?" Ali Baba asked.

"Gift? That is even worse than the other word." The chieftain laughed nervously as he brought forth something from within the bag of riches. It was also something so small that Ali Baba could not immediately determine its true nature. "Very well, we will give them this tiny gold eggcup." The chieftain smiled with the way he had conquered his decision. "Very tasteful, don't you think?"

Ali Baba, who still fully measured himself to soon be among the dead, mentioned, "That is still not much of a gift."

"What? How dare—" The bandit leader's rage stopped as he saw how the eggcup became lost in his closed fist. "Oh, I suppose it isn't. Very well. A gift. My, My." He stared back within the bag. "I saw a larger plate in here that I might be able to part with. It was in extremely bad taste."

This last comment came as little surprise to Ali Baba, who was familiar, if at a distance, with the tastes of his brother. The chief of thieves dug again within the sack, and, with a prodigious grunt, brought forth a plate of considerable size and weight.

For perhaps the first and only time, Ali Baba found himself in complete agreement with the leader of the thieves. He might call this plate remarkable, but that did not even begin to hint at its truly overbearing qualities. Perhaps it was the gold-inlaid nymphs, chasing each other around the border, that were too much. Unless it was the elaborately jeweled reproductions of everyday life among both farmers and villagers that adorned the plate immediately inside those borders. And then there was that reproduction of the cosmos, using only larger jewels, of course, for the sun and five planets. But mayhaps it was the etched silver portrait of maidens taking a bath that tumbled it beyond the edge of respectability, or could it be that obsidian relief of a vase inlaid at the plate's very center that, when pressed, opened to reveal the name "Kassim" spelled out in diamonds? It was either that, or one of the half dozen other features that Ali Baba had not yet had the stomach to digest. And that, of course, was not even considering the additional workmanship upon the platter's other side.

Their chieftain pulled his eyes away from the plate with difficulty. "Yes. I believe this should be the very gift. The sooner it is out of my sight, the better."

"Are you impugning my tastes?" mentioned Kassim, who, when one thought upon it, had even less to lose than his brother.

"When you come to regarding this dish, I attempt no opinion whatsoever," Thief Number One admitted. "There are, after all, simply certain things which the mind will not accept."

"Exactly why I had that plate fashioned!" Kassim stated with pride. "Although it was a shame that the kilns of my city could not accommodate any of my large designs."

"No doubt," replied the chieftain, who now seemed to be attempting not simply to avoid looking at the plate but to avoid overly touching it as well. "It will certainly make a unique presentation." He forced himself to glance back down at the offending platter. "But, before I give it to you, perhaps I will pry out a couple of the larger jewels."

"Ho!" the sentry called from the other side of camp. "The caravan is now going away!"

The chieftain grabbed the platter and thrust it toward the woodcutter. "Oh, very well, take the entire plate, although I know I shall regret this generosity when I am destitute in my old age!"

Ali Baba accepted the reluctant gift. It was a full four hands across, and heavy with jewels and inlaid stones. Somehow, he managed to balance it atop the basket which contained Kassim, and with a powerful groan, lifted both of them to the level of his waist.

Now, if he could somehow manage both his parcels, and negotiate his way lightly uphill to that ridge beyond which the caravan was currently disappearing, he could fulfill that which the chieftain wished.

If only he did not encounter these few small problems. How did somebody walk with a scimitar bouncing against his knee? And his brother, though now cut into parts, was still no lighter than when he was but a single entity. Even a woodcutter's muscles were strained when carrying both brother and plate.

And, furthermore, Kassim would not go quietly. "Am I to go out there unarmed?"

"You are right," Thief Number One agreed curtly. "We will hide a short sword in the basket."

So he would have still more weight? Somehow, Ali Baba would learn to smile and bear it.

"Use this basket to your advantage," the chieftain instructed as he deposited the short sword. "Perhaps his parts can search for booty while you keep the caravan distracted."

So it was that Ali Baba was sent forward to attempt the foul scheme of Caravan Redistribution. Somehow, as the chieftain described it, it all seemed not only possible but somehow inevitable. As he approached the caravan, however, the woodcutter began having doubts of an ever-graver nature. Surely, a wise man somewhere has said, it is difficult to be filled with confidence when you are unable to walk properly.

But he would win no battles with such an attitude. He was thinking the worst. Perhaps those members of the caravan would give him a chance to talk, and the redistribution would commence quickly, with as little pain as possible. Ali Baba had to remember that not everyone was as quick to judge as the leader of the forty thieves.

With that he reached the top of the ridge and saw the caravan in the distance. And, furthermore, the caravan saw him.

"Thieves!" called a voice. "Thieves! I would recognize that black robe and beard anywhere!"

This was not going well. He knew to turn around would mean certain death. But to go forward seemed to promise a sword between the ribs as well. If only he might be able to speak before larger weapons came into use, he might have some chance. He wished now that he had the benefit of the smooth tongue of Marjanah.

As he approached he could hear the merchants and camel drivers debating. It was odd, after living among men who dressed in nothing but black, to see men with robes of many colors, and even a number of traders in purest white. Some of those men looked in some way familiar, so that the woodcutter was certain that they must have sold their wares in his city before. But all other thoughts fled as Ali Baba noticed that the debate between the merchants and camel drivers was occurring with drawn swords. For the briefest of moments, he thought they might be fighting each other, but the swords seemed to be involved in a great deal of waving about in the air and absolutely no clashing of metal against metal. There could be only one conclusion from this turn of events. The swords were meant for him.

"I tell you, he must be a thief," said a merchant. "Who else wears that sort of black?"

"Either he is a thief," agreed another, "or in mourning."

"To me," mused one of the camel drivers, "he looks like a woodcutter."

The merchants all had a good laugh at that one. They no longer seemed to be holding their swords aloft.

The camel driver decided to extend his witticism. "How could he be a thief, unless they are letting in woodcutters?"

"It is truly amazing," one of the merchants agreed, "that he doesn't cut himself with that scimitar."

Ali Baba was truly astonished. One way or another, he had managed to convince them of his innocence. But that remark concerning mourning had blessed the woodcutter with a certain idea.

"We are pilgrims," he therefore called to the assembled caravan, "upon a quest!"

"Pilgrims?" one of the merchants called back. "That I might believe of your unassuming presence. But there is no holy place nearby."

There was not? The woodcutter thought there were holy places everywhere, but perhaps that came from a life of city dwelling. In the desert, there would be no holy places. In the desert, there was only desert.

But, since there were no holy places, what could his answer to that observation be? Ali Baba was becoming of a desperate nature.

"That is our quest!" he therefore responded, not sure quite what he meant.

"To go where there is no holy place?" shouted one among the caravan in astonishment.

This at last impressed the merchants. All the swords were resheathed at once.

"You must be truly holy to have such a goal," said the camel driver who had once called him a woodcutter. "It will take you a lifetime, and still you will be nowhere. I wish I could summon that gift of sacrifice!"

But this observation had provided the woodcutter with even further inspiration. Therefore he said: "It is that very sacrifice that I wish to practice now." He bobbed his chin to indicate that which he carried before him. "I have an offering."

"Ah!" the camel driver cried in delight. " I have always wanted a wicker basket!"

This was not precisely what Ali Baba had meant. Further, he did not think they would be so eager to accept the basket if they knew of its true contents. But he would not discuss those contents, for his task was not to disgust this group, but to gain their trust.

"Alas, no," he therefore said. "This basket contains all my worldly possessions, and the reason for my pilgrimage." In a certain way, the woodcutter realized, both those statements were very true. "Instead, I have brought you a plate of great value."

With that, he placed Kassim upon the ground and lifted up the large and ostentatious offering. The merchants had to shield their eyes, so bright was the plate beneath the light of the sun. And they continued to shield their eyes even after Ali Baba lowered the angle of the platter, and the sun was no longer upon them. For the longest of moments thereafter, the merchants were speechless.

"Surely, you are speaking of some other plate," one of the merchants managed at last.

A second, who seemed to have lost all the color that had once filled his face, asked: "You expect us to accept something like that?"

"But it is of inestimable value!" Ali Baba tried to look admiringly at the plate in his hands, but found his eyes would not rest upon it for long, either.

"Yes, I would do no estimating at all about that plate," one of the merchants agreed.

"No, no, the parts of that—object might be worth money," one of the merchants blurted with obvious difficulty, "if they could be properly removed and all word as to their origins suppressed."

"Indeed," the camel driver agreed, "we could melt it down."

"If someone could gaze long enough upon it," another of the merchants agreed, "to do so without retching."

"Of this plate among plates?" Kassim announced loudly from within his basket. "This art among art? Are you impugning my tastes?" Perhaps, Ali Baba considered, it was an error in judgment that they should attempt to give away Kassim's favorite possession.

"What was that?" the camel driver said in astonishment. "That did not sound at all like you. That voice was forceful and direct. Now, that could be the voice of a thief!"

"Did you talk then with another voice?" one of the merchants asked with interest.

"Perhaps he is possessed," another suggested.

"A pilgrim who is also possessed?" a third merchant called in awe. "Now, he must certainly be holy."

"Or perhaps as crazed as a loon," the first merchant mentioned.

"Or even further," the camel driver suggested, "perhaps he is a lying thief."

It was frightening, Ali Baba thought, how close they came to the truth. He had better say something further, and as quickly as possible, before they had time to continue their thinking.

"Please, take the plate!" he beseeched the members of the caravan. "As a pilgrim, I must make a sacrifice!"

"No," the first of the merchants firmly replied, "I feel that taking that plate would be a greater sacrifice."

But Ali Baba could be every bit as firm, for it was, after all, his life if he was not. "I must give you this plate," he therefore said.

But the merchants continued to be as reasonable as they were obstinate. "No, you are a pilgrim," said the second. "We would not think of taking something for nothing."

The third merchant reached into his purse. "We insist that you take these copper coins."

"And while you are at it," the first merchant concluded, "you may keep the plate."

But Ali Baba would outsmart these clever merchants yet. How could he accept their money when his hands were filled with this ugly platter?

"I will place the coins in the basket for you," the third merchant offered generously. Before Ali Baba could indicate to the contrary, the man had stepped forward to the basket. It was fortunate indeed that this merchant only lifted the basket lid to a height sufficient to slide the coins inside. Still, the wise man says that good fortune cannot last forever.

"Hey!" Kassim objected as the coins hit him atop the head.

"What was that noise?" the closest of the merchants asked with a frown.

The woodcutter attempted a smile. "It is a nervous affliction I have gained from spending too much time in the desert," he answered, further adding: "Hey! Hey, hey!" He jumped about a bit to add to the effect.

"Not to mention too much time spent in a basket!" Kassim further remarked, as if, now that he had found his voice, there would be no way he could cease talking.

"When you are nervous," the first merchant asked, "you produce another voice from the basket?"

"I swear that sounds like a thief," the camel driver concluded, "and a thief I have known."

Ali Baba's hopping did not seem to be having the desired effect. "Surely," he managed weakly, "you are mistaken." This was not going at all well. He had not taken a single step toward the Caravan Redistribution. Rather than the vast quantities of gold that his chieftain wished to discover, all he had seen thus far were a few coins pulled from this other man's robe. Therefore, in desperation, he asked: "You will not take the plate. What will you have from me?"

"We will ask the quest—" the camel driver said, as though he were thinking of something else. "Sorry. Rather, do that trick with the basket again!"

Kassim was silent for the moment.

"Perhaps," one of the merchants suggested, "we have to drop something else inside. Something larger might work even better, such as one of those brown gourds, of which we have filled innumerable sacks."

"Gourds?" Kassim replied rather more loudly than was necessary. "This is not a trick! This is me in my entirety, and temporarily, this is my home, and I will not have individuals indiscriminately dropping objects upon my head!"

But before this conversation could progress to any further point, there came a great cry from the distant ridge.

"We appear to be under attack," the camel driver observed.

Ali Baba turned about, and saw the remainder of the forty

thieves, all mounted on their jet-black stallions, rapidly traversing the sand.

"You have given the signal!" their chieftain called from where he rode at their front. "Now we shall steal!"

"Thieves!" the members of the caravan cried as they ran about the camels. "Thieves!"

This was the very least that the woodcutter might have expected. But there didn't seem to be the usual level of moaning, pleading, and general misery that might attend a potential massacre of this sort, almost as if the shouts were somehow rehearsed. And not a single member of the caravan had yet drawn a sword, but instead all seemed intent upon running, again not in those usual meaningless circles, but instead to two very definite directions upon either side of the caravan, almost as if they wished the thieves to ride unimpeded into their middle.

Why was Ali Baba of the opinion that everything here was not precisely what it seemed?

◆

Chapter the Twenty-first,
in which there are certain reversals of fortune,
in the most literal sense.

"Where is the gold?" the primary among thieves demanded as he pulled his horse up before Ali Baba.

"I believe there is something you should know," Ali Baba replied, looking back and forth to those members of the caravan disappearing behind their camels.

"There is no time for explanations!" Thief Number One demanded. "There is only time for gold!"

Ali Baba had had enough of this. He had not spent his entire life in honest labor to the belittled by a man such as this. "I might have been able to procure your gold if not for your untimely charge!"

"What untimely charge? We responded to your signal!"

"It was not my signal," Ali Baba replied bellingerently.

"It was mine!" Kassim shouted, for once coming to his brother's defense. "I will not have things dropped upon my head."

"This is so?" their chieftain shrieked as he found a new, basket-encased focus for his anger. "I do not allow such effrontery, no matter what they are dropping upon your head. I shall drop your head! I shall have your pieces cut up into pieces!"

But Kassim was even more angry than Ali Baba. "Why do you bother?" he asked in derision. "This scheme of yours will never work. They knew my brother was a thief from the moment they set their eyes upon him!"

"Is this so?" Thief Number One asked in surprise, as if this thought had not previously occurred to him. "Then dressing in black is, for once, a disadvantage?" This idea was apparently so fundamentally opposite to the purpose of his entire life that he appeared shaken. "Perhaps it is time for a counsel!"

Ali Baba took this pause in their leader's ostracizing to look

165

about him. At present, though they were still surrounded by camels, he could not see a single human among them. Might this absence be a more important topic for discussion?

"Pardon—" he attempted to speak.

"A counsel!" Thief Number Two immediately cried. "A counsel! A coun—" He abruptly paused at a look from his leader.

"The Caravan Redistribution Program is not working!" Thief Number One stated abruptly.

The Thief once known as Achmed stepped forward in response to that. "Perhaps we need to revise our approach," he reasoned. "Too many people know of the forty thieves."

Their leader seemed to take umbrage at this, even in the midst of counsel. "We are feared throughout the land!"

"My point precisely," Achmed agreed. "How, then, can we talk these people into accepting our program? You do not have polite conversations with those feared throughout the land."

Their chieftain frowned at this. "This subterfuge business is a tricky thing. I will have to think upon it. But this is a counsel! Better yet, we will all think about it."

"Perhaps," Harun suggested as he warmed to the idea, "we can learn something from my earlier years among the higher classes. Instead of going to the caravans, we can have the caravans come to us. Then, as a first step toward a change in our image, have a series of Brigand Hospitality Socials, serve chilled rose water and small cakes—"

Whatever further planning there might have been was lost beneath a fearsome and bloodcurdling cry as a hundred men dressed in white rose up about them.

Oh, yes, Ali Baba thought as he saw the hundred brandish their scimitars, this was the very sort of thing he had wished to discuss. He wondered if it was now perhaps too late.

"We are surrounded!" the first among thieves mentioned for the benefit of any of those who had not bothered to look. "But we will not surrender without a fight!"

The man whom Ali Baba had taken for a camel driver threw his head back and laughed. "Fight and be destroyed! We have three times as many swords as you! And all of my men know how to use their weapons!"

"Well, there is that," Thief Number One agreed after glancing briefly at Ali Baba. "But we shall resist!"

"And I have not yet introduced you to our bowmen," continued the man who could no longer be considered a camel driver. The ine behind him parted to show half a dozen men dressed in blinding white and armed with crossbows. "Therefore can my bowmen pick your thieves off at will, and there will be no way that your thieves may touch us!"

"There is that, too," Thief Number One acknowledged. "But we can make no end of surly remarks as you take us prisoner!"

The surrender thus negotiated, the thieves waited as the hundred men in white moved forward to take them prisoner. Even then, however, Ali Baba noted that the first among thieves was not overly upset, and instead seemed to be involved with an exchange of knowing looks with that dark-complexioned thief that Ali Baba had remarked upon previously.

"You may wonder who might be bold and brilliant enough as to capture the forty thieves?" the former camel driver asked. "Allow me to remove my disguise." He proceeded to tear away layer after layer of brown rag until he revealed robes that, if possible, were of an even whiter hue than all those around him.

"It is Goha!" Kassim remarked from his position within the wicker.

"It feels so good to be recognized," Kassim's former boss acknowledged, "and even better to return to my signature white." He waved graciously in the direction of Ali Baba. "And I do rather appreciate that trick you do with the basket."

Ali Baba briefly considered revealing the secret of the basket, but decided that Goha might not appreciate the fact that an employee of his now resided therein in six separate parts. And his free movement was currently in the process of being further restricted by other men in white and numerous ropes, so that whatever revelations he might have would of necessity be kept to himself.

"Watch carefully and quietly," Aladdin whispered to Ali Baba's side. "We might get our chance for freedom."

"You!" the first among thieves cried in fury as a pair of burly men in white wrestled him to the ground.

"Pardon me while I change my robes," was Goha's only reply. "My last set has been sullied by camel spittle."

Other members of the brothel keeper's retinue rushed forward with the spotless replacement garments, and had the robes changed in mere seconds.

"Much better," Goha remarked as he straightened the creases upon his sleeves. "When one is preparing to gloat over his conquest, it is so important to be dressed properly."

He clapped his hands. "But what would a conquest be withou[t] spoils? Let us see what is in those sacks!"

The first among thieves cried wordlessly, as if the very mentio[n] of the contents of those sacks stabbed him in the heart.

"There is nothing in this one," one of the men in white calle[d] back, "save vegetables."

"Perhaps these are not thieves, after all," Goha said with [a] smile. "Perhaps they are farmers."

This time the cry from the first among thieves was equal part[s] anger and anguish. His hands now tied behind him, Ali Bab[a] found himself herded with a group of thieves to one side of thei[r] horses and the sacks of booty.

"Find what is in the other bags!" Goha demanded.

"This one is filled with anything but vegetables!" another o[f] the men in white called. "The sack is filled with large an[d] ostentatious items made of gold!"

"Aha!" Goha shouted in triumph. "At last, you will give m[e] what I deserve!"

"The workmanship on these things is hideous," the other ma[n] in white further announced. "One might almost imagine thes[e] things once belonged to Kassim!"

"Alas," Goha said with a sigh, "he speaks of one of my valued employees, who has now been lost to us."

"Is that so?" the voice came from the basket. "And yet, nothing may last forever."

"That trick with the basket again?" Goha acknowledged. "While I appreciate your attempt to cheer us all, nothing can take the place of a comrade who is no longer among us."

"Perhaps," the basket further remarked, "I have information that may be of value to you."

"Might that be so?" Goha inquired. "We do wish we might find him, so that we might torture and kill him for desertion."

"But what do I know?" the wicker confessed. "I am naught but a basket."

More shouts came from Goha's minions as they found more sacks filled with gold. Their leader seemed ever more pleased with himself. But he still was somehow not relaxed, as he shifted from foot to foot and looked from time to time at the leader of the thieves, as if there were still some ritual that had to be performed before his triumph could be complete.

Goha walked forward at last toward the first among thieves. "But this is much too fine an opportunity to restrict myself to mere gloating." He looked down to where the other man had been forced to his knees. "There are certain choice items of information which I doubt the members of your band have become acquainted with."

He glanced first at the thieves huddled together in two separate groups, then at all the men in white who guarded those in black. "Know you this, all those present: Once, thieving and brothel keeping were kept under one tent. Once, the master of thieves and the master of brothels worked together as one. That is when I gained the name of One Thumb"—he held up the hand that was so transformed—"and that is where the leader of the thieves received his name as well."

All the thieves gasped as one.

"Never has such a thing been revealed!" Harun confided in a harsh whisper. "Thief Number One has always been Thief Number One!"

"Oh, this is such fun," Goha chortled. He paused with great meaning before adding, "Isn't it, Grubby Sheets?"

"Grubby Sheets?" the first among thieves roared. "How dare you! It is such—such an unfair name! How can one possibly keep his laundry clean when one is always thieving on the road?"

"Thus, no doubt," Goha allowed graciously, "your change of attire."

Thief Number One nodded grimly, attempting to save the last scraps of his dignity. "Black robes show nothing."

"Not even blood?" Goha asked.

All the thieves gasped again.

"You do not think we would be satisfied with this gold, which, though fairly substantial in quantity, is extremely hideous in execution?"

"Are you impugning—" Kassim began before he thought better of it.

"You were wise to stop," Goha said softly to Ali Baba. "There will be plenty of time for basket jokes when our business is finished. That is, if you still have a basket, or a voice."

He turned back to their leader, whom Ali Baba, and no doubt all the rest of the band, were attempting very diligently not to think of as "Grubby Sheets."

"But I do not wish to make idle threats," One Thumb further mentioned. "I wish all my threats to be quite substantial." He kicked out a foot, spraying sand over Grub—Thief Number One's robes. "I have always felt, when asking questions, one should start at the top."

"You see, we are privy to other information, and we know this to be only the beginning of your gold, for before Kassim disappeared, he had mentioned a cave filled with untold riches!"

Ali Baba felt no surprise. He could always depend upon his brother to give away every secret. Yet, at this moment, the basket was strangely silent.

"You expect to torture me?" Thief Number One said with a lightness of tone that was sure to mean defiance.

"Oh." Goha shook his head sadly. "Oh, no. Nothing as simple as torture. I know you too well from our past association to expect you to respond to mere torture. No, I think we shall begin with hours of general derision. Then I will tell a number of embarrassing stories about your childhood. This will be followed by a listing of every bad decision you ever made during that time when you were in my employ. Only then, once you have been totally broken down, will we be so gentle as to torture you."

But Goha's most recent bout of gloating was interrupted by another shout from one of his men. "There is even more than gold! I have found some women! And they are beautiful women!"

At that, Goha laughed again. "Excellent. The brothel can always use a few new recruits." He winked broadly at those around him. "Those already in my employ have to work so diligently, it ages them prematurely."

"The brothel?" Achmed said near Ali Baba's ear. Never!"

"Quiet out there!" One Thumb declared as he pointed his forefinger at Ali Baba's group of thieves. "We will, of course, have to test the women personally, once we have removed ourselves from this wild climate."

Achmed made a strangled noise that came from deep inside.

"Should your master refuse to speak," One Thumb continued, "or should he die before he gives us the information we require, we shall return for each of you. There is nothing for you to look forward to, save torture and death!"

"Come!" Goha said to those around him. "It is time to ridicule and deride!"

As he was lifted from his feet, the chieftain twisted about to look at the most mysterious of the thieves. "The plan!" was all he managed.

"Remember my warnings!" Goha remarked as they dragged the struggling leader of the thieves to a tent that must have been recently constructed. "Torture and death! And that only if we decide to be merciful!"

So it was that the two groups of thieves were left there upon the sand, with only a pair of sentries to guard them.

"We have been left out here in the night," Aladdin remarked.

"If our leader will not speak"—Harun shuddered—"then we shall all be tortured, one by one!"

"Left out in the night," Aladdin further remarked, "to get our minds from our troubles."

"In the sure knowledge that all our gold is forfeit," Achmed added in not the most cheerful of tones, "and those sweet women within our troop will shortly be severely abused!"

Yes! The women! Ali Baba had not truly considered the meaning of One Thumb's discovery. What would such a man do to Kassim's wife? Far worse, what would he and his men do to Marjanah?

"Left out in the night," Aladdin even further remarked (surely, he was a man whose camel had but a single hump!), "to tell stories!"

Faced by that singleness of purpose, the other thieves realized that further resistance was useless.

"I, for one, am looking forward to this," another voice added. "On with the telling!"

It took the woodcutter a moment to realize that voice had come from a certain stone that resided in Aladdin's pack.

Aladdin cleared his throat in preparation.

Ah, well. Even Ali Baba supposed there might be a worse way to spend his final night.

♦

Chapter the Twenty-second,
in which Ali Baba becomes annoyed that
a subsidiary story is taking up so much of the plot.

"So it was that the younger Aladdin," his older self began again, "sent his mother forth with great expectations of marriage to the beautiful princess.

"But nothing is so simple as it might first appear, and Aladdin's life was no exception to this rule. For, as you might recall, the evil magician had returned to Morocco, where he had stored his great library of sorcerous knowledge and the many arcane devices that made him preeminent in his art. And, when he consulted these many spells and philters, he discovered that the boy Aladdin had not perished in the cave as the magician had first thought, but had used the djinni of ring and lamp to bring about a life of great comfort for himself and his mother, and further did this lad look forward to improving his life by union with a princess.

"Now, nothing in all of this world or the next infuriates a wizard more than when that wizard makes a mistake, and so it was with this foul mage, as he rained curses upon the fair Aladdin and his hardworking mother and the entire country of China in which they did dwell. But curses did not buy the duckwort, and so it was that he decided to return to that city where Aladdin did still reside and wrest the all-powerful lamp from him forever. It was in short, the dire and evil wizard thought, time for another journey.

"But Aladdin and his mother knew nothing of this ill omen and so went about their simple plans. Therefore did Aladdin take what money remained from the sale of dinnerware, and outfitted his mother in the finest manner available in all that city. And further did he have his mother take a fine white plate, and upon that plate did he put all those fantastic fruits that he had taken from the enchanted cave. Surely, they were of such novelty and beauty that the king would take notice and hear his mother's petition.

"So it was that his mother went to the grand audience of the king, in the great hall of the king's palace.'' Aladdin paused then, and waited for Harun's approval, but the elder thief had been so taken by those recent events surrounding their capture that he did not appear to be truly listening. Therefore, the other thief continued without further interruption:

"Then did his mother stand in that line where the various petitioners waited to give their offerings. And, as she heard the king and the grand vizier discuss those offerings before her, then did the woman's head begin to fill with doubts.

" 'Ah, a mere golden tray,' said the king of the first gift. 'Toss it in the bin with all the others of its kind. The petition? Yes, yes, hand it to my vizier. What have we next? A diamond without compare? Very nice. I shall put it in this bucket here with those jewels of a similar nature. Petition to the vizier. And let us look at this next lovely gift. Why, it is a marvelous mechanical bird, made of rare metals and fine jewels, which opens its mouth to sing and flaps its wings upon its perch. You are astonished that I may discern so much with only a look? That is why I am king. Place that over on yonder table, with the seven others of its like. Hand over the petition and off the dais, please. And what have we here?'

"With that, the mother of Aladdin realized that she was that next petitioner about whom the king must then be referring. And while she desired at that instant to be a bird herself so she might not have to confront the king with so little a gift as these child's toys, so did her fear root her feet to the ground and her gaze to her toes, so that she looked like nothing so much as a woman who knew the proper mode of supplication before the monarch.

"And the king, much impressed by her courtly demeanor, spoke in a gentler voice than he had used on those who had passed by before.

" 'What would you of me, kind mother?' he asked.

" 'I would only that you accept this poor offering that I bring to you from my son,' was her quiet reply, 'and further give a moment to his petition, for it comes from his heart.'

" 'Certainly, kind mother,' the king replied, for who cannot obey a mother when she asks a question so? 'Will you not show me what you have brought?'

"And with that, Aladdin's mother lifted off the cloth with which she had covered her offering, and brought forth the platter cluttered with the marvelous fruit. And she was quite astonished with the reaction this revelation received, not only from the king and vizier but from the immediate court about them, for everyone joined in gasping as one.

"Then did both the king and vizier marvel at her gift, and she received the first inkling of the true nature of what she held in her hands. For these were far more than toys upon that tray, and in fact, were so wondrous and valuable that even a woman as pure of heart as Aladdin's mother had a passing wish that she had put a couple of them aside for her even more elderly years.

"'Never have I seen such jewels,' said the ruler when he was done with his extensive marveling. 'Truly, they shall make me a king among kings. But what of your petition?'

"With that, Aladdin's mother held out the small scrap of parchment on which she had written her son's wishes in her cramped and fatigued hand. 'Here it is, O mightiest of kings!' she said to him, casting down her eyes as she thrust the paper forward. 'Please read this most humble of requests at your leisure.'

"But the king shook his head, saying, 'We will have none of that, kind mother. When we are presented with such a gift, our curiosity demands that you speak your petition aloud and at once!'

"So did Aladdin's mother, with trembling voice, relay her son's wish, that he be granted the hand of Princess Badabadur in marriage. Many in the court gasped again at the audacity of such a request, but the king continued to smile upon her even when she was done.

"'But who is this Aladdin,' the vizier cautioned, for he had been hired by the king for that very reason, 'and why have we not heard of him before?'

"But the king would have none of this caution, and replied instead, 'I look with favor upon a lad who does not make much of himself in public, and instead spends his time seeking out jewels such as these to give to his king. I can think of no better man to marry the princess.' And, in a lower voice, he confided to his vizier, 'When you know a man who produces the likes of these, it is best to keep him in the family.'

"So did the king give Aladdin's mother leave to go, and share the wonderful news with her son. And the king further informed her that the wedding should take place as soon as arrangements could be made, which would be in one week's time.

"Now, when Aladdin heard the good news from his dear mother's lips, he went almost mad with joy. He decided he could no longer stay within the confines of his modest home, and instead resolved to spend one final evening with the friends of his childhood so that he might have one last game of kick the fez before he was famous and exalted forever.

"Then was Aladdin's mother left home alone, and perhaps all would have remained well, for her husband had died many years before, and she was quite used to spending time in solitude. But this evening was different, for a mere hour before, the wicked mage from Morocco had returned to their city, and had resolved that he would stop at nothing to obtain the magic lamp.

"Therefore, he strode through the streets in that quarter of the city where Aladdin and his mother dwelled, disguised as a seller of lamps, and shouted in his loudest voice:

"'New lamps for old! New lamps for old!'

"And Aladdin's mother, at this very moment, had become fretful, whether in reaction to her own experience or through the vile machinations of a wizard's spell, it is impossible to say. She began to think of the fine palace she had visited that day, and the many fine gifts that had been put before the king. No doubt, the gifts would be even grander on that day when her son would marry the princess. But what kind of gift could she, a once poor woman from a poor quarter of the city, give that would in any way match those other fabulous presents from far places and distant lands?

"Then did she hear the magician's cry.

"'New lamps for old! New lamps for old!'

"That, she thought, might be the very gift. Her son seemed so fond of his old lamp. He was very attached to it for some reason. She could not remember precisely why. She did recall that it had something to do with her fainting. But surely her dear son would keep nothing in the house that would cause her to faint? And how much more becoming would be a new lamp! If her son treasured that beaten piece of copper refuse in the corner, how much happier would he be with a pristine lantern of modern manufacture.

"'New lamps for old!' came the cry again. 'New lamps for old!'

"She opened the door, and there, immediately without, was the lamp salesman, almost as though he had known what actions she would take. When he smiled, he looked somehow familiar, but she could not remember where or how she had seen that face before, for there was sorcery at work.

"So sudden was the appearance of the wizard that she took a step back in fright. Perhaps a new lamp was not the perfect gift, after all. She reached forward to close the door. But the lamp salesman had acted first, and put his foot within that space between the door and the wall.

" 'New lamps for old!' he said in a merry tone. 'New lamps for old!'

"Now, Aladdin's mother had lived for many years, and was wise to the ways of the marketplace. There was but one way to properly remove a foot from a door. So it was that she relented, and resolved to listen to at least a bit of the man's presentation before she pushed him from the door.

" 'Tell me, then,' she said, 'about these new lamps.'

"With that, the magician smiled the most ingratiating of smiles, and began such a torrent of words that Aladdin's mother found it impossible to put two thoughts together in her head, much less speak those thoughts.

" 'Look at this wondrous lamp!' the mage said as he held forth a sample of his wares. 'Bright, shiny, and new, it will do all things that your old lamp did and more. It comes with our exclusive adjustable flame. And a special compartment in the back where you might store extra wicks, as well as our special cleaning cloth, already coated with a fine layer of ash to make that polishing take mere minutes!'

"This lamp that the seller held in his hands did seem like a wondrous thing; that much Aladdin's mother had to admit. Yet something still bothered her. Wasn't there some quality of her son's lamp that she should remember?

" 'And, wondrous as this lamp is,' the seller continued, 'it will cost you next to nothing. Because of the graciousness of this lamp's manufacturer, I am currently able to take in exchange any lamp within this household, with no further monies owed by you. Yes, though you may be astonished at my inducement, I will happily accept any lamp whatsoever, even that extremely tarnished object I see back in the far corner.'

"Aladdin's mother looked upon that lamp the seller had indicated, and frowned. Truly, the man must have remarkable eyes to see that dull lamp lost in shadows! Oh, yes, she recalled it now. That lamp had something to do with her son. She had tried to clean that lamp, hadn't she? Why had she never finished with its polishing? The tarnish upon it must have been too heavy. It was surely too much of a bother. But why could she not remember it clearly? And what had she been thinking about her son a moment before? Was age affecting her mind as well as her bones?

"But it was not age that was confusing her, but the sorcerer's spells. As surely as he had entered that house with but one thought in mind, the procurement of the lamp and its djinni, so had he arranged his spells so that any thought concerning this one special object would be beyond the woman's comprehension.

" 'A new lamp?' Aladdin's mother murmured, so befuddled now that she could not shape her words into a sentence. "I have doubts—such a decision."

" 'It is no decision at all. Merely pick up that lamp,' the seller suggested as though that might be the most natural thing in the world.

"Somehow, Aladdin's mother felt the cool copper in her hands. Yes, she had held this lamp before. Hadn't it produced a great quantity of smoke? She wondered, somehow, if she could attempt to polish it again.

" 'Merely give the lamp to me,' the seller suggested as if that would be the only truly sensible course of action.

"Somehow, she found a new lamp within her hands. The shock of this almost brought the elderly woman to her senses.

" 'But,' she asked of the lamp seller, 'what shall I tell to my son, Aladdin?'

" 'Trust me,' the lamp seller replied before she could frame her thoughts further. 'Between these two lamps, there will be no comparison.'

"And with that, the lamp seller was gone so quickly that Aladdin's mother had no knowledge of his leaving.

"And so did Aladdin lose the lamp, and with it all his dreams of happiness, for the wizard, vengeful man that he was, used that very lamp to lure away Aladdin's own true love. But the boy resolved that he would get that lamp again, and with it the fair Princess Badabadur!"

"That is it?" Ali Baba demanded. "It is not a very happy ending." Now that he thought of it, if matters kept to their present course, none of their stories would have happy endings.

"I know not of happy endings," Aladdin said with a ragged quality to his voice. "I only know the truth! And the truth was that I went searching for that lamp, and came to be captured by the forty thieves."

"Actually," said the deep tones of the stone which resided among Aladdin's belongings, "there was a very refreshing note of tragedy within that story. I may have spent millennia as a part of a cave, but I still know very little of tragedy."

"As a rock," Achmed added with a frown, "I would not expect that you would know much about anything."

"Actually," replied the stone, his voice betraying the slightest bit of hurt, "I am a great authority on sedimentation."

"I am sure that is the sort of topic that might keep us fascinated for hours," the thief answered. He nodded at some of their fellows, who had already nodded off during the long telling of Aladdin's tale.

"Achmed?" another voice called from the other side of their group of prisoners. "I would recognize that tone of voice anywhere. Is that you?"

"Is that Sinbad?" Achmed asked in return.

The other voice assured Achmed that he was indeed Sinbad.

"It is good to find you again, Achmed," Sinbad further said. "It is so difficult to recognize people when everyone wears a beard."

"We have found ourselves in another awkward situation," Achmed acknowledged.

"We are thirty-four," Sinbad mentioned. "They are one hundred and twelve."

"Sinbad has always had a gift for numbers," Achmed explained. "Sometimes, as in our present situation, I wish that he did not."

"We have known worse," Sinbad rejoined. "At least we have escaped from the Queen of the Apes!" He shivered, although the evening was still reasonably warm. "But I have spoken up for more reason than to become reacquainted. I wish to speak to the one once known as Aladdin, and shall be known as Aladdin again, for I have a plan by which we shall all regain our names."

"Your facility for figures has put grand ideas within your head, then?" Achmed asked lightly.

But Sinbad answered in all seriousness. "Only ideas that I know may be brought to fruition. You see, I believe I know the location of Aladdin's lamp."

Chapter the Twenty-third,
in which things begin to jump and people do as well.

Until that moment, the woodcutter had not realized he had been drifting off toward sleep. But then he heard of Aladdin's lamp. Here was something to cause Ali Baba first to awaken and then apprehend his attention. Here was a magic lamp complete with djinni, something even greater than all the gold within his kitchen. Perhaps here was a way to save himself and his fellow thieves, not to mention Kassim's wife and Marjanah besides.

"You know of the lamp?" Aladdin demanded. "Is it somewhere safe?"

"I can think of no place safer!" Sinbad said reassuringly.

"And will that place be readily accessible?" Aladdin further asked.

"Well, should we be able to escape from our bonds, we will be able to reach the site easily enough. Regaining the lamp might be a trifle more difficult."

From the distant tent, the thieves all heard a repeated chant:

"Grubby Sheets! Grubby Sheets! Grubby Sheets!"

There was a hoarse shout of defiance, and then the chanting began anew.

Ali Baba looked over at their two guards, who had built a small fire to protect them from the approaching chill of the night. For some time, they had been involved in a game known as hump the camel, which seemed to involve a great deal of rolling of dice on one guard's part and a great losing of dinars on the part of the second guard, along with periodic cries of "I have been humped!" As long as they believed the thieves were tied, these two would be no trouble.

"Where, then, is my lamp?" Aladdin insisted.

Sinbad frowned at the two guards, and at the tent beyond. "I will tell you when we are away from here. I do not wish the incorrect people to overhear.''

"This is all very encouraging," Achmed interjected, "but there is still the matter of our entourage being held prisoner by armed guards. We will need swords to cut our ropes, and further protect ourselves against whatever number of Goha's men confront us.''

"Then we are trapped here forever!" Aladdin stated in not the most positive of tones.

"Well, there is a certain ring," Achmed allowed, "that might help us if its owner might acknowledge its origins.''

Aladdin looked at him in noncomprehension, as if the word "ring" were entirely foreign to his vocabulary.

"If you do not wish to rub it," Achmed further stated with some annoyance, "hold out your hand and I will be happy to do so.''

But, rather than holding out his hand, Aladdin recoiled in horror. "I do not engage in such activities! I was soon to be a married man!''

Ali Baba, who was none too sure of the exact course of this conversation, had thought of another way through this dilemma.

"I can think of one," he therefore said, "whose arms are free, perhaps more free than he would like." And with that, he called to the basket some half dozen paces distant, cast aside by men in white who did not discern its true importance. "Kassim!''

"Hmm?" said his brother in the basket, as if he, too, might have drifted off to that land of dreams. "I am not sure that I am presently conversing with anyone. It was not enough that I was cut into pieces, certainly not! And then all my worldly goods were taken from me, but that was not the end of it, either! Now people inpugn my taste? There are simply certain things too odious to bear.''

"But the guards pay no attention to us," Ali Baba replied quickly. He simultaneously glared at Achmed before the lad could make some comment concerning owners of particular plates who would certainly be familiar with the odious. Achmed only smiled and shrugged.

"This is our chance to escape," he insisted to his brother. "With your help, we may be free of this place.''

"I am not sure that I am interested," Kassim replied sharply. "To free you, my parts will have to crawl over some quantity of sand. Besides what unpleasantness that might cause to my wounds, I stand a much greater chance of discovery. If there is one thing I do not desire, it is to have my parts chopped into parts. Perhaps you should request help from someone whose tastes more resemble your own."

The woodcutter glanced over at their guards, but both had turned to listen to a new chorus of "Grubby Sheets! Grubby Sheets!" from the tent beyond.

"But with your help," Ali Baba insisted of his brother, "we may regain Aladdin's lamp!"

"In this," the voice from the wicker acknowledged, "our tastes might meet at last. Is this lamp everything that the thief has said it is?"

"I have seen no limit to its power," Aladdin admitted.

"Then the lamp could make me whole again?" Kassim asked, renewed hope within his voice.

"Who is to say what the djinn can or cannot do," Aladdin admitted, "but considering they can transport you through solid ground or produce great quantities of food and gold within an instant, I imagine they might reassemble you within an instant."

"At the very least," Achmed added before Ali Baba could glare at him again, "he should be able to conjure a blind tailor."

"One has to allow for a large range of tastes in this world," Kassim admitted. "Do you think the darkness is sufficient to cover my movements?"

Ali Baba looked about. Night had indeed fallen as they had conversed, and now there was naught but a thin band of red at the very horizon. "There should be no trouble," he replied. "The guards' eyes will be blinded by the brightness of their fire, and they should be looking for no trouble from a basket."

"Grubby Sheets!" came the call from the distant tent. "Grubby Sheets!"

"No!" was the answer from the first among thieves. "I can bear no more!"

"You know," the stone spoke from within Aladdin's belongings, "this new activity sounds even more interesting than telling stories. I really should send out parts of me more often."

Kassim grunted softly from where the basket sat. "You will have to pardon me a moment," he said, the strain evident in his voice. "The lid is placed upon here very tightly. I am afraid I pulled it down after I received those coins upon the head. Thus must I pay for my own anger. I believe, to extricate myself from my present predicament, I believe I shall have to tip myself over. It will take me a moment while I swing my arms."

"Take your time," Achmed called. "We can always talk to the stone."

"I'll have you know," the rock replied haughtily, "that I have many areas of interest."

"Sedimentation," Achmed agreed.

"Perhaps," Kassim mentioned, "if I also swing my legs."

The basket teetered back and forth. The guards were busy with their game and took no notice.

"I know a fair piece about fossils as well," the rock mentioned jauntily.

Ali Baba heard another yell. At first, he thought this noise also originated from the tent, but, with a second cry, he realized the commotion originated among the other cluster of thieves.

"I can talk about magma for hours," the rock volunteered.

"I almost have it," Kassim called. His basket rocked wildly back and forth, but somehow still managed to remain upright. Fortunate were they that there was a disturbance among the other thieves, for the guards' attention was turned in that direction. "Tip over, tip over, tip over, tip over!" he urged the basket.

"Perhaps I could share some of the stories of stalagmites I have known," the rock concluded. "Say, do I hear some noise?"

"Aha!" Kassim cried in triumph as his basket tipped fully over, dislodging the lid at the same time. "Now I can go about my business!" And with that, his various parts began to crawl forth.

Ali Baba decided, even after his prior familiarity with the current state of his brother, he still did not want to watch the action across the sand. He instead turned his attention to the other group of thieves, who now seemed to be shouting with some regularity as an eerie green glow erupted in their midst.

The odd illumination was attracting the attention of everyone. This, the woodcutter decided, was a good sign. However, the unnatural light and the noise it caused among the guards and other thieves was bringing reinforcements from around the distant tent. This, the woodcutter decided, was not that good as a sign.

But the cries redoubled with what happened next. For the green glow rose above the others until the woodcutter could see it took the shape of a man.

"It is a wizard!" Aladdin called, saying the thought that all of them shared.

And with that, the wizard laughed, and flew in a great loop above the guards and prisoners, so that he passed directly above Ali Baba and those huddled about him.

"It is *my* wizard!" Aladdin further realized.

The magician whom Aladdin now recognized flew on toward the tent, and swooped down among the flaps to a renewed series of screams and cries of alarm from within. He reemerged but an instant later, but this time he carried the chieftain of all the thieves.

"See whose sheets are soiled now!" the first among thieves exclaimed triumphantly to those below, as the magician and his passenger rose swiftly beyond the range of One Thumb's bowmen.

There was a moment when all stared in wonder at the magical escape. And then that moment passed, and the men in white were among Ali Baba and his companions.

"Do not entertain any idea of escape!" they called. And further: "We will know the location of the gold, even if we must torture every one of you in turn!"

But more had changed here than a mere escape. Now that the wizard was gone, Ali Baba realized he might escape from these minions of One Thumb, shave off his beard, and someday resume a normal life. Harun al Raschid laughed and said that he recalled a humorous story. Actually, he recalled a great many of them.

"That was my wizard," Aladdin repeated triumphantly, "and I have a ring!"

"Speak only when spoken to!" the men demanded as they kicked Harun and cuffed Aladdin upon the side of the head. "We will ask the questions!"

And they had a question immediately. "What is this empty basket? What was within this wicker?" The guardsman who held the basket brought it closer for examination. "Ugh! The smell within here is foul!"

The wizard was gone, then, thought Ali Baba, and so were his spells. Much could happen now, if only they could get themselves untied. But where was his brother?

"You there!" one of the men in white shouted to Ali Baba. "Cease your movement, or it will go badly for you!"

But Ali Baba had not moved whatsoever. Yet what might that strange sensation be across his back?

He realized with some surprise that there was something, or someone, within his robes!

◆

Chapter the Twenty-fourth,
in which working with a djinni
helps give our heroes small gains.

Only in retrospect could Ali Baba sort through what happened next.

"I thought I told you not to move!" one of their surly captors continued. "Although how you can manage to move your body in that manner is beyond me."

But Ali Baba temporarily escaped this man's further ire when the guard spotted a worse offense. "Wait! What are you doing down upon the ground?"

"You will never catch me!" replied the brazen voice of Kassim. "I shall roll away!"

"So you say," the guard replied confidently. "But I shall wring your neck first!"

He dove for the head.

"You have no neck!" the guard exclaimed.

"I am free!" Achmed called at Ali Baba's right. "And I shall fight for my freedom!"

"I will grab your chin!" the enraged guard screamed.

"I am free!" Harun al Raschid remarked. "And I shall fight for my right to tell amusing anecdotes!"

"Ow, ow!" The guard pulled his hand away from the ground. Rather than his taking hold of Kassim, Kassim had taken hold of him, and with his teeth besides.

The woodcutter felt the ropes go slack about his wrists. "My brother! You *could* have been six thieves at the same time," Ali Baba said in admiration as the arm flopped onward to free another.

"Give me back my finger!" the guard declared.

But the other parts of Kassim continued their task. "My hands are free!" Aladdin shouted. "Allow me to rub my ring!"

There was immediately a great deal of purple smoke, and out of that smoke boomed a great voice:

"Though slave to the ring and the owner so blessed,
I am master of much, and what is this mess?
What will you, master, what will you?"

The smoke cleared to reveal a being of such a dark color that light refused to reflect off his form. He opened his eyes to reveal twin pools of red as bright as the sun.

"Djinni, this is my wish!" Aladdin fended off one of his white-robed captors with a well-placed foot before saying: "I would have you remove us from our bondage, and take us to the far end of this desert!"

The djinni of the ring nodded at this, and replied: "It is a simple enough command, except that you have not defined who you mean by 'us.'"

"Ah," said Aladdin as he tripped another of his enemy and punched a third in the stomach. "Then the quality of the wish depends upon how it is specified?"

"A djinni is only as good as his orders," the black-skinned being answered. "It is a worthy observation. You have matured greatly since last we met."

"I have left kick the fez behind," Aladdin agreed. "But you need a definition. What do I mean when I say 'us'?"

"Would you hurry up about this?" Achmed requested as he knocked two white-turbaned heads together.

"This, then, is 'us.'" Since Aladdin was a generous man by nature, even after all the time he had spent as a thief, he said: "All men dressed in black."

"All thirty-four of them?" the djinni rumbled in a voice not quite so certain as before. "And one of them in separate parts?"

"Wait!" Ali Baba called. "There are more!"

"More?" the djinni replied in a voice verging upon despair. "Do you wish me to transport these men in white as well?"

"Certainly not," the woodcutter chided. "But what of the women?"

"Of course!" Aladdin agreed immediately. "We must bring the women."

"Seven more?" The djinni paused for a moment to make a rumbling noise deep within his chest. "Very well. Your wish is my command. I will transport you to the limits of my ability."

And with that, Ali Baba and his fellows were surrounded by smoke.

But the smoke cleared almost immediately.

"They have jumped away!" came a cry from much too near.
For all they had done indeed was jump, for the men in white now
stood but a short distance from them!

"We have hardly moved at all!" Aladdin exclaimed.

"I would say about eight and a half cubits," was Sinbad's
estimation.

The men in white growled a growl of war and turned to attack
anew. To further their troubles, Ali Baba noted, the djinni was
gone.

But not all about the woodcutter were panicking. Achmed
seemed much taken with the young woman who had appeared
beside him. "Is this, then, Marjanah?"

"Are you a friend of my master's?" was her humble reply as
she turned her gaze down to study the toes of her shoes. Never had
Ali Baba seen his slave act so meekly.

"They will not get away this easily!" One Thumb cried,
waving his mangled hand above his head. "Attack!"

Aladdin rapidly rubbed his ring a second time. Purple smoke
filled the air.

> "To him with the ring I will grant a boon,
> But I must ask a question: Whyever so soon?
> What will you, master, what will you?"

But before he made a wish, Aladdin had a question. "You are
only able to transport our group but eight and a half cubits?"

The djinni shrugged. "There are many of you. And there are,
unfortunately, certain limits to my power. Personally, I believe it
comes from being trapped in a ring for millennia. That sort of
thing is certain to stunt your conjuring."

"I am sorry that we are overtaxing you," Aladdin apologized,
"but might you move us once again?"

"Your wish, as they say, is my command," the djinni replied in
a voice both bold and resigned, "or at least as much command as
I can muster."

Purple smoke surrounded them once more. But it cleared, if
anything, even more quickly than before. And there, a scant eight
cubits or so distant, was the increasingly angry mass of One
Thumb's fighting men.

"They will not escape us this time!"

But escape them they did.

> *"As slave to the ring my might is your gain,*
> *But this constant work is a bit of a pain.*
> *Shall it be the usual?"*

"Of course!"

Over and over again did this procedure repeat, until Aladdin had to pause to suck upon his ring finger to reduce the chafing. And, as the chase progressed, and One Thumb's troops began to feel an ever-greater fatigue as they ran beneath the desert sun, while the entourage surrounding Aladdin was much refreshed by having their entire number moved by an outside power, so did One Thumb and his men fall ever farther behind, and their bloodthirsty threats and calls for retribution were increasingly punctuated by heavy breathing and cries for water.

"They will not—" One Thumb managed, for by now most of his minions were beyond speech. "We will get—they will regret—rivers of blood will—that is, oh, bother!"

And with that, One Thumb collapsed as well.

Ali Baba spent a moment looking back at the trail of white bodies that littered the desert behind them.

"There is a copse of trees in the distance!" Harun called to the rest of them, for he was gifted with that farsighted vision often common among the old. "We have reached the beginnings of fertile land. The djinni has saved us."

"Perhaps, then," was Aladdin's reply, "we shall give both the djinni and my finger a rest, and walk for a distance. Quickly now, for I feel there is a chance that some of our pursuers might yet recover."

"O my brother-in-law!" Kassim's wife bounced up to Ali Baba. "Finally, there comes a moment when I can begin to thank you for your part in saving the women from the vile clutches of One Thumb." She shivered, a motion that showed off all of her parts to good advantage. "I look forward to the opportunity that we might show you how thankful we truly are. And may I mention how handsome you look at present, now that you have grown a beard?"

"No, you may not!" shouted the head of Kassim. "It may all be very well for the rest of you to walk from this place, but what of me? Shall I flop my way out of this desert? It is your duty as my wife to carry me out of this place!"

"I do not believe I could manage that with my delicate frame," his wife replied, "not to mention my delicate stomach. You have been out in the sun for a few days too long, O husband, and you have ripened.''

Ali Baba looked quickly about the assembled group. The djinni, in moving them, had apparently left Kassim's basket behind. "I am afraid," he therefore said, "that we have lost your conveyance."

"Will I have to flop around like this for the rest of time?" Kassim asked in despair. "Think, O thieves! You would not have escaped without my assistance. The least you can do to thank me is put me back together."

All agreed that Kassim's point was certainly valid, and that this was indeed the case.

Aladdin nodded at this consensus among his brethren.

"Perhaps, considering the circumstances," he mused, "I can call upon the djinni one final time."

So he rubbed the ring again, and a certain quantity of purple smoke erupted therefrom, although Ali Baba could swear that that smoke was nowhere near as great as it once had been. And when the smoke cleared, there, once again, stood the great, dark djinni, although now he appeared to have something of a slouch. And this is what the djinni said:

> "As slave of the ring I will do my best,
> But could I ask, please, might you give me some rest?
> I have sat within that ring for years, and now this!
> I tell you, I am sincerely out of conditioning.
> Oh dear! I am sorry.
> What will you, master, what will you?"

"We have but one final boon of you, O mighty djinni," Aladdin said. "This man, who has been reduced to six pieces by the cruelty of our former master, has helped us all to escape from certain torture and death. In return he has asked to be made whole again. Is this a task you might perform?"

"I might," the djinni agreed, "if I had not spent the entire day carrying Forty-one souls across a blazing desert." The djinni sighed, the sound of a soul escaping an aged body at the moment of death. "I am too careworn to conjure. Let me ride about upon your finger for a bit. I shall recover myself in virtually no time whatsoever."

Kassim was not at all pleased by this answer. "Then I have no choice but to flop about from place to place?"

"Oh, come now," the djinni replied. "Pull yourself together. Sometimes I do not know about you humans. I see many an empty waterskin about. With so many men with strong backs, surely, you can be carried!"

This, thought Ali Baba, was the voice of an obedient djinni? He had heard many stories in the past concerning these spirits, and how they had turned upon their masters when asked too much, or were influenced by men with evil in their hearts.

"Perhaps," he therefore said, "this is a good time to give our magical benefactor the rest he so dearly requests."

The dark being nodded in approval. "This is a difficult spell at the best of times, more suited for one of my senior brethren. You know, the kind you find in lamps. Although the matching of living tissue to living tissue is always tricky work, especially after he's been groveling through so much sand."

"But can you not simply snap your fingers and say, 'Behold, you are whole!'?"

"It is not as simple as all that," the djinni said, his voice reasoned, with perhaps but the slightest trace of annoyance. "Perhaps you would be better served retaining the services of a blind tailor.

"I am still too spent to spell. Please call me in the morning."

And with that, the djinni vanished.

Aladdin turned to gaze upon the distant trees. "I believe it is time that we walked."

His observation was answered by a dry and half-hearted cry from somewhere out in the desert. A cry that no doubt came from their exhausted but still pursuing enemy.

"And I suggest that we walk quickly," Aladdin added.

♦ ♦ ♦

BOOK THE THIRD:
being
EVERYONE'S STORY

♦

Chapter the Twenty-fifth,
in which, although there is still no cash,
yet does something get carried.

"But where are we?" Ali Baba asked, for even his woodcutter's senses were befuddled by their djinni-aided flight.

"I have been this way before," Harun remarked. "When you have been with these thieves as long as I have, you have been every way. I believe we are but a little distance from the cavern that contains all our gold."

"What shall we do now?" Achmed asked of the others. "We could leave this life behind, shave our beards and trade in our robes for respectable clothes." He looked to Marjanah, who, for some reason, had been spending a great deal of time in Achmed's presence. "We could find new reasons to start afresh."

"But what of that gold?" one of the others mentioned. "Not that any one of us wants to be a member of these thieves forever. But as long as that gold is there, who better deserves to have it than those who labored so to obtain it?"

"There are also some among us," the thief once named Sinbad (and could now probably again be called by that name) remarked, "who are none too certain they want to remain in one locale for too long a period of time."

"Surely," Achmed objected, "you could not still be worried about—"

"The Queen of the Apes is everywhere!" Sinbad said, his eyes wide with fright.

"Oh, come now," Achmed chided, "I was with you on those many months of flight before we were captured by the thieves. In all that time, the Queen of the Apes only caught you on six occasions." He paused to think. "Or was it seven?"

But the other man would not be comforted. "It is easy for you to say! You did not have to feel those paws! And those hairy kisses!" Sinbad began to look as if he had spent far too much time out in the sun. "And then, when she put all her weight atop me!" It was evident, from his expression, that he could bring himself to say no more.

Achmed answered with a question. "But if the Queen of the Apes was so set upon having you, why has she not found you again in all these months?"

"In this," Sinbad replied, "the thieves saved me. I believe that she was scared away by our numbers."

"But we must go on," Achmed insisted. "All our voyages, all we have accomplished, cannot end like this!"

There it was again, thought Ali Baba, that thing about voyages. He had asked somewhat after this before, and received a somewhat oblique answer. But, now that they were free of their vile leader, he could no longer hold back on his questions, for now he trusted these others as closely as his own brother; more closely, actually, seeing as his actual brother was Kassim.

"Are you, then," he asked of this Sinbad, who was actually a bit upon the scrawny side and not at all the type he would have chosen as a wealthy merchant, "the Sinbad of legend?"

But, as Sinbad still seemed to be feeling the ill effects of thinking of the Queen of the Apes, Achmed answered for him. "Oh, no, no, that was a much older gentleman, who used to serve as my master. We went out on this voyage, don't you know—"

"It seems," said the stone from within Aladdin's belongings, "that there are more stories to be told around here."

So it was, as they strode en masse from the desert, that Achmed began to tell the tale of the miraculous eighth voyage of Sinbad the Sailor, and how it finally put right numerous wrongs performed upon the previous seven voyages, including the capture of a particularly obnoxious djinni named Ozzie.

And at that time, Sinbad joined in the storytelling to talk about the woman in the palanquin, that same woman he had come to love. Her name was Fatima, and what did he know of her? Her laugh, perhaps, and the sound of her voice, and the delicate wave of her hand. What more did a man need to fall in love? But then, through a great disturbance involving magic and unnatural beings, he lost her under extremely mysterious circumstances, and found in her stead the Queen of the Apes.

"The Queen has dogged my steps ever since," Sinbad concluded. He paused for a moment before he continued. "Well, that is, she has until the last year or so, however long I have been in the thieves."

"That is a truly marvelous story," Ali Baba agreed, "but we have marched for some time now. Where precisely are we walking?"

"I am leading us back to that magic cavern," Harun called from the front of their group, "for, although we never stayed at that place for more than hours at a time, it is still the closest thing we know to a home." He paused to give the sort of discreet cough Ali Baba was sure he must have used when he had inhabited palaces. "Also, I am hoping to take away my fair share of the booty."

"It is where we must go," Sinbad agreed, "for that is where I saw Aladdin's lamp."

"It is there?" Aladdin shouted in wonder and disbelief. "Then such must be the reason for the presence of that vile magician, for he has made it his life work to obtain that magic lamp. Strange it is how all our stories are coming together."

"But very satisfying," the stone within his belongings replied. "I am getting far more entertainment from this than even I had imagined."

So they would return, then, to that spot where Ali Baba's adventure had begun. Many was the time as he had ridden endlessly on horseback that he had thought to curse the day when he first spied upon these thieves, and so began the events that changed his destiny forever. However, now that he thought upon it, things had not resolved themselves so badly, and further he still had some substantial quantity of gold hiding beneath his kitchen.

"That is also very near the Palace of Beautiful Women," Marjanah mentioned softly from where she walked by Achmed's side. "Which, from your former chieftain's description, can be found in the deepest part of the cavern."

"So the cave is filled with gold and beautiful women?" Ali Baba asked in disbelief. "Whyever so?"

He heard a sigh come from amidst Aladdin's belongings. "Alas. That cave was always thus. Large as it is, I fear that the cavern has always felt inferior. Thus does it seek embellishment."

"Forgive my less-than-perfect ears." Ali Baba was astonished at this revelation. "You say that this cave has emotions?"

"Caves are no different from humans," the stone replied. "Well, actually, they are somewhat draftier. And they sport many more hard edges. But, as one might look at emotions, caves desire the same things that all who think may desire: attention, a feeling of importance, and perhaps even love."

"But why should the cave feel inferior? I have been inside, and it is truly massive."

"All you say is true, but this cavern does not share all the best of features of grottoes underground. It has no great domed ceilings, for one, and its stalagmites are by and large second-rate." The stone sighed again, an act that Ali Baba found disconcerting. It was bad enough that the object talked, but how could something that did not breathe then breathe out? But still the stone continued:

"Any and all of us could find ways we wished we were better. I myself would prefer to be made out of quartz."

But Ali Baba had further questions about this strange and emotional hole beneath the earth. "I have heard that the cave has reanimated my brother's parts, and has further twisted men so that their faces look behind, and their arms sprout out where their ears should be. But what hold does this cave and this palace have over the thieves?"

Now it was Harun's turn to answer. "None over most of us. Its true hold is over the first among thieves."

"Then it has cast a spell over him?" Ali Baba mused. "I remember a story once where a man's heart was trapped in a tower, so that none might kill him."

"That was my story, actually," one of the thieves mentioned.

First Aladdin, then Harun al Raschid and Sinbad, and now this. Ali Baba was amazed.

"Does every member of the thieves have a story?" he asked.

"Actually, they do," yet another thief replied. "Mine concerns a magic fish I found when casting my net three times in the Dead Sea."

"And mine largely has to do with a magic carpet," replied another, "and three maidens in a hidden garden."

"Mine has to do with a garden as well," still another added, "and a flower with very special characteristics. Not to mention a ring, an intricate box, and a sly serpent."

And on and on the thieves recited, mentioning tales filled with wonders and dangers, until Ali Baba began to feel the slightest bit inferior, for his successful theft of gold from the magic cavern seemed as nothing to the drama and variety of the stories around him.

"Yes," Harun concluded. "All men have stories."

"Or at least all men in the forty thieves," Achmed amended.

"Whatever," the stone chortled. "I shall have a wonderful time."

"But you were telling me of the chieftain of the thieves, and how he was in servitude to this enchanted cavern."

"Ah, well, you were almost correct in your conjecture about our leader, for the cavern does hold a piece of him."

"But it is not his heart."

"Far worse," Harun replied. "The cave has captured his liver."

Ali Baba opened his mouth in silent astonishment.

"The ancient Greeks, I believe, thought that the liver was the seat of love," Harun explained. "Or perhaps it was the spleen. Or it could have been the Romans. Then again, who is to fathom the true motivations of an enchanted cavern?"

"But how does he function?" Ali Baba asked.

"He has a brother who is cut into six pieces," Kassim's head mentioned from a nearby water bag, "and he asks how someone functions without something as inconsequential as a liver!"

"Far be it from me to interrupt your learned discussion, O master," Marjanah interrupted, "but I thought I might mention that it was growing dark, and we would be wise to soon seek shelter."

Ah, thought Ali Baba, that sounded more like the Marjanah he had known over the years: humble, yet to the point. Perhaps whatever ill effects she had suffered when captured by their chieftain would wear away with time. Still, he would only be truly reassured when he had had a moment to talk with her, and perhaps longer to speak to some older, wiser, but still-not-unattractive person such as Kassim's wife, who might put the whole incident into a proper perspective.

"I can sense your concern, young miss," Achmed replied boldly, "for I am sure you have led a cloistered existence, and do not know much of the wild. Let me reassure you now that you are under my protection, as well as that of more than thirty other individuals who, while all good men, were forced to live the life of thieves for months or years."

"Forced," agreed another of the former thieves. "That's it exactly."

"And, now that we are free of the first among thieves, we shall never steal again," added one more.

"That is, of course," concluded a fourth, "after we remove the gold from the cavern."

"But that isn't stealing," another thief argued. "Not really. I mean, you can't really steal what you've stolen already, can you?"

"I see your point," said the man who was forced. "Well, that makes everything fine, then."

"And I am so glad you pointed out how all of you might protect me," Marjanah said to Achmed, staring up at him with eyes that seemed far too large. "Knowing that, I feel much safer."

No, Ali Baba thought, all was not right with his young slave. What foul torture, he wondered, had brought her to this awful pass?

"Still," said Aladdin thoughtfully, "it was not a bad thought to find some place to rest for the night." He paused to look about him, for they had now traveled far enough to be in the midst of the trees. "We are approaching the cavern, are we not?"

"I believe we are reasonably near," Harun replied.

"Then perhaps as soon as we find some protected grove, there we should stay," Aladdin reasoned, "so that we might arrive at the cavern with strength and good spirits."

"You are right," Harun agreed. "We will have more than the cavern to contend with."

"Then you expect to find our chieftain," Ali Baba asked as the thought struck him with amazing suddenness, "and the wizard?"

"All of us have spent so long as thieves," Harun reasoned, "there is nowhere else for us to go."

"Not quite correct!" another voice shouted, a voice Ali Baba now identified with everything evil. A hideous green glow, all the brighter for the approach of evening, flashed overhead.

"You may not have any gold," shouted the first among thieves from where he rode upon the wizard's back, "but you do have women."

He laughed at that. "Or should I say that you did have women, for now they are ours."

♦

*Chapter the Twenty-sixth,
in which we talk to the trees,
and they do listen to us.*

Ali Baba looked about him, and realized that their former chieftain was quite correct. The women had disappeared. Marjanah! he thought. And the wife of Kassim! Never had he realized how much he looked forward to the company of these women until they were gone.

"The palace accepts seven more within its gates!" Thief Number One cackled. "My liver is safe for another day!"

So, Ali Baba considered, what the others said was true. And while he could not say he was truly sympathetic with such a vile fiend, at least now the woodcutter might begin to understand him. Yet how could such a man be without a liver, and yet be so filled with bile?

And with that, the thief and his wizard were gone.

"Marjanah!" Achmed called at their sudden disappearance.

"Kassi—" Ali Baba stopped himself. He might find his brother's wife among the fairest of the fair, and she might give every indication of having some reciprocal emotions, and also might her husband be cut up into six pieces, but still there was a time and place for all things, and this was none of that! Besides, he had a wife at home, whom he might of course never see again due to unpleasant circumstances having to do with swords and wizards and magic caverns, but he did not wish to think upon that, either. Oh, for the days when the whole of his life was but a tree and an axe!

"My wife will do well in a place like that," Kassim said dismissively. "Her tastes were always far too expensive."

"What shall we do?" Achmed asked, his normally steady young voice betraying hints of panic.

"We could call upon the djinni of the ring," Harun suggested. "Surely, he would have a solution."

Ali Baba once again thought about those stories he had heard. "But when last we summoned the djinni," the woodcutter reasoned, "he appeared less than pleased."

Sinbad agreed. "I, for one, have had many negative experiences with djinn."

Half a dozen of the others murmured agreement, saying if there were but time, they would tell unpleasant stories about the djinn as well.

"But Marjanah!" Achmed implored.

Aladdin looked in a kindly way upon the youngest of the thieves. "I know how you are feeling now, for I have felt that way, and still do within my heart, for the Princess Badabadur. Therefore do I call the djinni. Truly, he can feel no anger when he sees that we make this request for love."

Love? Ali Baba thought as Aladdin began to rub his ring. Was that what so strangely afflicted a number of those around him? Seeing how peculiar it made their behavior, the woodcutter was glad that he was married and beyond such things.

Aladdin pulled his hand from the ring. "The djinni comes."

This was, Ali Baba thought, the first time anyone had had the time to announce the spirit's arrival. And not only the speed but the nature of that arrival had much changed, for rather than emerging as a great cloud of smoke, the purple burst from the ring in irregular puffs, like a fire that would go out for lack of air.

Still did the djinni appear, although, from the way he moved his head and folded his arms, he did not look all that overjoyed to be here. And when the djinni spoke, he sounded less than pleased.

> *"Though slave to the lamp, I am out of my league,*
> *For, all truth to tell, I am done by fatigue.*
> *What would you anyway, master, what would you?"*

"The women have been spirited away by that vile magician!" Aladdin explained as he pointed toward the north. "Somehow, we must rescue them!"

The djinni raised one of his hands to stroke his chin. His eyes were no more than slits of fire, and closed repeatedly as he talked. "Oh, even such a supernatural being as I can see that is serious. I wish I had some energy so that I might help you. We will have to pursue this problem in the morning, if I have sufficiently regained my strength."

And with that, the djinni disappeared.

All things, Ali Baba thought, had limitations.

"We will never see Marjanah again!" Achmed wailed with the foolish abandon of youth.

"There is more than one way to the Palace of Beautiful Women," another voice spoke up. It took Ali Baba a moment to realize it was the voice of the stone, speaking with the authority of the cave that had been its home.

"You have entertained me with your stories," the stone said further. "Now it is time for me to tell a few tales of my own. Take me out of your sack and hold me in your fist so that I might better see the way."

"There is no view from a water bag, either," Kassim complained.

Aladdin did as the stone bade, pulling it from the bag and holding it aloft in his fist. No one made any move to do anything with any part of Kassim.

"Night is falling swiftly," Aladdin said as he held forth the stone. "Will you be able to see?"

"Stones do not look in the same way as humans," was the rock's reply. "We are a part of the earth, and every pebble, every grain of sand, does our seeing for us. The wizard flies through the air above us now, but when he lands upon the earth, I will know, for the other parts of me will tell me so."

Ali Baba marveled that such a thing could be, as many of those around him murmured of Destiny.

"But come," the stone called. "We should be on our way even before they reach their destination, for we want nothing ill to happen to the women."

"Marjanah!" Achmed declared, but this time the name was less a word and more a sob.

"In which direction did the magician depart?" the stone inquired.

And with that, thirty-odd thieves pointed to the sky. Unfortunately, they also pointed in five or six completely different directions.

"To err is human, to forgive is the rock," said the being that rested on Aladdin's palm, "or so says the wise stone. We shall not worry, for I have methods of determining their flight.

"Brother trees!" the stone called. "Brother trees! There has been magic out tonight."

The trees about them rustled, in that way that trees will when they are blown by the wind off the desert, save that this night there was no wind.

"Listen!" the stone instructed.

Ali Baba listened to the rustle of the trees on this most still of nights, and thought that he heard words among the leaves.

Burning magic in the air, were the words he heard. *Burning magic in the air.*

"Brother trees!" the stone called out again. "The magic has fled. Tell us where it has gone."

To the north, the trees replied. *To the father of all caverns.*

"Brother trees!" the stone said for a third time. "Guide us, so that we might right a wrong."

And the trees answered.

We will tell when your path is true.

In all this time, Ali Baba had never before heard the voices of trees.

"We travel north," the stone announced. The rock held before him, Aladdin began to walk, and the others followed.

Ali Baba listened to the rustling as he walked.

Is that not the woodcutter?

He has taken our brothers! May lightning strike him!

But he has cut down the old and infirm, and allowed the young to grow.

He does what he does. That is all that can be said, for tree or man.

But pass us by today.

Do not cut us yet.

Leave us to the sun and the rain for another season.

Goodbye, woodcutter, goodbye.

Walk on, they said to all. *Walk on. Your path is true.*

Ali Baba heard the rustling voices fade as they walked beyond the grove.

"I have not heard such a thing before," he said aloud.

"You did not yet know how to listen," the stone replied. "You will learn many things this night."

But they now walked along a barren patch of ground, and for a space there were no more trees to guide them on their way.

"Will we not lose our way?" Aladdin asked.

"The stars will be with us shortly," the stone replied. "They will be glad to show us north." Many of the men murmured assent to this wisdom.

"But for now," the stone said again, "we have other helpers." Thereupon he called out again in a loud voice:

"Hares! Mice! Beasts of the night! Have you looked up?"

The stone paused a moment, and then called again:

"Owls! Nightingales! Birds in flight! Have you looked down?"

And when the stone was sure that all had heard, it spoke again:

"There was magic in the air tonight. Where has it gone?"

Small, high voices called from the hidden places in the field around them, and Ali Baba could understand their words as well:

They have come from the south and gone to the north.

But not true north, no, not true north.

We thought they were bound for the cave.

The father of all caverns.

But not true north, no.

And from the sky above came the lonely call of the owls, and the sweet songs of the nightingales, and the two mixed together, and formed words:

They have veered away from the entryway.

They do not land at the stone that moves.

They go beyond. They go beyond.

True north no more.

"Let us go," the stone instructed. "A step or two to the left, and then straight on."

Thus did the rock lead them all for a time in the growing darkness. But it called Aladdin to stop again.

"They have landed," the stone said. "We are near." And then it called out again.

"Brother ground. There is magic here tonight. Has it touched the earth?"

And Ali Baba heard another sound in return, a faint and subtle noise, like the sound of a sandal, scraping across stone.

It has.

They are here.

Come.

Show you.

"We will find them now," the stone said with confidence. "They may have magic, but I am of the earth."

And with that, the stone led them down a hill into a shallow ravine.

"Here is where they passed below," the stone announced.

"It is another entranceway to the cave!" Aladdin shouted in astonishment.

"Then the wizard and first among thieves took the women this way?" Ali Baba asked. "Should we follow them?"

"Strange things have happened to those who have spent too long within these caverns," Harun warned.

"Please," Kassim said from within his water bag. "Let us not belabor the obvious."

"But many of us have passed in and out of this cavern a hundred times, with no ill effects," Achmed insisted. "Who is to say that this time will be different?"

"Caves can be so whimsical," the stone added enigmatically. "I do not know if I can help you more. Not only will you fight the first among the thieves and a mighty wizard, but the father of all caverns as well."

There was a moment of silence and decision then among the former thieves.

"I wish to go within," Aladdin announced, "and find the lamp."

"I need to go within," Achmed added, "so that my life might be complete with Marjanah."

"I have always wanted to go within," Harun admitted, "so that I might see the palace."

"I feel the necessity to go within," Sinbad added, "so that I might escape the clutches of the Queen of the Apes."

"I would go as well," Kassim volunteered. "After you have been cut into six pieces, what else might a magic cavern do to you?"

"We would like to go for the gold," others among their troop agreed, "although we believe we will adjourn to the main entrance for that purpose."

And what of Ali Baba? "I believe I need to follow the others through this opening. In a way, my story began when first I encountered the thieves and entered this cavern. I feel that it is my destiny to enter this cave again and put an end to these things."

"Well said," the stone added heartily. "If you are all to die, at least you shall do it in grand style."

Aladdin lit the first of the torches he had fashioned from the cloth and oil they carried. "Let us proceed."

Ali Baba looked down at the dark hole before them. Then again, perhaps his destiny rested back in his kitchen, and the repeated counting of his gold. But it would make a terrible ending.

Achmed handed him a torch, and Ali Baba followed Aladdin within the entryway, cursing his highly developed sense of story.

◆

Chapter the Twenty-seventh,
in which we enter the cave
and learn some deep secrets.

They entered the cave, one by one, for the passage, though tall enough to accommodate a man, was so narrow in spots that Ali Baba and the others had to turn so as not to scrape their shoulders.

"Is it wise," asked Harun from somewhat down the line, "to immediately rush into this place without formulating a plan?"

"We do it now," Aladdin replied, "while we have the courage."

That was what they called it, then. Courage. To Ali Baba, it felt more like a sour sensation at the very pit of his stomach.

"Do you think," Harun mused, "that we should wait until morning, when the djinni is rested?"

"Marjanah!" Achmed called out to the darkness before them. He pushed upon Ali Baba's shoulders urging him to hurry.

"The element of surprise will be with us now," Ali Baba mentioned thoughtfully.

"I do not believe a magician may be surprised," was Harun's less-than-enthusiastic reply. "It has something to do with the basic definition of their profession."

"It is not true," Aladdin said firmly from his place at the head of the line. "Think upon my story, and how my adversary mistakenly returned to Morocco. Even the greatest of mages could not know everything."

"Very well," Harun replied with a sigh. "If you feel it is for the best. I am afraid I know too much about these sorts of caves, and how sometimes they may crash down upon you when you make the wrong sort of noise, or emit noxious gases that will poison you as you walk. Sometimes I wish I weren't quite so learned."

"There is more to it than that," the stone said reprovingly. "Cave-ins and gaseous emissions do not happen for no reason at all. It amounts to but one thing: Does the cave look favorably upon you, or no?''

As if in response to the stone's musings, Ali Baba heard a rumbling somewhere in the far distance.

"Ah," the stone remarked, as if it could understand the language of the cave. "I see. I believe I should be in the woodcutter's hand now."

"Whatever you request," Aladdin said as he passed the stone back to the woodcutter's surprised and not-altogether-willing fingers. "This means, though, that you should take the lead."

"My brother?" Kassim asked incredulously from that point where his head was slung over Achmed's shoulder.

"Remember," the stone remarked. "The woodcutter took gold and the cavern let him live—unharmed."

"You need say no more," Aladdin replied as he pressed his back to the side of the cave to allow Ali Baba to pass.

But the stone was not yet done. "Caves play favorites as much as anyone. You were blessed enough to take a lamp from one. But this cave favors Ali Baba."

It did? Then why, when Ali Baba pressed his torch forward, could he see nothing but a wall before him?

"The cavern's passageway seems to end here," he mentioned to the others.

"For some, no doubt, it does," the stone almost agreed. "But for others, there is a way beyond."

Once again, Ali Baba wished he had Marjanah near, for she was always the one within the household who was good at riddles. Unless, he thought, this was not truly the end of the passageway, but a hidden doorway to the way beyond. And if this were so, the woodcutter realized, Ali Baba had a way to open that door.

"Open, Sesame!" he therefore said.

A slab of rock rolled out of the way, revealing a wider and higher passageway beyond. Somehow, Ali Baba thought, he heard a second sound behind that rumble of the wall, something like a deep-throated chuckle.

"Move forward," the stone in the woodcutter's hand urged, "for what we seek still lies beyond."

Ali Baba did as he was bade, for he realized he had been staring into the all-encompassing darkness before him.

"We will persevere," Achmed said behind him, "and find all that we desire."

Ali Baba paused again. "But not immediately," he said in

reply. "We seem to have come to a set of steps, carved in the solid rock, that lead forever down."

"When will this tunnel end?" Kassim complained. "Will we have to walk forever?"

Ali Baba once again realized he had had more than enough of his brother's company. And Kassim was not even walking!

"Perhaps," Harun said in a more congenial tone, "we could use something to lighten the tone. To gladden our evening, perhaps I shall relate the story of the King's Ass and the Wonderful Fart."

This, then, was one of those stories that Harun al Raschid was famed for from the distant past. Ali Baba wished he might pause and truly listen to it, save that he was charged with leading the way deeper within this cavern. From what bits he did glean, the story had a great many people exclaiming "It is your ass!" while the beast of the title gave forth gaseous emissions of various musical tones.

They climbed down a hundred steps. Harun's story ended, with a few polite laughs from the company, but the stairs continued.

"On we go?" mentioned Harun. "Perhaps it is time for another story, say 'The Queen's Magician and the Fart of Destiny.'"

Onward spoke the tale spinner as they continued on their downward course. This current story had something to do with a majordomo who could not control his gaseous emissions. Ali Baba was pleased that he had to pay attention to what lay before them upon the stairs, and so could not pay truly close attention.

Some time later, Harun completed this story as well. The laughter was a bit more abrupt than the time before. They walked on for a time in silence.

"Will we climb to the very center of the earth?" Kassim demanded.

"Mayhaps we could take your head," Achmed suggested gently, "and roll it down what steps remain. When you reach bottom, you might call up to us."

"Actually, I am simply making conversation," Kassim replied with a forced laugh. "I'm a head in a waterskin. What else can I do?"

"We must be careful not to fight among ourselves," Harun cautioned. "We must be united when danger strikes. Perhaps it is time for one last humorous tale, say 'The Elderly Painter and the Fart of Art'?"

With a sudden yet deep perception, Ali Baba began to appre-

ciate that time under the magician's spell when Harun al Raschid
was a depressed old man. Fortunate it was for all of them, then,
that the steps ended just below.

"We are near," the stone announced.

"Near what?" Aladdin asked. "The lamp? The palace? The
treasure hoard?"

"We are near that place," the stone replied, "where this cavern
wants us to be."

That answer did not give great encouragement to Ali Baba.
"How are we to fulfill our destiny," he said aloud, "when we are
following the dictates of the magic cavern?"

"Unless," Sinbad said, "our destiny is to follow the dictates of
the magic cavern."

"It is a tricky business," Harun agreed. "But I was about to
begin my story."

Before he could say another word, the cavern around them was
filled with a great roar of voices, not unlike the sound of an angry
army.

"Was that the cave?" Ali Baba asked, his voice tinged with
awe. "I do not like this business."

"I think not," replied the stone. "Caverns are, as a rule, more
polite than that."

There was another noise behind them. The sound of many feet
pounding upon rock.

"They are some distance from us still," the stone explained.
"The cavern is allowing us to hear their progress."

"You do not escape One Thumb that easily!" a voice echoed
from nowhere and everywhere. "I would have caught you sooner,
save that I had to obtain clean robes!"

Ali Baba liked this business even less.

"When will we find this place where we are supposed to be?"
he asked, unsure that he even understood his own question.

"Every step brings you closer," was the stone's less-than-clear
reply.

"Then let us step quickly," Achmed encouraged, "so we might
find Marjanah before something terrible befalls her!"

Ali Baba appreciated the lad's singleness of purpose, although
he had no idea of whether they would find the palace here or no.
He lifted his torch before him, and saw that the corridor, while
wider and taller than any space they had seen before, still seemed
to stretch on toward no discernible destination.

He felt as though they had been walking for an eternity. He

came to a place in the cave where the wall curved away, and decided it was time to rest. Without the cavern's assistance, they could no longer hear One Thumb, and he felt that they were in no immediate danger of being overtaken.

"Let us rest for a minute," he said to the others. "Then we shall find the palace."

But a different voice greeted him than those of his compatriots.

"Well, what do you know?" It was a woman's voice. "I swear it looks like a woodcutter. Care to show me your hatchet?"

It was, Ali Baba realized, not simply any woman.

♦

Chapter the Twenty-eighth,
in which we learn that you can't get
to the palace from here.

Ali Baba would know that voice anywhere.

It was the wife of Kassim.

He looked up, and saw her gazing down at him from a window carved high in the cavern wall. She smiled. No matter how one looked at her, even at this odd angle, she was beautiful.

"Is that who I think it is?" Kassim's head said in an uncertain tone.

"Is that my husband that I hear?" she replied in a voice that dripped with disinterest. "I'll have him know that I have been moved into a palace."

"Yes," Kassim agreed, "it certainly sounds like her."

She waved to the men below, and her long arm was covered by golden bracelets and jeweled bangles. "Now, this is the sort of luxury I could become accustomed to. Once we move out of this place, I'll show you how I really want to be treated."

"Now," Kassim further remarked, "there can be no doubt."

"Even though you are within the palace," Ali Baba called, "we are still within the cavern. Do these two places meet? How do we get into you?"

Her smile broadened at this most recent remark. "I thought that you would never ask. But you will have to guess."

Guess? Ali Baba was no better at these riddle games than before he had held the stone. And yet, if you were in an enchanted cavern and the way appeared blocked to you, what might you say?

"Open, Sesame?" he therefore ventured.

A stone block came crashing down before them, mere inches from Ali Baba's nose.

"I know not if this was designed as a means of entry," Harun mentioned at the stone's sudden arrival, "or a means of assuring

210

a quick demise. But it appears that a way has been opened to us to the palace.''

And indeed there was a large opening in the cavern wall where once that potentially lethal slab had stood. Light spilled from that opening, bright enough so that Ali Baba might no longer need his torch. He took a cautious step over the fallen slab, wary of other traps. But all was quiet, save for the singing of birds.

Birds? Ali Baba thought as his head peered within the opening for the first time. But all thoughts and feeling save wonder left him when he saw what was upon the other side.

He stood now at the beginning of a great space, that stretched for a thousand cubits before him, and perhaps half that distance into the air before it came to the great domed roof above, a space so large it was almost as if there were a whole separate world spread out before them, a world underground.

At first, it puzzled Ali Baba that, despite the fact that this great domed place was far below the ground, it was lit as bright as noon, so that he could clearly see the copses of trees to either side of him, as well as the formal garden immediately before him. A path of golden stones led through the garden, and beyond it to the first of many buildings that made up the palace, although to call this great structure merely a palace would do it a gross disservice, for it was ten times the size and ten times the height of any palace Ali Baba had ever previously witnessed, with so many fanciful windows and minarets that it might take as long to count them as it would the gold beneath the woodcutter's kitchen. And, speaking of gold, the palace was roofed with it, and the doors and windows framed by lines of precious stones, which all shone in the unnatural light.

''Now, this truly is a palace.'' Harun spoke for all of them. ''Perhaps there is a new story in here somewhere.''

Ali Baba thought there was far more than a single story here, for he had at last discerned some of the sources of illumination. For the leaves upon the trees and bushes seemed to glow with a light of their own, putting forth a many-colored radiance into the area around them. And the birds that flew above the trees produced rays of light whenever they fluttered their wings. And when they opened their mouths to sing, they produced rainbows.

''Truly, this is a marvelous place,'' Ali Baba murmured. ''What more fitting place could there be to contain my magic lamp?''

''Perhaps we should enter and approach the palace,'' the stone in Ali Baba's hand suggested. "As good as caverns are at waiting, it is best not to keep them waiting overlong."

"And so we shall," Ali Baba replied as he took his first hesitant steps upon the golden path. He waited for some other response within this strange, new world, but all he heard was the delicate singing of the rainbow birds and a further dainty tinkling, for as the wind blew the glowing leaves it made them ring like ten thousand tiny bells.

"I have but one question," he asked of the stone before he ventured farther. "How can the palace be now so far in the distance, if I so recently spoke with a woman in that palace, and she was then positioned almost directly over my head?"

"It is not wise to question the particulars of your surroundings when you are in an enchanted cavern," was the stone's stern reply.

"We must go to the palace," Achmed insisted, "to rescue Marjanah!"

So it was that they strode forward upon the bright and broad golden path, Aladdin to one side of Ali Baba, Achmed to the other, with Sinbad, who carried the head of Kassim, and Harun, who carried some parts of the body, walking close behind.

They did not have far to go, however, before their first confrontation.

"Beware!" called a chorus of high voices. "There are intruders in the sacred garden!"

"Do the women call out?" Ali Baba asked.

"Those are not women," Aladdin replied with a sourness of tone. "I recognize that sort of voice from my former life. We are to be challenged by the palace eunuchs."

"They have eunuchs at the Palace of Beautiful Women?" Ali Baba asked in surprise.

In response, three great, fat fellows sporting scimitars so long they almost looked like sheaths stepped upon the path before them.

"Well," said one of them, "the Palace of Beautiful Eunuchs simply does not have the same ring."

"Not that it matters to you," said the second, "for you will soon be dead."

The third one opened his mouth, but before he could speak, emitted a raucous and multi-toned gaseous eruption from the other end of his digestive system.

"Me and my weakness for pickled Rukh egg!" he exclaimed apologetically.

"Yes," Harun commented, "there is definitely a new story here somewhere."

Aladdin looked upon these three in astonishment.

"These are not simply eunuchs," he said in wonder. "I have seen them before, and told you of them in my tale. These are the guards who protected the Princess Badabadur!"

"Oh, so," said the first of the three, "then do we need to protect the princess directly this time."

"This young man looks somehow familiar," stated the second of the three. "If you were to take away his heavy beard, would he not resemble someone whom we have met before? Someone we have met but not beheaded?"

The third eunuch belched prodigiously. "Oh, pardon, you mean, he is"—he paused to look at his two fellows—"the man who got away?"

"Yes," replied the first with evident delight, "the very same who besmirched our perfect record of beheadings and disembowelments!"

"It is fortunate, is it not," said the second, "that that record may now be corrected."

The third farted in agreement. All three of them raised their swords and stepped forward.

"Yes," Harun mentioned, "there is a definite story here, should we live long enough to relate it."

"This is my fight," Aladdin said with a great nobility mixed with a certain amount of foolishness. "The rest of you must go on to rescue the women."

"Oh, most certainly not," replied the first of the eunuchs. "Our task is clearly to kill you all."

"These things are never as simple as one would hope," the second eunuch agreed.

"Come, let us get on with it!" insisted the third. "It is nearly time for dinner!"

The first eunuch shifted his sword, moving his great weight with the grace of a tiger rather than the power of an elephant.

"We should thank you, really," the second eunuch said brightly. "It does get rather boring down here."

"That is true," agreed the first. "After all, when you protect a palace a mile beneath the ground, who can possibly find you?"

"The food is quite good, however," mentioned the third.

"Mayhaps," suggested Achmed to Aladdin, "it is time to call upon the djinni of the ring."

"Beware!" cried the eunuchs as one as they halted in their approach. "We remember that djinni!"

"But I—" Aladdin began to protest.

"You do not wish to call upon that fearsome being for reasons of mercy?" Achmed said so quickly that Aladdin could not finish his original thought. "Your feelings are misplaced. Truly, these three are going to murder us!"

"Ah," Aladdin said abruptly, stopping himself from confessing that the djinni was no doubt still far too exhausted to be able to fulfill any but the smallest wishes. "You do have a valid argument. Perhaps I should restrain my merciful impulses and release the djinni to wreak his horrible and quite inhuman vengeance."

The eunuchs paused for a moment of close consultation among themselves. When they looked again at Ali Baba and the others, their smiles were less certain than before.

"Actually," the first of the three said, "now that you mention it so politely, perhaps we might negotiate some different outcome to this encounter."

"What does it truly matter, actually," added the second of the group, "that one man more or less was not beheaded? Surely, this is a private matter, only worthy of discussion between our two small groups."

"Yes," the third added helpfully, "and furthermore, I believe it is extremely close to the dinner hour."

It was truly amazing, thought Ali Baba. The merest mention of the djinni, and the three eunuchs were not so eager for death and dismemberment. But that was but the first step upon the path to the palace, for, while the eunuchs did not brandish their scimitars in so cavalier a fashion as before, still had they not removed themselves from that point where they were blocking the further progress of the others.

This was the very subject that Achmed was next to address. "So you are no longer planning to murder us," he summarized, "but you still block our path?"

The leader of the eunuchs answered firmly, but with great respect. "The presence of a djinni may give us second thoughts about the proper enactment of our duties outside the palace. However, in the protection of Princess Badabadur, we are un-wavering. We will use every means possible to dissuade your further advancement upon the path."

"Is she, then, within these walls?" Aladdin insisted with a fevered brow.

"That fevered brow does not argue well for our dissuading," the third eunuch mentioned with a touch of nervousness.

"But have you truly thought upon this?" Achmed insisted. "Why are you protecting your princess?"

"We have always protected the princess," the first of the three insisted in return. "It is part of the eunuch code!"

"But is this palace not a prison?" Achmed inquired.

"It is, in truth, a palace of a prison!" answered the first of the guards.

"And yet," the second added, "we understand that every need of the women is taken care of within those walls."

"They do fairly well by us as well," said the third between burps.

"Of course," the first reasoned, "it might be nice to have an occasional head to remove from a body."

"We do get out of practice," the second added as he gazed wistfully upon his scimitar.

"It seems that it is hardly worth polishing our swords," the third commented regretfully.

"But Princess Badabadur is here," the first stated boldly, as if that were all the explanation that was needed.

"And so are we," the second furthered the explanation.

"And we are fed very well," the third managed around his gaseous emissions, "although the food tends to be a little rich."

Ali Baba could see no way around the logic of these three eunuchs. Perhaps, he considered, his destiny was to give up this quest and turn around the other way. But where did that leave Marjanah and the wife of Kassim? Well tended, no doubt, but still prisoners.

Achmed, however, was not prepared to admit defeat.

"But from the stories I have heard," he therefore said, "I understand that she often liked to take long walks among the streets of her city."

The eunuchs appeared to agree with this.

"That is indeed the truth."

"I miss those walks as well."

"They gave me many excellent opportunities for beheadings."

Achmed smiled then, for he knew that now that he had gained their attention, he might soon have their approval. Therefore he said: "Would not her imprisonment, then, prevent her from one of those activities she treasured most?"

"I had not thought about it in that way," the first eunuch mused.

"We are here," added the second with little conviction, "therefore we protect."

"I wouldn't mind resuming those walks," the third added with more enthusiasm. "Well, not the walking part particularly. But sampling foodstuffs from those empty stalls?" He closed his eyes and emitted a most contented sigh.

"And you say that the princess is but one of many women within those palace walls?" Achmed continued to press his argument.

"There are untold women within that palace," the first eunuch agreed, "perhaps a hundred times a hundred."

"What will one woman be," the second wondered, "more or less, in that huge and crowded palace?"

"Much better that she should be under our direct protection," enthused the third, "so that we might get to oversee her welfare and participate in frequent beheadings."

"Beware!" the first eunuch called to the others. "It is time to free the princess!"

And with that, the three eunuchs turned to lead the way.

Sinbad looked after the three guards.

"Hundreds upon hundreds of beautiful women?" he asked of no one so much as himself. "Much as all the thieves seem to be the tellers of tales, might not all the women therein be the subject of those tales?" He paused, as if his next thought were almost too great for him to express. "Might even the fair Fatima be in there as well?" He tugged upon Ali Baba's sleeve, as if he wished the woodcutter's agreement. "As you may recall, I told you that she disappeared under mysterious circumstances."

Ali Baba nodded his head at the thought. It was a fascinating conjecture. And, in an enchanted cavern such as this, nothing was impossible.

"We will free our beloved women!" Achmed called to the others as he hurried to follow the eunuchs. "Nothing now may stop our success!"

"Stop where you are and prepare to die!" came another voice from their rear. "No one escapes the terrible vengeance of One Thumb!"

♦

*Chapter the Twenty-ninth,
in which we learn that,
when you do reach the palace,
you should be careful concerning
the nature of your invitation.*

Then they were to die now, Ali Baba thought, when they were so close to their goal.

"Oh, how pleasant," came a high voice from the very most forward point of their entourage.

"This is indeed proving to be an interesting day," agreed the high voice of the second eunuch.

"With all certainty," the third added with a belch of delight. "Here are heads we might cut off with impunity!"

"If you gentlemen will excuse us," said the first of the three as they quickly placed themselves between Ali Baba's band and the still-large contingent of men in white. "Continue toward the palace. We will meet you there, after we have whetted our swords with blood!"

So it was that that portion of the cave was quickly filled with blood, screams, and the strange, high laughter of the eunuchs. Ali Baba saw one white-turbaned head fly one way, and then another, as the three guards proved they had not lost their devastating technique.

Ali Baba was now doubly grateful for Achmed's silver tongue, and the way his clever arguments had enlisted the eunuchs. It had not escaped the woodcutter, further, that Achmed and Marjanah shared a certain attraction. Love, he thought, was almost as mysterious a force as Destiny, but perhaps here, he might see a match truly made in paradise!

But he had to hurry, or the others would leave him behind upon the golden path! So did they all move swiftly, past fantastic formal gardens, and bushes and shrubs in the form of animals, not to mention animals in the form of bushes and shrubs, for some of the vegetation seemed capable of moving from place to place, and various lesser shrubs could be seen walking sedately across the

manicured lawns. As for Ali Baba and his fellows, they marched
for so great a time that the carnage behind them faded to no more
than a distant murmur. But still did the palace seem no nearer than
before.

"I believe," Ali Baba called ahead to Achmed, who, though
they had been traveling for some time, showed no sign of
slackening his pace, "that there is some form of trickery involved
here. We walk and walk, and the palace appears no closer. The
building is large, but it cannot be that large."

"The man has discerned the truth," said someone nearby in a
silvery voice.

"It is so unusual for one of his species to be so perceptive," a
similar voice answered.

"They move about so quickly," a third called in jest, "they
have no time for study."

Ali Baba could not abide this further mystery. "Who speaks?"
he demanded.

"We are merely a few of the magic talking bushes that litter this
estate," one of the voices mentioned dismissively, as if this were
a fact that any woodcutter should already have known.

So these bushes not only were filled with light but spoke as
well?

"The bushes do not talk to everyone," the stone in Ali Baba's
hand mentioned. "You should feel rightfully honored."

"We have to admit," replied the bush, "that when we saw he
carried a talking stone within his fist, we decided his was of the
upper class of humans."

And with that, the bushes and the stone seemed done with the
exchanging of compliments.

"To reach yonder palace," stated one of the magic shrubs,
"you must have the patience of a bush."

"Wait here for a while," another added, "and the palace will
come to you."

Ali Baba looked to the others in his group.

"I have heard of stranger things within the stories I tell," Harun
agreed. "I think that we should heed the advice of the vegetation,
and see what the palace does in turn."

This decision was obviously of great concern to others in the
group.

"Marjanah!" Achmed called.

"Princess Badabadur," Aladdin whispered.

"Fatima," sobbed Sinbad.

Ali Baba was not sure which name he wished to call out. Perhaps that was why he was left holding the stone.

"It may well be that it is time to tell another story," Harun suggested, "say that clever little tale I call 'The Magic Potato and the Fart on the Cart.'"

"I fear that we might offend the eunuchs with such stories," Sinbad interjected. "Let me tell you, rather, in detail, how Fatima and I were parted, for perhaps it shall give us some clue as to how we may regain the women."

When it was agreed that this was as positive a way as any to pass the time the bushes said was required, Sinbad began his painful description:

"We were being attacked by the most fiendish of demons, known as He-Who-Must-Be-Ignored. I may only say his name once, for to say it three times will call him back from whatever foul place he may dwell. Of all of us, only Fatima could withstand this demon's horrible humor. But, as she conquered this foul creature, there was a great explosion, with severe magical consequences, and myself and my companions scattered about the field of battle. When I came to my senses, I crawled over to the palanquin, which was the last known spot we had heard from Fatima. But to my astonishment, Fatima had disappeared, and had been replaced by the Queen of the Apes!"

"What happened next," Achmed continued, for he saw that Sinbad was too overcome to speak further, "is best left unexplained."

"The palace!" Harun called. "It has indeed come much closer!"

Ali Baba turned, and saw they were perhaps only a dozen paces away from steps that led to a great and central door.

"The bushes have advised us well," he commented, and took six full paces forward, before he noticed that those steps remained precisely that same dozen paces away.

"We are not there yet," he said with a sigh. Perhaps, he thought with discouragement, they would have to keep talking until they found themselves in the palace's vestibule.

"There you are already!" came the voice of the first eunuch as the three guards approached them upon the path. "We thought you would have gone much farther by now."

"Perhaps they do not know the way," the second eunuch commented. "Surely, one of us should have taken the time to guide you."

"Those men in white were hardly fit opponents," the third remarked dismissively. "Eventually, they ran away screaming. Since we are dedicated to the rescue of Princess Badabadur, we were loath to follow."

"For now," the first of the three agreed, "the clean decapitation of twelve to fifteen souls will have to suffice."

"There were a couple that were not so clean as well," the second remembered grimly.

"The shame of an unpracticed hand," the third added, staring at his oversized feet.

"But what are we waiting for?" the first announced. "The palace is here. We have only to climb the stairway."

Ali Baba looked down and noticed he stood upon the first of the steps. He followed the eunuchs up toward the great door, which, in the general manner of all around it, seemed to be made of beaten gold with great diamonds set in place for the doorknobs.

"Beware!" the first eunuch called out. "Men approach!" He glanced apologetically at Ali Baba and his fellows. "You will have to forgive me, but it is the task I have been assigned."

"Men?" came the sound of women's voices. "There are more men? We have not seen men in ever so long." This announcement was followed by a hundred shrieks, not of fear, but of anticipation and delight.

"From the tone of their voices," Harun said darkly, "I think it is we who have to beware."

Ali Baba looked upward and saw a hundred windows, and within each window the face of a maiden, looking upon their approach with great anticipation.

The great doors swung open by themselves as the nine approached, as if they, too, were anticipating what was to come. But Ali Baba was surprised to see that there was already some sizable commotion taking place upon the floor of the great hall before them.

Two dozen women stopped their activity to look at the newcomers as they entered. They smiled at Ali Baba and his fellows, and turned to them with open arms. But there were more present in these halls, for behind the women the woodcutter heard a pair of distinctly male groans.

The women parted and Ali Baba could see a pair of male figures upon the floor, their once black robes in rags.

"Thank goodness you have arrived," said the first among thieves. He rose shakily, and seemed to have a great deal of trouble placing one foot in front of the other. "Excuse me. I need water. Fluids of any kind."

"Aladdin!" croaked the other as he, too, rose up, first upon hands and knees, and then, quite shakily, to his feet. "At last we meet without disguise!" He tried to laugh, but only made a dry, strangled sound. "Know now, that I shall have the lamp and defeat you." He attempted to take a step, but managed more of a stumble. "At least I will as soon as I get some rest."

And then the women closed their ranks, and the sight of the two was lost to the woodcutter. But what would happen now? He had thought, at the very least, to look for Kassim's wife, although he had to admit that many of these other women immediately around him were every bit as attractive, enticing, seductive, comely, luscious, shapely, and desirable. How could he, lost amidst all these women, find his destiny?

Ali Baba had a thought. The way the women looked upon him, perhaps this was his destiny.

♦

Chapter the Thirtieth,
in which we learn what lies in the cave,
and perhaps a truth or two.

As great as was the desire of the women, the desire of three of the men was greater.

Achmed was the first to push himself through the throng, ignoring the articles of clothing that were torn from his body.

"Marjanah!" he called.

And somewhere, from the very rear of the hordes of women who were now filling this great hall, came an answering cry.

"Achmed!"

Aladdin, emboldened by his compatriot's success, pushed his way past the hundred grasping hands and kissing lips to call out the name of the one that he desired.

"Princess!"

"Pardon?" said a women who stood upon a balcony overhead. "Are you referring to me?"

"Princess Badabadur!" Aladdin therefore called her more specifically.

The beautiful princess frowned at that. "Have we met?"

"It is I, Aladdin!" he exclaimed, undaunted, as he climbed the steps to take her away.

"I was betrothed to a boy named Aladdin once," she acknowledged, "before that horrid wizard took me away."

"Fatima," Sinbad called, his courage also strengthened by the success of the others. "I know you are here somewhere!"

He was rewarded only with a laugh, both delicate and distant.

And he laughed in turn. "I saw that flash of hand at the top of the stairs," he shouted excitedly. "I would recognize that laugh out of a hundred laughs! I would spot that hand in a sea of hands. Fatima! It is your Sinbad! I am coming for you!"

There was another laugh amidst the pillars of the landing above. Sinbad took the steps two at a time.

"Where are you, my beloved?" he called as he reached the landing. "Hiding behind that curtain?" He approached on tiptoe. "I can hear you breathing. Such a passionate sound! Open up the drapes so that I may see you."

"Ook ook! Scree scree!" came the answer from the other side of the curtain.

Sinbad screamed as a hairy paw emerged from the curtains and dragged him from sight.

Achmed looked up from where he and Marjanah had been exchanging deep gazes. "So that is what has happened to the Queen of the Apes."

In their haste to find their mates, the others had left the water bags containing Kassim littered about the marble floor.

"Women!" Kassim's head called to those about him. "There will be no crowding with me! And no waiting in lines! I may be divided six different ways!"

"Careful now!" Harun called as the women approached him. "I am elderly and need to be handled with prudence!"

Ali Baba had none of these problems. His only worry was the twenty or so women who were currently circling him. And, true to the name of this place, all of them were beautiful. He had a certain idea of what they desired and he had to admit that, married man though he was, he might not be averse to such activity under the proper circumstances with any one of these women. For a chance, he might even have a good day.

But here were twenty of them, and all of like mind?

Even the best of experiences, Ali Baba realized, may have a bad aspect.

But before the women could do more than push him down upon the cold marble and tear off half of his black robes, he felt another, greater tremor beneath him, as if the very earth shook.

"WHAT TRANSPIRES HERE?"

He had heard that sort of voice before, if never quite so loud and forceful. It sounded like this great cavern had at last elected to speak. And that meant, of course, that the very earth had indeed shaken.

"ENOUGH! THIS IS BORING. IT IS TIME TO HEAR SOME STORIES!"

By now, all had paused, whatever their pursuit, frozen by this interruption. The dramatic effect was no doubt heightened by the fact that their surroundings shook prodigiously with every word that was spoken.

"Isn't it time for introductions around here?" said the stone, which somehow had managed to remain in Ali Baba's hand. The rock, for one, did not appear to be cowed in the least.

"I AM THE GREATEST OF CAVERNS," the great voice rumbled and shook, "A CAVE TO SWALLOW LESSER CAVES. YOU MAY CALL ME—MORDRAG!"

Mordrag? Ali Baba thought. It did not sound at all like a friendly name. Before this moment, the woodcutter was not even aware that caves could have names. It certainly sounded impressive.

"Not a bad name," the stone acknowledged. "Does it come from a particular side of the family?"

"ACTUALLY, THE NAME DOES NOT MEAN A THING. BUT I THOUGHT IT SOUNDED IMPRESSIVE."

"Indeed it does," the stone acknowledged. "Oh, by the way, Uncle Sid says hello."

"TELL HIM THE SAME."

"Why don't you tell him," Ali Baba said softly to the stone, "that this visit has been very pleasant and all, but now we really must be going?"

"BUT YOU ARE IN MY CAVE AND UNDER MY CONTROL!" Mordrag rumbled before the stone could utter another word. "ALL HERE IS MINE!"

But Ali Baba had had enough of being bullied about, whether it was by a leader of thieves (whom, now that he might think of him as Grubby Sheets, the woodcutter now regarded in an entirely different light) or the most immense enchanted cavern in all of the world. He would have an end of this tyranny, and his succession of very bad days.

"I think now," was therefore his only reply.

"Will you then fight the will of the cavern?" the stone asked him with great excitement.

"I believe that I must," Ali Baba replied, almost regretting his decision already, "although I do not know where my fight shall lead."

"I have the feeling," the rock said generously, "that great things will happen, and all these many people and ploys that now swirl about you will crash together in such a conflagration that it will make the very earth shake. But then, I am only a stone. What do I know?"

"WHAT DO YOU KNOW, INDEED?"

To Ali Baba, this was nothing more than another example of

petty bullying. "Enough of this!" he therefore said, bending over to scoop up a part of Kassim. "We are leaving!"

"So soon?" his brother wailed. "Before a single woman has opened my water bag?"

"SO YOU THINK!" the cavern rumbled darkly.

"I don't think about any of this!" Kassim complained. "I know none of the women have opened any of my water bags! Do you know how frustrating it can be when your parts are so far apart that you cannot keep in contact with yourself? And then to be deprived of the touch of others? It is too much."

"YOU TALK AT VERY GREAT LENGTH. I DID NOT REALIZE WHAT A SERVICE HE HAD DONE WHEN YOUR BROTHER FIRST REMOVED YOU FROM THE CONFINES OF MY UPPER TREASURE CHAMBER."

"And I shall now remove him again," Ali Baba said calmly. "If you all shall excuse me. I suggest that the others of my party should follow me."

So it was that the woodcutter was quickly joined by Achmed and Marjanah, walking arm in arm, then Aladdin leading the way for the Princess Badabadur, with the three eunuchs protectively guarding her rear. After this came Harun al Raschid, rearranging his robes so that he might have some dignity, although he also seemed to have gained a woman upon either arm. And then very quickly down the stairs rushed Sinbad, trying desperately to tie what little remained of his robe into a functional loincloth.

Another woman stepped forward from the group. "Would you forget about me?"

Ali Baba looked about and realized that she was the wife of Kassim. And yes, truly, he had become so upset with the attitude of the cavern that he might have forgotten about her, at least until he had reached a place of greater calm.

"Never, dearest one," Kassim reassured her from the water bag now slung over Ali Baba's shoulder. "You are the primary reason that we have sought out this palace."

"Very well," she said as she sauntered over to the woodcutter. "Perhaps we may use this opportunity to finally get to know each other better."

"NO ONE IS GOING TO GET TO KNOW ANYONE ANY BETTER," the cavern roared, "WITHOUT MY PERMISSION!"

Ali Baba did not feel the slightest urge to reply. Instead, he

looked about at his ever-growing group of compatriots and said:
"Shall we begin?"

"I WILL SHOW YOU DIFFICULTY," the cavern thundered,
"WITH EVERY STEP YOU TAKE!"

And, as Ali Baba started down the steps, he saw that the cavern
had made good upon its threat. For there, standing in the midst of
the garden, were a dozen men in once white robes with scimitars
at the ready. This time, however, there was a certain additional
difference about these adversaries, for none of these men sported
a head.

♦

Chapter the Thirty-first,
in which the day becomes not only bad
but thoroughly confusing.

"At last!" Kassim called from his water bag enclosure. "Here
is an opportunity for me to show my worth!"

"Pardon?" Ali Baba said, for his thoughts were upon their
headless foes.

"Take me out of this bag and throw me in their midst!" Kassim
explained with enthusiasm. "I shall rest upon their necks, where
their own heads should be. At the very least, it will confuse them.
At the best, perhaps I can control them and turn their swords to our
advantage!"

Ali Baba decided he would do as his brother bade, if only so he
would not have Kassim's head continue to shout into his ear.

"Beware!" called the three eunuchs as they advanced upon the
headless warriors. "Where we once cut off heads, we now remove
arms and legs and torsos!"

"Well, brethren," Aladdin said to his fellows in black, "let us
see how well we learned to fight while we were among the
thieves."

Ali Baba lifted Kassim's head from his sack.

"It is good to look upon you again, brother," Kassim remarked.
"It gets exceedingly boring within the sack."

"No doubt," Ali Baba replied as he found he still had some
difficulty speaking with a head, even that of his brother, when
there was no body attached. "I will attempt to toss you true."

And so he did, as a call came from amidst the women.

"Wait!" Ali Baba recognized the voice as that of his slave,
Marjanah.

Kassim's head landed upon the shoulder of one of the headless
men. He grabbed the white cloth with his teeth, shouting a string
of muffled syllables that might have said: "I am almost to my
goal!"

"Why are we so quick to fight?" Marjanah insisted. "It is a male trait, I am afraid, and not well considered. And furthermore, Mordrag, why do you so confront your guests at the first sign of conflict?"

The cave rumbled beneath her. "WHAT DO YOU MEAN? WHAT SHOULD I HAVE DONE?"

Kassim attempted to pull himself up closer to the severed neck, using a combination of tongue and teeth. The body would have none of it, however, and proceeded to shake its shoulders in an attempt to dislodge its unwanted guest. Kassim uttered another string of syllables muffled by the cloth, that this time could possibly have said: "This is more difficult than I had thought!"

"You collect gold and women as divertissements," Marjanah continued to the cave, "and want to hear nothing but novel stories. From everything I know of your existence, your greatest enemy is boredom."

"CAVES ARE NOT KNOWN FOR THEIR VERSATILITY," Mordrag admitted. "BEFORE I KILL YOU ALL AND START WITH A NEW BATCH, WHAT WOULD YOU HAVE ME DO?"

The body upon which Kassim rode now attempted to poke at the head with its sword, an awkward maneuver at best, since the body had no eyes to guide it. Kassim once again called out a new line of virtually nonunderstandable syllables, although he might have said: "*Get me off of here!*"

"You are always looking for adventures," Marjanah explained. "Instead of attempting to stop us in ours, why not let it run its course so that you might revel in its richness?"

"WOMAN, YOU HAVE CONVINCED ME, FOR NOW," Mordrag acknowledged. "BUT REMEMBER, SINCE CAVES ARE NOT GENERALLY KNOWN FOR TALKING, WE HAVE DEVELOPED NO TRADITION FOR KEEPING OUR WORD."

And with that, the dozen bodies fell back to the earth. Kassim rolled free with a yelp. After he had regained his breath, he mentioned, "At least all I do, I do with dignity."

Ali Baba scooped up the head and placed it again in the water bag before Kassim might comment further.

"Then what will you have us do now?" asked Marjanah boldly of the cave. Now that the bodies no longer threatened, Achmed returned to her side to look upon her with great admiration.

"THERE ARE OTHERS BESIDES YOU WHO WANDER THESE HALLWAYS. WHY NOT GO FOR YOUR ADVEN-

TURE?'' The cavern chuckled, that same sound Ali Baba had heard the first time he discovered the treasure trove. "OH, YES. OPEN, SESAME!''

And with that, another stone slab crashed down upon the still slightly twitching bodies of the headless warriors. Sinbad, who was closest to the fallen slab, took a cautious look outside. "It appears to be the same corridor through which we entered. Although how you might precisely tell one cave from another is quite beyond me.''

"RETRACE YOUR STEPS,'' Mordrag instructed, "AND YOU SHALL FIND YOUR ADVENTURE.''

Ali Baba decided that he would once again lead the way. He looked down at the smooth piece of granite within his hand. "Are you ready for this, O guardian stone?''

"I think the scope of this is larger than what I am used to handling,'' the stone replied with some uncertainty. "Then again, what I am used to handling is generally sitting in the same place for thousands of years at a time, pressed down by gravity. I shall do what can.''

The others followed the woodcutter into the passageway, relighting their torches to pierce the darkness. At the end of a short corridor, there was once again a stairway leading up.

"Shall we?'' Ali Baba said to all those who followed.

"AFTER YOU,'' the voice of Mordrag bellowed all around.

They began to climb the stairs. But the stairs only went for a short way, followed by another corridor of some distance that twisted to the left, and only then another set of stairs. In short, the passage up did not appear to conform to what Ali Baba remembered of the passage down.

"Could the cavern be playing with us?'' he asked aloud.

"COULD BE,'' Mordrag rumbled from the floor, ceiling, and walls.

"Must you toy with us in this fashion?'' Aladdin asked. "Will you ever let us go?''

"IF I TOLD YOU THAT, THIS SITUATION WOULD LOSE ALL ITS SUSPENSE. I WILL TELL YOU THIS. I QUITE AGREE WITH THE YOUNG MARJANAH. THERE IS STILL A CERTAIN DRAMA TO BE WORKED OUT.''

At that instant, Ali Baba wondered if his young slave's intercession had helped them or hurt them.

The steps ended quite suddenly, to be replaced by yet another corridor that seemed to stretch far beyond the range of their torchlight.

"Where are we?" Achmed said to those around him.

None of them had any idea.

"We are lost forever!" Kassim wailed.

"You always were a bit on the spineless side," his wife remarked.

But Ali Baba was beginning to have some inkling as to that way in which things work within an enchanted cavern. "There seems to be hope for he who has a positive attitude," he said to the others. "Things have changed in the corridors and cavern below when I have asked questions or made decisions. Therefore, I must make a decision now."

He felt a bit foolish attempting this in a place where there was no indication of another passageway whatsoever. But why not? It had worked before.

"Oh," he therefore called, "open, Sesame!"

The three eunuchs yelped as a trapdoor opened beneath their feet.

"Where have they gone?" Harun asked as he thrust his torch into the new opening. "I believe I see—-gold!"

"Then is this another entrance to the treasure trove?" Achmed asked.

"It must be!" Sinbad agreed. "And the magic lamp is within there as well."

"I believe," Aladdin said to those around him, "that it is time for us to follow our brethren." And with that, he, too, jumped through the opened space.

What could Ali Baba do but follow?

◆

Chapter the Thirty-second,
in which a certain cavern becomes crowded with more than gold.

The drop was not far. Ali Baba and the others hit the piles of loose coin with a series of resounding chinks.

"Beware!" the eunuchs called from nearby. "We are not alone within these treasure rooms."

"Then the magician and our chieftain have preceded us!" Sinbad surmised. "Aladdin, quickly! Before they find the lamp! You must use the ring, and pray that the djinni has rested enough!"

In this, at last, Aladdin agreed, and quickly rubbed his ring. This time, a suitable amount of purple smoke erupted therefrom, and then as quickly dissipated to reveal the obsidian djinni. The creature's eyes were bright in the dim light of this back corner of the treasure room, and he opened his fearsome mouth to say the following:

> "Though slave to the ring and still sore fatigued,
> I am ready to serve you in what you need.
> What will you, master, what will you?"

"Somewhere within this hoard," Aladdin explained, "there is a lamp that contains another of your kind. Find that lamp and bring it here!"

But this time, the djinni hesitated. "I am not certain I can do that, O master. We of the spiritual sort are governed by strict rules of noncompetition and interference. Djinn are by and large creatures of solitude."

"Perhaps," Achmed said reasonably, "we should first extinguish those torches which are still lit. There seems to be a fair amount of light in the main chamber beyond, and I think it would behoove us to hide our presence as long as possible."

It was true, thought Ali Baba. Although they had fallen into room of some considerable size, so filled with gold coins that hi legs sank down to his knees within the piles and still he felt n bottom, this appeared to be but an antechamber of the mai treasure hall. Through the large arched doorway that led into th area he could see the reflections of flickering torchlight, that sam torchlight, no doubt, that he had witnessed when first he had foun that treasure, and that, while only a few days past, now seeme like a lifetime gone.

Ali Baba felt a pair of smooth yet strong hands grasp one of hi own. "It is so dark in this corner without the torchlight," said th husky voice of Kassim's wife, close by his ear. "I am so fortunat to have strong arms to protect me."

"I am sorry to disappoint you, O wife," Kassim called from where his head was slung over Ali Baba's shoulder. "But I believe my arms are in two entirely different water bags."

Harun pulled his legs forward with effort through the mass o coins, his every move surrounded by a great jangling of gold. "I escapes me," he mentioned, "how we might secretively approach anyone if we must travel through this morass."

"Very well," Aladdin said. "O djinni of the ring!"

The great dark spirit nodded. "I hear and obey. Within certain limitations, of course."

Therefore did Aladdin ask: "Might you transport us to the middle of the great treasure room beyond?"

The djinni made a quick count of all in his presence. "This is easily within my powers. Consider it done!"

Ali Baba blinked and found himself in a room filled with torchlight, transported instantly with all his companions, the three women, and the three eunuchs. All of them stood upon a great platform made of gold. And all about them was more gold, coins and bracelets and statues and ingots and large raw nuggets of it, the sheer monotony of color broken up here and there by occasional islands of jewels of every conceivable hue. In the distance, Ali Baba could see a series of vestibules which ringed this palatial chamber. Surely, it was from one such vestibule that the djinni had brought them, but from that first room Ali Baba had had no idea of the size and scope of the wealth contained here, for, if the room where they had been were a golden pond, they now looked out over the ocean.

"I had no idea," Harun spoke for all of them. "Such wealth puts even all my palaces to shame."

"It was little wonder that the thieves were finding it difficult to collect gold," Achmed said. "It appears that this room might contain everything of value from our part of the world."

"Twenty-three billion four hundred million seven hundred sixty-three thousand and seventeen dinars," Sinbad announced. "And that is only upon the surface."

"Perhaps it does contain everything of value from the entire world," Achmed added with a low whistle.

"I have heard of caverns with great longings," remarked the stone still cradled in the woodcutter's hand. "Caves are, after all, nothing but great holes longing to be filled."

Ali Baba felt a shapely leg pressed against his side. "Longing is something I can understand," Kassim's wife whispered.

"But I must admit," the stone continued, "that Uncle Mordrag has become something of an overachiever."

"But where, among all this," Ali Baba despaired, "might we find the lamp that contains the djinni and the key to our fortune?"

It was, the woodcutter agreed, a daunting sight. A cavern that was amassing all the wealth within the world? If the cavern was as successful with its other pursuits as it was here, Ali Baba wished he might have had more time to examine the Palace of Beautiful Women. But, then again, there was one beautiful woman who was very near. Ali Baba suddenly wished that he had not chosen to carry the water bag that contained Kassim's head. It was difficult to consider his brother's wife with a portion of his brother so near.

"Why not call forth the djinni from the ring?" Sinbad suggested. "He would not bring us the lamp, but he said nothing about helping to locate it."

"A fine idea," Aladdin agreed, as he once again rubbed the ring.

The djinni appeared after the required smoke:

> *"I'm slave to the lamp, and so cannot rest,*
> *But all this work I begin to detest.*
> *What wish you, O master, what wish you this time?"*

Perhaps, Ali Baba thought, they might overtax this djinni at last.

"A thousand pardons, O spirit of the lamp," Aladdin said solicitously, "but we have another request. While we know you may not fetch us another djinni, we were wondering if you might be able to indicate where within this large room one might reside?"

"I am certainly able to do that," the djinni agreed. "Is that all you wish?"

"Certainly not," Aladdin snapped in a way that showed how frayed his emotions had become. "We require that you point to wherever that djinni may reside."

It was hard to read an expression upon a face that reflected all light, but still did Ali Baba believe the djinni frowned.

"After all this practice, one might think you would have learned how to phrase your wishes." He grunted, a sound without enthusiasm. "I suppose there is nothing within the djinn's code of conduct that should keep me from indicating another of my kind, although such a request does do some damage to my pride of profession. Very well. At least I will receive some rest." He pointed to his right. "The nearest djinni is in yonder pile, and a powerful one he is indeed."

"Where?" Aladdin demanded. "I see no copper lamp!"

"This djinni does not reside within a copper lamp," the spirit answered smugly, "but in yonder colorful bottle."

Ali Baba saw both Sinbad and Achmed take a step backward upon the platform at the very mention of such a container.

"Do you recognize that bottle?" Achmed asked.

"I most certainly do," Sinbad answered. "It is the same in which we captured the great and terrible Ozzie, a djinni of far too much power."

"So Ozzie is imprisoned here as well? Perhaps all the wealth of the world truly does reside within this cavern," Achmed repeated with wonder.

They heard a deep, appreciative chuckle from the cavern walls.

"A cavern is nothing without a reputation," the stone in Ali Baba's hand remarked.

"But that is not the djinni we desire!" Aladdin exclaimed. "Is there another here as well?"

"Three or four, in actuality," the ring spirit replied. "A couple of them are quite minor. There is a button djinni almost at your feet. There is even less room for a djinni in a button than there is in a ring. And upon the far side of the room is a thimble djinni, and in the antechamber behind us resides a head-of-a-pin djinni."

"Button djinni?" Kassim called from his bag. "Thimble djinni? Would either of them know anything about tailoring?"

But the ring spirit did not acknowledge Kassim's question, for Kassim did not hold the ring. Instead, he continued to search about the gold. "Lamp, did you say? Well, there is that other djinni halfway across the room." He turned about to wave behind them all. "While nowhere near as powerful as this fellow in the bottle close by, he is behind yonder pile of gold"—the ring spirit pointed once again—"close to a couple of other gentlemen. I suppose you can see none of them from your vantage point."

"Beware!" one of the eunuchs called out triumphantly. "What did we say about others being in the room?"

With all this wealth and strangeness about him, Ali Baba had quite forgotten about their adversaries, and no doubt the others had as well.

All upon the platform turned about to look at the other half of the ocean of gold. They were rewarded by a cry of triumph from behind that particular gold pile.

"One of the two gentlemen now has the lamp," the ring djinni explained. "Pardon. Both of them now have it."

The cry of triumph was quickly followed by other shouts, these more angry in nature.

"Oh, no, you don't!"

"It is you who won't!"

"I thought we agreed to share all things equally!"

"Most certainly! Then why will you not share your half?"

As the voices continued, Ali Baba saw first one hand, then another, then two different hands holding a lamp, rise above the golden pile.

"I shall cast a spell upon you!"

"I shall be forced to use my deadly scimitar!"

The top of the golden pile exploded outward as the two men rolled forward, arms and legs entangled, the magic lamp somewhere in their midst.

"I have it now!"

"Oh, no, you don't!"

"My hand was there first!"

"Only on top of mine!"

"Hold!" the chieftain called as they reached the bottom of the pile. "We are not alone!"

"I am fully familiar with that sort of trick to distract my attention," the mage replied with heavy sarcasm. "You forget who it is that performs magic tricks—oh, we do have visitors, do we not?"

Both bandit and mage had noticed Ali Baba and his band.

"You there!" the chieftain called. "My loyal followers! Destroy this foul wizard, for he is the source of all our troubles!"

Ali Baba found he had no desire at all to perform any service for his former leader. Those at his side seemed similarly inclined, for no one made a move of any sort.

"Your mastery no longer imprisons us," Harun said to the chieftain, "without the extra pressure of the magician's spells."

"Oh, there is that, isn't there?" The chieftain frowned. "Magician! Renew your spells quickly so that I may compel these men to tear you—oh, dear. That doesn't appear to work, does it?"

"Soon, nothing will work for you," the magician declared as he slipped and slid upon the coins beneath him. "Drat! How may you have a decent struggle if you may never gain any footing?"

"Nothing will work for either of you, soon," Aladdin called, "now that we know the magician's true identity!"

"And, furthermore," Achmed added, "we can now think of our former leader as 'Grubby Sheets.'"

With that, the bandit chieftain roared, and, fueled by a great and terrible anger, wrested the lamp from the magician.

"Mine!" the chieftain called. "At last, my liver shall return to me. The lamp is mine!"

"I think not!" the magician replied in a voice that indicated he was not in the least impressed. "Firstly, though, I have to clean up this place a bit!" He shouted three mystic words and made a pass above his head.

The chieftain yelped as the coins beneath his feet disappeared. The lamp went clattering out of his hands.

Ali Baba was amazed at the magician's power. With the simplest of gestures, he had taken the gold, and rearranged it within the room so that there was a great wall of coins, stretching floor to high ceiling around much of the perimeter, and immediately in front of this wall were neatly sorted piles of jewels and other valuables which, because of size and shape, might not be properly stacked. The only gold which hadn't moved in the room seemed to be the large central platform on which Ali Baba and his compatriots still remained. So it was that, abruptly and amazingly, the magician's spell had revealed over half the cavern floor.

"I should hire you upon a regular basis," the voice of Mordrag rumbled from the walls. "Imagine how much more gold I might place in here now than before!"

But the magician was intent on something more valuable than gold. With the surprise of the spell working to his advantage, he rushed for the fallen lamp.

"The lamp!" Aladdin declared. "But it is too far! I shall never reach it!"

"Call your djinni!" Achmed suggested strongly.

"Oh, of course!" Aladdin replied, for the djinni had resumed his earlier habit of returning to the ring at the first possible notice.

"It is too late!" the magician called in triumph. "The lamp shall be mine!"

"I think not!" boomed a voice from the far end of the cavern. Everyone in the great chamber looked quickly to that part of the room.

There, surrounded by his expert bowmen, stood One Thumb.

"I have twenty men," One Thumb remarked with practiced gloating, "each of whom can easily loose an arrow before you might take a step and speak a spell. It was awfully kind of all of you to show us the way to these untold riches. Now that we see the gold, of course, it is ours, not to mention a very interesting lamp!"

"I think not!" a woman's voice called from the extreme opposite end of the cavern.

Ali Baba and everyone else turned back in amazement to look at this most recent intruder.

"Oh, woe!" further said the woman. "I feared the worst had happened to you, my husband!"

Ali Baba could not believe his eyes and ears. The woman at the end of the cave was his wife, and she was further accompanied by a man who wore the high helmet and bright uniform of the captain of the guard.

Then did the woodcutter's curiosity overwhelm him. "How do you come here, O wife?" Ali Baba called.

"It was simplicity itself," the captain of the guard replied in her stead. "You had given her some basic directions, which started us upon our way. Once we reached the vicinity, all we had to do was follow the trail of exhausted and dehydrated men in white robes."

"Oh, woe!" his wife further remarked. "I could think of nothing else to do, for without you to talk to, what is my life?"

"Perhaps," Kassim's wife said close by Ali Baba's ear, "I might be your second wife, and take care of all those needs your first wife may not."

"I heard that!" Kassim yelled from his water bag. "How can you marry him when you are already married to me?"

Kassim's wife put her shapely hands upon her even shapelier hips. "Wasn't it you yourself who said, 'Now that I am cut into six pieces, I shall not have long to live'?"

"A husband has a right to be melodramatic!" he whined defensively.

"And a wife has a right to plan for her future!" she said defiantly.

"It was my early depression talking," Kassim explained. "Perfectly understandable, considering what had happened. I am but a little disorganized."

At that, his wife nodded sadly. "It gives one very little solace to hug a water bag."

"Oh, woe!" His wife's newest cry brought the woodcutter's attention back to her. "Now our adventure is over, and I must return to being a common housewife!"

"And we, of course, get to keep all the gold," the captain of the guard remarked. "One of the sultan's laws covers this, I am sure. Or, if not, he will be glad to invent one." He took a step around the nearest wall of gold coins. "With gold to this extent, even the sultan may at last balance his budget! And we must retain everything else for evidence, including, what was it, a lamp? Yes, very certainly, the lamp is ours."

"I think not!" the wizard exclaimed as he shouted out a half dozen words. The captain of the guard froze where he stood, and an instant later appeared to have turned into a statue of solid gold.

"The same will happen to anyone else who takes a step toward me, or looses any arrow or spear!" He walked slowly and deliberately toward the fallen lantern. "I have struggled for this lamp for twenty years, including a pair serving beneath the most disgusting of bandit leaders." The bandit chieftain cried in outrage, but made no further move.

"I worked my spells," the magician continued, "to make certain we would find ever-more-inept thieves to join our band."

The thieves around Ali Baba cried in outrage. After a moment, Ali Baba joined them. Inept? He was among the very best of woodcutters!

"Can you imagine?" The wizard chuckled. "Inducting a man who has already been cut into six pieces?"

Kassim cried in outrage. "If I wasn't trapped within a water bag," he muttered thereafter.

"And all along, I watched and waited for my opportunity to be shown the lamp, and take it for my own. Once we had been attacked by the overbearing One Thumb and his men in fussy white, I knew I had my chance!"

One Thumb and his men cried in outrage. "Go and tear him limb from limb!" One Thumb screamed.

None of his men took his advice, preferring, no doubt, to regard the newest gold statue of the captain of the guard.

"So it was," the magician continued his explanation in the manner of villains everywhere, "that I managed to endure the vile company of the leader of the thieves long enough for him to show me the location of the lamp. What sacrifices I have made! No one but I deserves this prize. Now it is mine!"

"We think not!" Ali Baba looked over to the third of the cavern's many entryways. There stood hundred upon hundreds of the occupants of the Palace of Beautiful Women. "We have endured days, months, even years of imprisonment within this enchanted place. Some of us let our base desires overwhelm us when you first appeared, but no more. If anyone deserves the spoils of this cavern, it is we who were used so badly. There are many wise women among us as well, who will be glad to counter any spells you may have devised!"

"Enough talk!" the wizard yelled as he dove to the floor. "I have the lamp!"

Chapter the Thirty-third,
in which djinni meets djinni,
and there is a cave to pay.

Achmed jostled Aladdin. "So why haven't you rubbed your ring?"

"Oh, yes," Aladdin remarked as he set to work. "I become easily distracted by large groups of people."

But the wizard was busy as well, so busy that two plumes of purple smoke erupted from the two different sources almost simultaneously, and two booming voices filled the room.

"I am the djinni of the magic lamp—"

"Slave of the ring and once again here—"

"I've been in there so long I might have—"

"It appears you have called me once too often—"

The two djinni stared at each other and exploded simultaneously:

"I cannot hear myself!"

They both paused to glare for a moment before they added:

"No one makes a noise when a djinni talks!"

"Destroy them!" the wizard called to the spirit of the lamp.

"Wait a minute, O master," the lamp djinni replied. "I had not even gotten to the 'What will you' part of my speech. There is a certain etiquette to be observed here."

"What can you expect from humans?" the ring djinni commented.

"And who are you?" the spirit of the lamp remarked, his shining golden nose high in the air. "A common ring djinni?"

The other's eyes flashed with a light of deepest crimson. "There is nothing common about ring djinn! We are among the most hardworking of all the spirits!"

"And among the most common," the golden spirit insisted dismissively. "Let us conclude this, O master, so that I may get away from these creatures and back to the peace of my lamp."

"Is that so?" the ring djinni replied. "I was angry enough when I came out of my ring, but perhaps my anger was misplaced upon the humans! Do you think it is easy to live your entire existence crammed within a tiny ring, being ever careful to tuck your powers around you so you will not lose any more than necessary?"

"Enough of this complaining!" the lamp djinni replied. "Perhaps I should destroy more than these pitiful humans who hide behind you. Perhaps you have outlived your usefulness as well!"

"You dare?" the ring spirit asked in amazement. "But what of the djinni conventions?"

"Well, yes, there are those," the lamp spirit replied, humbled a bit, it seemed, by the reminder. "Very well, I will only destroy those around you."

Ali Baba looked up at the great golden spirit. Did that mean they would be destroyed despite having a djinni?

But then Marjanah stepped forward. "Wait a moment, here!"

"You may proceed, O master," the lamp djinni remarked. "Or, in keeping to the letter of convention, perhaps I should say, 'What will you, O master, what will you?'"

"Are you, a mighty ring djinni, going to allow anyone to talk to you in such a fashion?" Marjanah quickly asked.

"What do you mean?" the ring djinni asked in a somewhat confused manner.

"So I can have them destroyed now?" the wizard asked of the djinni of the lamp.

"You are simply going to let that other snobbish spirit destroy us, and therefore assert that he is far better than a common spirit like you?"

"Why, no, of course not. I never meant to do anything of the kind. Nothing is further from the truth!"

"Why, certainly you can," said the lamp djinni. "Is that what you wish? After all this time, you must have thought about what you really wanted."

"Well, then," Marjanah continued, "do something to prove your point!"

The obsidian spirit frowned. "Might you have any suggestions?"

"Aladdin!" Marjanah instructed. "Tell the spirit of the ring to destroy the magician!"

So it was that Aladdin wished for the destruction of the mage at the same instant the mage wished for the destruction of Aladdin and his fellows.

"Very well!" both djinni said as one. "Your wish is my command."

"Wife of mine!" Kassim called. "We will surely die. Can we not be reconciled?"

"With one portion," his wife asked dismissively, "or all six?"

"Pardon me," the ring spirit said to that of the lamp. "I have to pass you to destroy your master."

"So sorry," the lamp spirit said in return, "but I cannot allow that until I have destroyed your master first."

The two djinn stared at each other for a long moment.

"Is that so?" the lamp spirit said at last.

"Who is going to make me?" the ring spirit replied.

"I will not be lectured by a common ring dweller!"

"You probably never think to polish your lamp!"

So it was that both djinn rose higher and higher above them, each shouting at the other, and doing nothing but shouting. By issuing contrary wishes, Aladdin and the wizard had neutralized both of them!

And with that, the cave rumbled around them. "Enough is enough. This was amusing for a moment. You were right to allow the drama to play itself out. But it craves resolution!"

"But what do we do now?" Ali Baba said aloud.

"I believe the women should return to their palace," the cave replied. "I will construct a similar structure for the men. Then both women and men will spend the rest of their days telling me diverting stories."

"In this way," the stone in Ali Baba's hand admitted, "at least one will receive his heart's desire."

"O wife!" Kassim called. "Might you hold me together for a final embrace? We are to be separated forever!"

"And none too soon," his wife replied as she watched the drama unfold above her.

"Forgive me, O master," Marjanah interjected, "but perhaps I should attempt some further conversation with those above."

"Isn't she among the most wonderful of women?" Achmed enthused.

"I warn you!" Mordrag cried with a distant rumble. "Any tricks, and it will go badly for you!"

"Djinn!" Marjanah called. "Why do you fight each other?"

"It is not my wish," said the slave of the ring, "but this obstinate fellow from the lamp will not be moved."

"It is neither my desire," said the slave of the lamp, "but what can you do with trying to reason with the lower order?"

"Mayhaps," Marjanah called, "it is time for you to rise above the petty wishes of these humans, and do something truly spectacular. Something that will set you apart from all other djinn."

Achmed, catching the direction of her argument, added with great enthusiasm: "Something that will be handed down in story and song, from generation to generation, both in the spirit realm and on the human plane!"

"That does not sound unreasonable," the lamp djinni murmured.

"I could see that it has possibilities," the ring djinni agreed.

"Of course," Marjanah continued, "you would need such as us to spread the tale, and thus assure that your fame was well known everywhere."

"Wait a moment," the cave rumbled. "This is going too fast for a mind made of stone. I will have quiet now so that you may resume your diverting stories."

But Marjanah had gone too far to be stopped now. "Quickly!" she urged. "Open the top of this cavern to the sky and raise up all within!"

"You will be famous forever!" Achmed exclaimed. "We shall call it National Djinni Day!"

"I don't know if I wish to be famous alongside a ring djinni!" the slave of the lamp announced.

"Is that so?" the ring spirit replied. "I would wager that you cannot find your way out of that drafty lamp in the morning!"

"Enough of this!" Mordrag reasserted. "They will argue forever!"

And Ali Baba realized that, despite the best efforts of the most clever of slaves, they would probably continue to do exactly that.

"So who will tell me a story before I lose patience? You, in six pieces. Surely you must have six tales to tell!"

"Leave me alone!" Kassim whined. "I have been having a bad day!"

"I have had enough of insubordination," Mordrag rumbled loudly. "I will show you what happens to those who do not obey an enchanted cavern!"

And with that, Kassim screamed.

All was silent for a moment.

"What have you done to my brother?" Ali Baba demanded.

"Beware!" the nearest of the eunuchs announced. "We will look within the bag upon your shoulder, for we are used to blood."

So saying, all three eunuchs huddled around that water bag which Ali Baba had handed to them. They opened it and looked within, their expressions of a uniform severity.

A squeaky voice, higher even than those of the eunuchs, called out from deep within. "Kassim does not forget! I will get you for this!"

The leader of the eunuchs quickly closed the bag.

"Those are his teeth who spoke."

"They are no longer connected to his face," the second added.

"His head is now in six pieces," mentioned the third.

"As are the rest of his parts," the cave finally added with a dark chuckle, "which now number six times six. But come! Do not make me test my strength again. Who will tell me a diverting story?"

And with that, everyone spoke at once.

"I can tell you of the story of the Great Island Volcano and the Even More Magnificent Fart," Harun suggested.

"That story may be too diverting," Mordrag murmured.

"Oh, woe!" cried the wife of Ali Baba. "He wants me, a poor bride of a woodcutter, to tell him stories?"

"One Thumb has not risen to his position of prominence by ignoring the needs of others. Perhaps we might make an arrangement."

"We will not go meekly back to the Palace of Beautiful Women! We want you to know that there will be some changes made!"

"There will be no stories here!" yelled the subcaptain of the guard. "Not until we collect the taxes upon all this wealth!"

"Mine is bigger than yours!" shouted the lamp djinni.

"Your mother was a succubus!" replied the ring spirit.

"Enough!" Mordrag cried. "I cannot deal with all of this! Why did I have to branch out into collecting humans, after all? Why could I not be satisfied with unlimited wealth!"

"Uncle Sid always said your reach exceeded your grasp!" the stone in Ali Baba's fist announced. "I never understood that, considering that caves don't have arms."

"Oh, woe!" called the wife of Ali Baba. "Such a large cavern, and he cannot bear to listen to a few simple complaints?"

"I will not be criticized!" Mordrag screamed, and the very earth shook all about them. "Especially by that woman. Should she spend any time at all down here, I should surely go mad. Perhaps I should let her go. Perhaps I should let you all go. But that seems like far too much trouble. Instead, I believe I will crush you under a thousand tons of rock, and start afresh!"

And with that, the cavern truly began to shake.

Chapter the Last,
in which life is saved,
freedom is lost,
and the story goes on and on.

"Uncle Sid always said that Mordrag had a temper," the stone in Ali Baba's possession commented.

"What will we do?" Ali Baba moaned. "We will all surely die!"

"Unless we can find some entity who might be stronger than this enchanted cavern, I fear this is so," agreed the stone.

"And yet both of the djinn are locked in their argument of contrary wishes!" the woodcutter lamented.

"But did not the ring spirit mention that there was a djinni of even more power present?" the stone asked.

Rocks began to fall around the periphery of the cavern.

"The spirit in the bottle?" Ali Baba looked up at the beginning of the end. "I suppose anything is better than death. But where is the bottle?"

"It is over slightly to your right, on top of a pile of similar bottles," the stone explained.

"Oh, so it is," Ali Baba remarked. "But how were you able to—"

"I do not have time to explain how something without eyes can see," the stone interrupted "We must save such explanations for another part of the story. What is more important is to take the top from that bottle and release the djinni inside."

Ali Baba shifted his feet to regain his balance as the earth rose beneath him. "How do you suggest that I do this?"

"Throw me," the stone replied. "You have the good muscles and eye of a woodcutter, and I might be able to shift and turn myself a bit to guarantee a direct hit."

The woodcutter quickly agreed. He lifted his arm.

"Are you prepared?" he asked.

"A stone can never be anything but ready."

245

With that, Ali Baba launched the missile. Despite the horrendous commotion around them, it flew straight and true, and knocked off the cork of the bottle's top.

Nothing further happened.

"What is amiss?" Ali Baba called. "Have we hit the wrong bottle?"

"It is the correct bottle," the stone called back, "but I did naught but shear the cork in two! I have failed, and now I can but sit here! It's a problem with being a stone! All the rest of you are doomed, for there is no way to open that bottle!"

Ali Baba stared hard at the stone. Why had he not thought of this before?"

"Open, Sesame!" he called.

And the cork popped out of the bottle.

"LOOK OUT, O WORLD OF MEN!" called a voice even larger than that of the cavern. "OZZIE HAS RETURNED, AND HE'S READY FOR ANYTHING!" And with that, purple smoke ten times the thickness of any Ali Baba had seen before erupted from the bottle and formed itself into a very large and unpleasant face of the deepest green.

"What?" Mordrag mumbled.

"You want this cave controlled?" Ozzie said. "Consider it a favor for a favor. It is the least I can do for he who has freed me. Mordrag will sleep for a hundred years."

The cavern stopped shaking abruptly. Ali Baba had saved them all.

"Ozzie!" came a call from Ali Baba's side.

"Sinbad," the djinni replied.

"That is my name," Sinbad seemed to reply automatically.

"I do love the way that works." The djinni chuckled. "Now, what shall I do to all of you? Surely, all of mankind deserves some punishment for locking me in a bottle for all this time!"

Punishment? thought Ali Baba. Perhaps he had also doomed them all.

"But we have just freed you—" he began.

"And I have saved you," Ozzie replied. "The slate is clean. Now silence, before I turn you into something who might dwell in this sort of place."

The djinni paused a moment in silent consideration.

"I like this storytelling," Ozzie said at last. "If I hear a story of sufficient amusement, I might spare you all. Of course, if I don't, I most probably will destroy you all in a singularly unpleasant and painful fashion. Nothing, I assure you, so simple as the fate of Kassim.''

''Beg pardon, O djinni of the bottle,'' said the spirit of the lamp, for the two other djinn had finally ceased their argument for enough time to recognize this newcomer. ''But we were in this place before you, and so must, by those rules that govern all of our kind, demand that you give us precedence—''

Ozzie materialized a hand and snapped his fingers before the other djinni could say another word. The two other spirits screamed as one as they were drawn together into the bottle.

''The least I could do was give them a chance to become truly acquainted,'' Ozzie said. ''Besides, I feel so much better with that bottle filled with someone else. Now, to this storytelling. I will accept three stories. And I will choose the storytellers. Oh, this is such fun! Let us see. Sinbad?''

''That is my name!'' Sinbad replied.

''So nice of you to volunteer,'' Ozzie answered. ''And for our second storyteller, I think I shall honor the man who freed me.''

''But I am but a humble woodcutter!'' Ali Baba protested.

''All the better,'' Ozzie agreed. ''Oh, I shall be able to devise the most incredibly unpleasant deaths. I have been working upon this ever since I was trapped in the bottle, don't you know.'' He paused to survey the others. ''And for our last storyteller? No, no, not you, Harun. I am sure no one wants to hear a dozen fart stories immediately before their deaths. Perhaps a woman.''

''I will volunteer!'' Marjanah called out.

''Oh, dear,'' Ozzie replied. ''No, I have been listening to you from inside my bottle. You are far too good at that sort of thing. I am afraid that you might win.''

He turned to look at the large group of women at the far entrance. ''Perhaps someone from the palace.''

A small but exceedingly fair woman spoke up from the middle of their ranks. ''Pardon me, O great and noble djinni, but I have been known to tell a story or two in my time.''

''Ah, and aren't you a cute little human,'' Ozzie chortled. ''Yes, I will enjoy hearing you last of all, before I kill every one of you. Unless one of you—a porter, a woodcutter, or a small, shy woman—can dazzle me with your prowess! Oh, I do like this game. And what is your name, child?''

''Scheherazade,'' was the woman's reply.

''It is a pretty name as well. Do not be too frightened,

Scheherazade, when you must attempt to tell a story to delay your death.'' And with that, the great green djinni roared with laughter.

But Scheherazade only folded her hands in front of her, and smiled.

But that is enough for the second day.
If you wish more, you must witness
The Last Arabian Night,
forthcoming presently.